KINDLE THE FIRES OF WAR

She's outnumbered 100 to 1.
They're going to need more men.

Kiku has gone rogue. Now hunted by the Russian mob and the Yakuza, Kiku heads to Hong Kong's underbelly to rescue her lover. Faced with impossible odds, Kiku must outwit, outfight, and outrun everyone trying to capture her and collect the two-million-dollar bounty. Rats fueled by greed or vengeance, driven by ruthless leaders, run rampant, all hoping to score. The mob, Yakuza, and Hong Kong's black market—they all wanted to fight. Kiku started a war.

WARNING: If you have plans, cancel them! Call in sick to work, get a babysitter, do whatever you must to steal away with Kiku. You won't be able to stop reading, so get ready to strap in, buckle up, and hang on for the action-thrill ride of your life!

Praise for Christopher Greyson's
Kindle the Fires of War

A winner!

I loved every minute of it!

Move over Bond, here comes Kiku!

If you like Mission Impossible, you will love Kiku!

This book is so action-packed I had to remind myself to breathe!

A truly fun and face-paced read! Kiku is a kick-butt action hero, but her character is balanced by a vulnerability that adds depth and complexity.

From multi-award-winning *Wall Street Journal* bestselling author Christopher Greyson comes this spellbinding tale with jaw-dropping secrets, a colorful ensemble of characters, and a protagonist you'll root for from the first page to the last. Christopher Greyson's novels have been read by millions of readers.

ALSO BY CHRISTOPHER GREYSON

The Girl Who Lived

One Little Lie

Pure of Heart

The Adventures of Finn and Annie

The Detective Jack Stratton Mystery-Thriller Series:

And Then She Was Gone

Girl Jacked

Jack Knifed

Jacks are Wild

Jack and the Giant Killer

Data Jack

Jack of Hearts

Jack Frost

Jack of Diamonds

Captain Jack

Kiku - The Yakuza War Trilogy

A Beautiful Place to Die

Kindle the Fires of War

Dance of Death

This book is dedicated to my sister Maia.
No matter what life throws at her, she always battles back with a smile and a laugh. As my grandfather said, she's a spitfire who's got a lot of moxie.

Kindle the Fires of War

WALL STREET JOURNAL BESTSELLING AUTHOR
CHRISTOPHER GREYSON

GREYSON MEDIA

1

"What brings you to Hong Kong?" the immigration official asked.

"I have a few days to kill." Kiku smiled impishly at the young man, amused at her own choice of words. "I decided to visit a friend."

The official scanned her passport. Everything about it was fake except the photograph, with which she was quite pleased. The fuchsia dress accentuated her large, dark eyes and raven-black hair. Her porcelain skin glowed in the soft lighting.

The young man glanced up at her and blurted, "Are you a m-model?" before turning crimson.

Kiku tilted her neck so her hair would ripple over her shoulders and thanked him for his compliment without answering his question. She was frequently approached by well-meaning strangers asking if she was a model. Once in a restaurant, a CEO had spontaneously offered her the role of spokesmodel for his company. It was a ridiculous proposition, but she'd been flattered all the same. At any rate, it was better to give no hint of what she actually did to earn her living.

The flustered immigration official stamped her passport and mumbled, "Enjoy your visit to Hong Kong," gesturing to the next in line. Kiku dropped her smile and followed the herd of people over to baggage claim.

As she watched the sea of luggage slowly rotating around the carousel, she hoped she could identify the suitcase she had stolen before getting on the plane in Maryland. She had procured the bag for appearances, since it was sure to trigger additional scrutiny if she tried to board an international flight without any luggage. Normally, she never forgot even the most insignificant detail, but everything had been a blur on the way to the airport, her mind in knots and tangles ... Now the only thing she could recall about the suitcase was that it had a red string tied to the handle.

Amateurish.

She'd let anger get the best of her. She crossed her arms and scowled. An even graver mistake was driving straight to the airport, not even bothering to take standard precautions against being followed—other than driving ninety miles per hour in a fifty-five zone.

But now she was once again the master of her emotions—outwardly, anyway. On the inside she still seethed, her temper raw from betrayal and frustration. She scanned the crowd for any threat. If someone *had* tailed her to the airport, one phone call and fourteen hours of flight time would be enough for anyone to arrange a welcoming committee to greet her. As she looked around casually, she covered her mouth with the back of her hand, playing up the weary international traveler image, but other than a couple of businessmen leering in her direction, no one drew suspicion.

A black suitcase with a red string came sliding down the ramp. This was the one she had stolen and checked as her own. She grabbed it off the belt, quickly made certain that nothing in it was contraband, then headed for the green channel with nothing to declare. Ten minutes later, she was strolling through the exit doors of the airport and into the miracle of history and reinvention that is Hong Kong.

Across Tung Wan Bay, all the glitz and bling and neon of the city was on display, sparkling in the warm rain. Hong Kong had a love affair with lights and glare, but it put Kiku on edge, and her silk dress was already wilting in the subtropical steam. She grabbed a tourism flyer out of a dispenser and held it over her head as she hurried through the rain toward a short Japanese man under an umbrella who was holding up a sign that read *Victoria Peak*. Jiro had arranged the ride for her, but she didn't recognize the driver. He'd tried to offset his weak chin with a soul patch, but it only brought attention to it.

"Excuse me, sir," she said with a small bow. "Do you have the time?"

The driver checked his watch and made a face like he was working out a math problem. "One twenty-eight?" he answered hesitantly.

It was 9:28 p.m. in Hong Kong. The driver had provided the current time in London—the code she and Jiro had agreed on.

Kiku bowed again. "Thank you for meeting me." When the man didn't offer her the umbrella or help her into the car, she headed for the trunk, fumbling to maneuver her luggage off the curb and cursing Jiro for sending this oaf as her driver.

He followed her to the back of the car and Kiku held her suitcase out to him. He popped the trunk, tossed his sign in the back, and reached for her luggage. "I'm Jimmy."

"It is nice to meet you." Kiku let go of the suitcase before he had a secure grip on it, and it bashed off the bumper and landed in a puddle. Swearing, he bent down to pick it up, sending a cascade of water from his tilting umbrella down the back of his pants. Cursing loudly now, he heaved the suitcase into the trunk, slammed the lid, and yanked the rear door open for her.

Kiku scanned the interior before entering the taxicab. The four-door Volvo was immaculately clean, but the pungent air freshener made her blink. Dripping wet, Jimmy shut his door and, to her astonishment, shook his shiny, medium-length black hair like a dog after a bath. Then he pulled down the visor to check the mirror, let loose a few more curses upon seeing his mane utterly disheveled, and proceeded to restyle it, while Kiku waited impatiently.

"Your package from Jiro is underneath the passenger seat."

Kiku reached down and removed the belt bag of cash from its box, slid her dress up, and strapped it around her waist in a flash.

After a few more muttered curses, Jimmy flipped up the visor and pulled away from the curb. "Where are you going?" he asked over his shoulder.

"I have not decided yet. Head toward the city, please."

Jimmy exhaled and ran a hand down his wet face. "I don't know who you are, lady, but Jiro told me to take care of you, and he pays very well. Hong Kong is no place to just drive around aimlessly."

"I am very familiar with the city and its dangers."

He angled his rearview mirror toward her and raised a skeptical eyebrow. "How do you know I'm not a danger?"

Kiku delicately folded her hands on her lap. "You are not a threat to me."

His male pride obviously wounded, he turned in his seat and glared over his shoulder at her. "I told you who I work for. If I were you, I'd be very afraid of me. You should be shaking in your high heels."

She already knew he worked for Jiro, and he was stupid for telling anyone, let alone her. Kiku had seen his tattoos through his wet shirt. He was *ninkyō dantai*—Yakuza. She was unimpressed. Maybe it was her casual smile or the chuckle that escaped her red lips, maybe it was that the look of pity on her face was one he'd seen before, but it set off his already wounded ego. He glared into the rearview mirror and leveled a finger at her reflection. "If I wanted to, I could kill you right now."

Unfazed, Kiku watched the city lights outside the windows. "That might be difficult without your gun."

Jimmy's face twisted in confusion. He pressed his back against the seat and moved back and forth like he had an itch he couldn't scratch.

Kiku smiled.

Jimmy's eyes widened and he reached around to his back, his mouth dropping open. He jerked up in his seat and swiveled to look at her. "You swiped my gun?"

Kiku pointed to the headlights coming at them. "You should focus on the road."

Jimmy shrieked and jerked the steering wheel to the left, narrowly avoiding a small truck, which laid on its horn as it blasted by them. When Jimmy overcorrected, he crossed the white line, nearly clipping the car beside them. More horns blared, and cars swerved to avoid them.

Jimmy smacked the steering wheel. "That's why you dropped the suitcase! You set me up to grab my gun."

He began mumbling to himself again, but Kiku's attention was no longer on him. There was only one way out of the airport in Hong

Kong, and if they'd been followed, the options for escape or diversion were limited. To their left, was nothing but shipping containers and the polluted water of the bay. To their right, was another two-lane strip and the enormous Disney World resort. Until they had cleared the Kai Tak Tunnel in New Kowloon and could disappear into normal, chaotic city traffic, they were exposed and vulnerable.

Her unease increased when, in the rearview mirror, she spotted a large black Escalade always maintaining the same distance behind them, even after Jimmy veered recklessly into oncoming traffic. That behavior wasn't normal. A typical driver would back off or even change lanes if the car in front of him swerved so carelessly. The license plate was Hong Kong, but anything out of the ordinary put Kiku on guard. And black Escalades were much prized, among the Yakuza and others, for their size and power.

Kiku lifted her chin. "Speed up."

"Lady, we're almost at the tunnel. The cops love catching speeders here."

Kiku took out Jimmy's pistol and scowled. "Shut up, Jimmy."

The Escalade was gaining on them, and then two motorcycles surged past the Escalade on either side.

"Always keep a round in the chamber." She racked the slide on the gun—a South Korean military tactical pistol—as they entered the tunnel.

"Keep the gun low." Jimmy waved his right hand up and down like it was on fire and he was trying to put it out. "They're illegal in Hong Kong."

"Save your speech for *them*." Kiku tipped her head back as she powered down her window.

Jimmy checked his side-view mirror, swore, and stomped on the gas.

Too little, too late.

The powerful V8 Escalade was roaring up behind them like a rhinoceros, and the two motorcycles were even closer, only thirty yards back, and the riders were reaching into their jackets.

Kiku slid over next to the door. "Faster, *please*," she said, irritation slipping into her voice. Jimmy was catching up to an eighteen-wheeler.

All its wheels were in contact with the road, which meant it was carrying substantial weight.

That will do.

Both motorcycle riders now held guns in their right hands. Kiku's mind raced. She knew that the best way to kill someone in a car while riding a motorcycle was to aim ahead of the target and then drift slightly backward as you fired. Kiku didn't know if her would-be assassins would follow best practices, but she wasn't going to wait to find out.

When the taxi cleared the front bumper of the truck, she raised her gun chest high and put three rounds into each of its two front tires. There was a time when she would have shot the truck driver and saved five bullets, but something inside her had changed. She ground her teeth. This kinder version of herself was an unpredictable stranger. In her world, mercy was weakness. One day her enemies would find a way to exploit it. Weakness gets you killed.

The eighteen-wheeler jerked hard to the right and smashed into the wall of the tunnel. Tiles and debris flew into the air, and chaos erupted behind them. Tires screeched, metal shrieked, and the echo was deafening.

"Right lane," Kiku ordered as a number of cars in front of them slammed on the brakes. "Give me your phone." She laid the pistol against the seat back so it was aimed at Jimmy's head, to emphasize that she wasn't making a request. Jimmy steered to the right, grabbed his phone off the seat, and handed it to her.

"Cut back left." Kiku pointed to the car slowing down in front of them.

"I know how to drive!" Jimmy shouted as he swerved around the decelerating sedan. The taxi scraped against the tunnel wall, sparks flew, and the side mirror snapped off and sailed backward.

"Then I suggest you drive like you do."

Jimmy swore as he pumped the brakes and narrowly avoided clipping a van. Kiku glanced back and smiled. The eighteen-wheeler had blocked off both lanes behind them. There was no way the Escalade could get through. The motorcycles were a different matter.

The phone's screen lit up, and she pressed "emergency call."

The operator answered in Cantonese: "Nine-nine-nine emergency response."

Jimmy's head wobbled around on his neck like someone had just tasered him. He mouthed, *Are you crazy?*, followed by a number of curses in Japanese and English.

He was freaking out because ordinary criminals never call the police. But he had no idea who Kiku was.

Kiku spoke in English, her voice rising dramatically. "We're in the tunnel from the airport! These crazy men on motorcycles are shooting at everyone! They have guns!" she wailed, and ended with a loud sob. "A truck smashed and—"

"Calm down, miss." The operator was now speaking English, too. "How many motorcycles are involved?"

"Two."

Emergency lights were already visible up ahead, and sirens were drawing closer.

"The men have red helmets and black jackets. They have guns and —" She clicked the phone off and handed it back to Jimmy.

"You called the cops?" he snapped.

Kiku held up a hand, cutting off his protest, and listened. Above the wail of the police sirens, two motorcycle engines revved loudly behind them.

"Slow down, please."

When Jimmy jammed his foot down on the gas instead, Kiku racked the gun, ejecting a cartridge high into the air. Seeing this on TV and in movies always drew her scorn—because one should always have a bullet in the chamber, ready to fire—but she did it now to emphasize her demand and was confident that Jimmy would listen to orders, if properly motivated.

It worked. He took his foot off the gas.

Two police cars sped toward them, coming the wrong way down the tunnel.

"Pull over."

Jimmy looked at Kiku like she had two heads, but obediently pulled over to the side of the tunnel behind a Mercedes that had already moved over and had its hazard lights flashing. The police cars zipped past them just as the motorcycles approached from behind.

Kiku unlocked the left rear door and scanned the view in back. The motorcycle riders had seen the police, and the police had seen them. The cruisers slammed on their brakes, and their tires smoked and screeched as they fought to turn around and give chase. The motorcycles' angry buzz intensified as the riders pinned down the throttles. The hunters were now the hunted.

Kiku allowed the first motorcycle to rocket past. But when the second motorcycle raced up, she kicked the door open.

The motorcycle's front wheel slammed into the door, ripping the door off its hinges and catapulting the rider high into the air.

"Hold this." Kiku dropped the gun over the front seat. She couldn't risk being caught with it if the police stopped her.

She slipped off her shoes, got out of the car, and ran fifty feet to her would-be assassin, now writhing in pain on the ground. His motorcycle lay on its side off to the right, its rear wheel still spinning.

"Are you okay?" she shrieked dramatically as she grabbed his jacket, rolled him onto his back, and ripped his pistol from his shoulder holster. She shoved it through her dress's neckline into her bra, then unbuckled his helmet, pulled it off, and retrieved the gun from her makeshift holster.

One look at his face, his military haircut, and his steroid-enlarged neck and she already knew whom he was working for. A tattoo of a flag whose country no longer existed was splattered in blood on his exposed forearm. That confirmed it. The man was Russian, working for Cade Novikov. But she asked just the same, pressing the gun against his throat for emphasis.

"Who sent you?" Her Russian was rusty, but his eyes narrowed in understanding before he spat toward her. Unfortunately for him, gravity sent the gray glob back to him and it landed on his own cheek.

She scowled. She'd been very sloppy indeed if the Russians already had her in their crosshairs. She ejected and palmed the magazine, then pulled back the slide of his gun to flick away the live round.

A police car skidded to a stop behind her and its doors were flung open. "Move away from him!" a policeman shouted in Cantonese.

Kiku dropped the empty gun back into the Russian's hands. "He has a gun!" she screamed as she covered her head and ran shrieking back toward the cab.

Bullets filled the air as the policemen opened fire. Kiku ran to the rear of the cab, the police rushing by her, their guns trained on the motorcyclist, who was no longer moving.

"Do you have any warrants?" Kiku whispered to Jimmy as she reached the cab.

"What? Me? No."

"Are you known?"

Jimmy shook his head. "I'm clean." From the look on his face, she knew he understood the implications of her question. The Hong Kong police kept close tabs on known gang members. If the police were aware Jimmy was Yakuza, they would need to flee the scene, which would be very complicated right now.

"Follow my lead and say as little as possible. Do you have a pen and paper?"

Jimmy grabbed both from the glove compartment and handed them to her. Kiku wrote instructions on the pad and handed it back to him.

"This cab will not be sufficient. Explicitly follow these details and get me that vehicle and everything else on the list. Make sure you get that exact license plate number."

"Whatever," Jimmy muttered. He stared at the cab's door, now lying in the road, and swore. "My brother-in-law owns this cab. I promised I'd get it back to him untouched."

"That was a foolish promise to make."

Jimmy glared at her.

Kiku smiled. Her arrival in Hong Kong had gone about as well as she had expected. But her visit was going to get much harder from here.

2

An hour and a half later, having given her witness report to the police and quickly convinced them that she was an ordinary tourist from Washington, D.C., Kiku stood at the window on the fortieth floor of her favorite hotel in Hong Kong, the Langham, and looked at the city stretched out in neon splendor at her feet. The billions of lights, the idea of tossing herself overboard and getting lost among the sea of people, used to give her comfort. But now she didn't want to get lost in the lights; she desperately needed to find one of them.

Takeo. The brightest light in her dark life. And she had no clue where he was down there, or even whether he was still alive. Her heart didn't ache, it burned. All she wanted to do was go from one Yakuza safe house to another, torching them to the ground until she found her love.

Her hand balled into a fist. She tugged the sheer curtains closed to soften the glare and paced the boxy room, her bare feet sinking into the carpet.

Love. She'd never admitted that feeling to herself, let alone to Takeo. For all she knew, he thought their trysts together were nothing more than sex driven by lust and need. As they once had been for her as well.

Discovering that Takeo had a young son and rescuing him had changed her ideas—about Takeo, about love, about everything ...

Kiku's phone buzzed and, seeing the number, she answered quickly. "Jiro."

"Where are you?" The mirth had disappeared from Jiro's happy-go-lucky voice after his kidnapping. The Russians had grabbed Takeo's brother to avenge the death of their own leader's son, but Kiku's daring rescue had ruined their plan. That was why Cade Novikov's men had moved on to target Alex, Takeo's son. An heir for an heir.

"Are you certain the line is secure?"

"Yes. It's a brand-new burner."

"Where are you?" Kiku trusted Jiro's sincerity, but his lax ways often left him open to security breaches.

"The parking lot at the mall. I ditched my guards in the food court."

Jiro had to be careful; his life depended on it. Kenzo may have declared Jiro the head of the American Yakuza, but he was only a figurehead, a puppet controlled by Kenzo. Even though Kenzo had returned to Japan with Takeo, he was still the one in charge. Jiro only had one rule to follow: don't do anything without asking Kenzo.

"I just arrived in Hong Kong. Have you found out where Takeo is being held?"

"I don't have any details, but I believe he is still in Hong Kong. I don't know who with."

Kiku resisted the urge to threaten to carve out Jiro's heart or to insult him for his ineptitude. He couldn't save himself from his kidnappers, let alone his girlfriend. Jiro was trying, but as the pampered second son, he lacked the experience and skills necessary to be of any real help now.

"And do you still believe Kenzo is trying to arrange a marriage for Takeo?" Just saying the words made Kiku's chest tighten and her mouth run dry. Marriage? Takeo would never go along with an arranged marriage. Would he?

Why not?

After all, Takeo believed that Kiku had disobeyed him and let his son die. Any feelings he might once have had for her had most likely died then, too.

"My father wants an heir. And you know how Kenzo felt about Takeo's mother—he wants his heir to come from her blood line. Takeo is the firstborn." There was a tinge of hurt in Jiro's voice. "Publicly, Kenzo blames Takeo for Alex's death, but ... I'm not sure about that."

"Continue." Kiku knew the truth, but she was uncertain how much Jiro knew. She purposely had not told him that Kenzo had ordered Alex's death. If Jiro found out, he might tell Takeo, and if Takeo discovered the truth, that his father had ordered his son's death, he would certainly attack Kenzo.

And then Takeo would die.

She heard Jiro's breath puffing into the speaker. His hesitation went beyond a son's loyalty to his father. He was afraid. Kiku had never met a more ruthless or brutal man than his father, Kenzo.

"Shin would never betray the Yakuza," Jiro said.

"Shin killed Alex." A lie. "I was there. I killed Shin." That much was entirely truthful. "How is that *not* a betrayal?"

"It's a betrayal of Takeo." Jiro cleared his throat. "Let me explain. Shin was head of Takeo's security, but ultimately he worked for my father."

Kiku took a moment, pretending that the news surprised her. "Why would your father have his own grandson killed?"

"He cares about two things: power and dynasty," Jiro whispered harshly into the phone. "Alex wasn't ... he was only *half* Japanese." And half made him nothing. The Nakumora family line was pure Japanese blood, and to the Nakumora, lineage was everything.

Kiku's fingers tightened around the phone, the ugly truth confirmed. Kenzo wanted to murder his own flesh and blood because he wasn't pure Japanese. He felt a mixed bloodline was dishonorable and made a person weak. Being half-Korean herself, Kiku couldn't wait to come face to face with Kenzo and demonstrate how wrong he was. The lights outside the window blinked and swirled behind the sheers. Kiku shook her head as if she'd been punched.

"And your father thinks Takeo producing a suitable heir will fix everything?"

"No, Takeo doesn't want anything to do with it. He's ... he's not doing too well. Our mother's death struck him hard, but the death of his son ..."

Kiku kept her mouth closed. No one could know that she had faked

Alex's death. Not even Takeo. *Especially* not Takeo. No matter how much pain it caused him.

"I tried to tell him that you did your best," Jiro said, "but you didn't bring Alex to Chicago as Takeo instructed. I know I told you not to—I had to warn you. But I can't tell Takeo my suspicions about our father. Not right now. He'd try to kill Kenzo, and we both know how that would end."

"That is a wise decision." Kiku closed her eyes. "Takeo blames me."

There was a long pause. "He believed you could do anything you set your mind to doing. To him, you were invincible."

"And yet I failed."

"It was his *son*. I'm worried about him, Kiku. If he is in Hong Kong, it's going to be like finding the right shadow in a graveyard."

Kiku pushed aside the curtain and with it the image of Takeo grieving and stared down again at the glittering cityscape. The Yakuza owned hundreds of buildings in Hong Kong. Takeo could be in any one of them.

"You have to find Takeo," Jiro continued. "He defied our father by trying to turn the American Yakuza legitimate, and Kenzo knows all about it. He wants Takeo to give him an heir, but after that, Takeo will pay for his defiance ..."

Kiku had already surmised that. Once Takeo produced a son *worthy* of carrying on the Nakumora name, he would be executed.

"I will find him, Jiro," she said, and hung up.

The lights below taunted her. Jiro was correct: in Hong Kong, it would be impossible for her to find Takeo by herself. But there was one man whose business it was to wriggle into dark crannies and ferret out secrets. Unfortunately, the last time Kiku had asked that man for a favor, it had not ended well. He had promised to kill her the next time he saw her.

Kiku stared past her reflection at the darkness beyond. What did that matter? Going after Takeo was a suicide mission in any case. There were a thousand different ways this could end in disaster. What was one more?

Let the Rat King try to kill her—he had failed more than once before. Still, this time she would be meeting him on his turf, on his terms. The odds were against her, but she was used to that. She was Yakuza. The name came from the game *oichokabu*, where eight-nine-three—*yattsu, ku, san*—was a losing hand. She knew that was what the world thought of the Yakuza—worthless losers—and what the world thought of her. But tomorrow she would do what she always did: prove them wrong.

3

Kiku stayed in the hotel all day, taking full advantage of the Langham's gym and spa. Having to wait to begin her search was brutal, but taking her frustrations out on her body during her workout helped. She would have loved a massage afterward, but the gunshot wounds on her side and calf were still too tender and would raise suspicions. She settled for a long soak in the luxurious bathtub.

When the sun was setting and the neon glitter began to come to life, she walked down the block and crossed the street to the taxicab parked outside the Imperial, another upscale hotel. One of the cab's rear doors was a different color; Jimmy had managed to replace it.

He was sitting inside the car, staring at the hotel entrance. When Kiku opened the back door and slid into the seat, Jimmy jumped and swore. He did a double take between her and the revolving doors. "What the— How'd I miss you?"

"I stayed at a different hotel last night."

Jimmy's confusion hardened into anger. "Look, I trusted you. I'm supposed to keep an eye on you. You said you'd stay in the Imperial. Jiro wanted me to stay with you."

"That was never going to happen." Kiku folded her hands in her lap. "Nor is it necessary. Head toward the Cattle Depot."

Jimmy turned around in his seat and started the engine. "You know they don't have any cows or stuff like that. It's a bunch of artist shops now."

"I am aware of that."

Even though rush hour had ended, traffic in Kowloon was still heavy. The cab drove for several blocks before stopping at a large intersection for the red light. A throng of people crowded the road as they crossed.

"We need to stop at Fat Man Market first." Kiku powered down her window. "Did you get the vehicle I requested?"

"Yeah. They're waiting for us three blocks from the Cattle Depot."

"Did you get everything on the list?"

Jimmy ran a hand through his hair in frustration. It was obvious he was not used to taking orders, especially from a woman. "I can read. I got everything you asked for, and my guys are ready."

"Please hand your phone to me."

Frowning, Jimmy took out his phone. "Why don't you buy your own? I've gotta make a call first."

Kiku scooted up to the edge of the back seat and smiled at Jimmy, revealing her sharp canine teeth. Her left hand flicked out, grabbed Jimmy's seat belt, and coiled it once around his neck, then she sat back, pulling the strap tight. Jimmy's eyes bulged as he frantically clutched at the strap.

"Calm down," Kiku said. She relaxed the tension enough that he could breathe again. "What you want is irrelevant. So are Jiro's wishes. You do what I say, when I say it. Though you may work for Jiro, the conversation regarding my killing you would be very brief. I would explain that you buzzed incessantly, and after several swats, I had no choice but to kill the insolent mosquito. Jiro would thank me and send me your replacement within the hour." She reached her hand forward. "Your phone."

Jimmy stretched his arm across the seat back. In spite of the look of hatred in his eyes, his hand shook. Kiku took his phone, flung it into the back of the truck parked next to them, and powered up her window. Jimmy's red eyes blazed as he glared at her in the rearview mirror.

"Do not take it personally. I do not trust *anyone*." Kiku released the seat belt and tossed an envelope over the seat. "There is ten thousand dollars for your services. There will be more when your job is complete."

Jimmy coughed, but a smile grew on his face as he rubbed his neck. "More? Like, how much more?"

"I reward obedience. Do as I say and you will be quite happy. But please remember, if you do not do as I say, you will not live to spend the money in that envelope, Ka." *Mosquito.*

Jimmy coughed again and nodded.

"The light is green." Kiku tipped her chin up. "Move into the right lane. The Fat Man is up ahead."

Kiku strolled through the front doors of Fat Man Market while Jimmy sat parked outside. The bustling shopping center was mobbed with jostling customers. She worked her way past the chic boutiques and clothing stores to the antiques shop in the far corner.

The old owner's eyes lit up when he saw her, and he hurried out from behind the counter. Kiku had found that people remember two things well—pain and money—and both could be used to manipulate people. With the shop owner, the latter had always been sufficient.

"And how may I help you today?" the man said. He greeted her by taking her outstretched hand in both of his. The simple act was common in the southern states of the US, but it was a rarity for Asians. "You look very happy today."

The flattery was nowhere close to the truth, but his smile was contagious and she grinned back. "I'm looking for a bottle of Pappy Van Winkle's Family Reserve. Twenty years."

The old man feigned surprise. He wasn't supposed to sell liquor—and didn't sell it to the general public. But if one wanted something unusually high-end, he had it.

"Pappy's is quite exquisite. But if you are in the mood for a whiskey, I may have a personal bottle of Mars Maltage I would part with." He patted her hand. "Just for you. It doesn't come cheap. It's a twenty-eight-year-old pure malt."

Kiku was unsure if the recommendation was just that or if the old man was out of Pappy's. Either way, the Rat King liked dark liquor, and the more expensive, the better.

"*Domo arigato*. That sounds perfect. Please select two tumblers as well."

Ten minutes later, the old man handed Kiku a bagged box and a bill for four thousand dollars. She handed over a credit card and added a five-hundred-dollar tip. He smiled and bowed, and she did the same.

Kiku had been coming to this little store for many years to purchase everything from alcohol and antiques to guns and other contraband, and in all that time she'd never given her name, nor asked his. Today was no different. The name on the credit card was not her own, of course.

"*Domo arigato*. Come again soon!" the man called out as Kiku strolled out and headed to the supermarket.

Here the aisles were even more crowded than the outside streets. People were pressed shoulder to shoulder as they made the slow journey around the store. Kiku made her way towards the baking section, where she grabbed a bottle of almond extract, then headed to the pharmacy for the last item on her shopping list.

By the time she exited the store, she felt like running into the night. She wasn't claustrophobic, but the sheer weight of the people pressing against her had sent all her senses into overdrive.

She slipped into the back of the cab. "Head to the Cattle Depot."

Jimmy nodded and pulled out into traffic. He glanced back at the bag on the back seat and rolled his eyes. His voice rose in stereotypical male condescension as he said with a chuckle, "You actually went shopping? Did you get everything you needed?"

Kiku took out the bag from the pharmacy.

Opening the syringe package, she resisted the urge to stick it into the side of Jimmy's neck. She would need it for later.

4

The closer the cab came to the Cattle Depot, the more apprehensive Kiku became. Even five blocks away, she was scanning the faces of the people they passed and felt sure that some were staring back.

"Are you certain you wish to accompany me?" she asked Jimmy.

"Jiro ordered me to. I'm going."

"Leave your gun and money in the car. Take them out now."

Jimmy frowned. "Who are you going to see? The cops?"

Kiku flexed her hands, trying to relax the tension rising up in her fingers. "The Rat King."

Jimmy swore, and jammed the envelope Kiku had given him under the dashboard. She hid her smile when he reached down and removed his ankle holster. Most people would have missed the faint bulge in his pant leg, but she hadn't.

The Cattle Depot was a collection of shops belonging to artists from all over the world. Some of the greatest craftspeople Kiku had ever seen had stores there with working studios within them. As Jimmy parked the cab, she wished she had the time to go into every one and witness the creativity in action. But she wasn't here to see the art.

Jimmy got out of the cab and stretched. He tried to act casual, but his head darted around like a bird able to hear a cat nearby. He looked ready to take flight at any moment.

His fear was well justified.

"Where exactly are we going?" he asked.

"Down." Kiku strolled toward the entrance, and Jimmy hurried to catch up. From the puzzled look on his face and his clenched jaw, it was clear that he'd never been underground. "You have never met him?"

Jimmy pulled back his shoulders and added a slight swagger to his stride. "Sure I have. He came to meet Jiro once."

Kiku wanted to smack the smug look off the fool's face. The Rat King would never go meet anyone, not even Kenzo. He would have sent an emissary to represent him. But if Jimmy was too stupid to know the difference, she wasn't going to take the time to explain it to him. He'd find out soon enough.

Kiku walked through the doors of one of the master potters. The group of people watching the demonstration didn't even look up at the tinkling of the little bell over the door. She and Jimmy strode past them through the front gallery to an upscale display room in the back.

A young girl, her hair up in a bun and her gray apron smeared with a reddish clay, brushed back a wayward strand of hair. "Can I help you?"

"I wish to pay my respects to Mong Wai."

"Certainly." The smile on the girl's face remained unchanged, but a vein in her neck began to throb. "Let me check if he is in." She pointed to a spot on the floor. "Please wait here."

Kiku stood on the spot and stared straight ahead.

Jimmy's eyes wandered around the room, and he began to stroll over to a large vase in the corner. Kiku snapped her fingers and pointed at the floor next to her.

Sticking his tongue in his cheek, he moved to stand next to her. "I'm not your pet."

"Know this: if something happens to you in here, not even Kenzo can help you."

Jimmy straightened up and exhaled. "Okay ... look, when you asked if I've met *the* guy, I thought you meant, like, *a* guy. They're a group, right? They're a bunch of losers who pick up information, but there's no real leader. The Rat King is just a story, like the bogeyman."

"Some monsters are real." Kiku tipped her head toward the wall.

"And in addition to the camera behind the picture frame, I am certain there are microphones. I would be more careful who you refer to as a *loser*."

Jimmy paled. His mouth opened and closed a couple of times like a mute ventriloquist dummy. Staring right at the picture, he said, "I was kidding. I don't ... I didn't ..."

"Stop talking." Kiku smiled for the camera.

Jimmy's stammering wouldn't undo his insults. Besides, his disparaging remarks were quite accurate—*losers*. Or at least that was how most people viewed the members of the Rat King's family. In a society that relegated the Yakuza to outcasts, the rats were beneath contempt. Addicts, prostitutes past their prime, vagrants, and beggars—the Rat King gave them purpose and treated them like his children. In return they were fanatically loyal to him. It was a family, but a very twisted and dysfunctional one.

The young girl reappeared and led them to a door. "Right this way."

Jimmy and Kiku followed her down a long, brick-lined hallway. The door clicking shut behind them was loud in the confined space. The passage ran ten yards straight back, stopping at a metal door. It swung open as they approached and four men appeared—all thin, wearing black suits, and of average height—followed by a short man who made Kiku's muscles twitch with the instinct to reach for her hairpin and stab him in the face. The four men were armed, but the real threat was the little man with the wide-spaced eyes.

He hurried forward, holding up a hand. "Far enough." His voice was raspy. He leered as he made a circle in the air with his finger as if spinning a basketball. "Backs to me. Arms out."

She fought down the bile rising in her throat as his gnarled hands groped every inch of her body. Those hands lingered far too long and grabbed way too much, but he had let her keep both her hairpin and the ornate belt at her waist. Two small victories to start the night.

Jimmy skittered sideways as one of the other men ran his hands up his legs but otherwise stayed quiet for once.

After he was done groping her, the little gargoyle of a man reached into Kiku's bag and lifted out the box holding the Mars Maltage.

"A gift for the Rat King."

The short man opened the box to peek inside. He unwrapped one glass, felt the other through the wrapped paper, and finally handed the bag back to Kiku, licking his lips. Without a word, he stomped away, and the four armed men surged forward to escort Kiku and Jimmy to the Rat King's lair.

A wide staircase wound its way down three stories. Framed art lined the stairwell but did little to dress up the gray walls of the former bomb shelter. The beauty of the art was undeniable—a priceless collection of ill-gotten gains—but just as a gilded tomb's incense and perfumes cannot mask the stench of death and decay, all the fine art in the world couldn't warm the chill of evil in this rat's nest.

However, the structure was perfect for staying out of sight and coming and going as one pleased. Several air shafts had been widened, and it was rumored that from here the Rat King's army could scurry to any corner of Hong Kong without going aboveground.

Kiku descended the steps with the grace of a woman entering a gala, despite the circumstances. She had to give Jimmy some credit: his eyes frequently locked with hers, and he seemed to pick up on her signals to slow down and let her lead. Still, she was not sure she had gotten through to him that if he did anything foolish, this would be his crypt.

The staircase ended in a large room outfitted with an eclectic mix of furniture and mismatched display cases, with a final result halfway between a hoarding grandparent's dining room and a bistro trying too hard to be trendy. The Rat King sat at the head of a long mahogany table in a high-backed chair. At the opposite end, almost twelve feet away, was one empty chair.

The Rat King crossed his long legs and waited, his eyes alert with amusement and sensual anticipation. Gaunt and pale, with sharp cheekbones and slicked-back hair, he was perfectly suited to his nickname—though it was a title passed down for generations. His real name was Cheung, but like all his fathers before him, he had been given the title of Rat King upon his father's death.

The gnarled little man moved in front of Jimmy to bar his passage and Kiku knew this was her cue to come forward, giving her nervous escort the slightest nod as she passed him. She stopped next to the empty chair opposite Cheung, put the bag on the table, removed the box, and unwrapped the crystal tumblers.

At Cheung's motion, the short man rushed over and fetched the box and the glasses, then bowed twice as he returned to Cheung's side. He carefully lifted the bottle out of the velvet-lined box and held it out for Cheung to examine like it was fine wine. Cheung scrutinized the label and the bottle, paying close attention to the seal at the top. Finally, the Rat King nodded approvingly. His troll poured two glasses and awkwardly carried one back to Kiku, who turned the glass slightly and pretended not to see the splotch on the rim where a little had spilled over the lip.

Cheung smelled the Mars Maltage, then took a big mouthful and swirled it lustily in his mouth before swallowing. "You stopped in to see Bok Hu on the way here."

Kiku nodded, feeling somewhat disappointed to learn the old shopkeeper's name. She'd liked the mystery and was sad her little guessing game had ended. She raised the glass to her lips and took a long, slow sip. Bok Hu's choice was exquisite.

Cheung motioned for her to sit.

She was surprised he would let her get as close as that, even with the two guards obscured in the shadows behind him.

She smiled as she took the proffered chair. So did Cheung, but there was malice in his grin and the muscles in his jaw were tight. Even at this distance, Kiku could make out the four long scars on the side of his face. She had put them there.

But only because Cheung had forced her to. At the time, she was twelve and he was almost thirty. He hadn't expected a twelve-year-old girl to fight like a demon, but that was what she'd done. She'd also left him missing a chunk of his right forearm, though his long sleeves hid that injury.

She took another sip of whiskey to wash away the memory of the taste of his flesh. She would have died that day if it hadn't been for Daichi, who had taken pity on her, and Kenzo, whose power and influence had saved her. On the street, they said that the Rat King didn't hold grudges, because it hurt business. But that was a lie. Twice since then he'd tried to have her killed, and the last attempt had almost started a war with Takeo. That was only a year ago now, and she hoped the truce was still holding. But she never counted on hope.

"I need information."

Cheung sneered, "I might be able to help you. The question is, do I want to?"

"Where is Takeo Nakumora?"

Cheung took a longer sip, draining half the glass, and tittered like an old hag, his bony shoulders poking up into little spikes. "So the great Kiku lost her boss's son and now she can't find him either?" He let his head roll back and laughed at the ceiling. The men behind Kiku joined in, guffawing boisterously.

Kiku's expression didn't change as she sipped the smoky liquor, holding it on her tongue until it warmed to caramel. She didn't care what these pigs thought of her. She hadn't failed; she'd succeeded spectacularly. Her reputation, though quite precious to her, did not depend on whether she was acknowledged for her contributions—for Kiku, like the samurai, continuing to exist was proof enough.

While she waited for an answer, Kiku tapped her right pinky against the table; she enjoyed the tiny tapping sound of the prosthetic, especially on wood.

Cheung's simpering giggles faded. He drained his shot and poured himself another. He lifted his glass and gave the slightest tilt of his head. "Since you are in such dire need of my assistance, Kiku, how can I resist making a deal with you?"

She loathed bargaining with Cheung. He always began with dramatic, exorbitant demands. But this time he surprised her.

"Takeo is no longer in Hong Kong. He's in Japan."

Kiku's heart sped up. Not because Cheung was giving her free information—though that alone was a very bad sign—but because if Takeo had gone to Japan, she knew exactly where he was.

Fumeiyo no ie. The house of disgrace.

The Nakumoras owned a hundred homes in Japan, but after his mother's death, Takeo had vowed he would never return. However, no one had ever lived in Fumeiyo no ie, and no one ever chose to go there. The small estate dated back five hundred years and served only one purpose: to hide a shamed man until he could restore his honor.

For Takeo, the options were few—marriage or death, both of them arranged for him—so Kiku had no doubt that Takeo was in Japan against his will. Kiku finished her drink and prepared to ask her next question.

Cheung held up his hand. "One more moment, if you would indulge me. I have heard another bit of information you will no doubt find as intriguing as I did." He too finished his drink, and placed the cork back in the bottle. "Cade Novikov has offered two million pounds for your head."

"I am fortunate that Kenzo values my head even more highly."

"Does he?" Cheung leaned back in his chair, gripping the armrests and barely able to contain his excitement. "You let his grandson die. You failed him. Perhaps this time the great Kiku is vulnerable."

She had to look away from the sight of his nostrils flaring, as if he smelled meat, but she spoke coolly. "I thought the Rat King did not hold grudges."

"I don't." He rubbed the scars on his cheek with the back of his hand. "This is business. Supply and demand." He held his hands out, palms up like a scale. "For example, you are in great demand for the Russians." He lifted his left hand high. "But the Yakuza?" He lowered his right hand until his forearm tapped the armrest. "Not so much."

He snapped closed both hands, and every man in the room except Jimmy drew his weapon and took aim.

"I'm still valuable to the Yakuza," Jimmy wailed, raising his hand like a kid in class, and one of the guards instantly placed his pistol at the back of Jimmy's head.

Kiku picked up her tumbler and wondered again if she'd injected too little almond extract into the bottle, but it was time to play her card now. She let an impish smile play across her lips as she nonchalantly sniffed the tumbler.

"There are still sides to the business that you fail to see, Cheung."

Cheung went pale as he sniffed his own glass.

"You forget that I recently rescued Jiro from certain death, for which Kenzo rewarded me quite handsomely. He has publicly absolved me of any blame for his grandson's death. He has let it be known that he seeks vengeance on the Russians and holds Cade Novikov personally responsible. You were absolutely right to point out the importance of impartiality in business transactions. So, how do you think Kenzo will view *your* handing me over to the Russians so you can profit from his innocent grandson's death? As something useful to him?"

Cheung's hands balled into fists.

"I think you should also remember," Kiku continued, "that Kenzo, unlike you, keeps track of transgressions and exacts a price for any and all."

Cheung planted his feet on the floor.

"But just in case ..." Kiku held up her glass. "Even you must detect the hint of almond?"

Cheung's hand went to his throat. "Cyanide!"

Kiku shook her head. "No. It *is* deadly, but also curable."

"What did you put in my drink?" Cheung stood. "I can make you tell me." He pointed at Jimmy, and all guns in the room zoomed in on the same target.

Kiku shrugged. "Go ahead. Disembowel him. I can call for another ride."

Jimmy swore, but the shotgun pressed against his back cut him off.

Kiku remained seated. "You know that I will not tell you anything. And if you do manage to live beyond twenty-four hours, Kenzo will burn you out of every hole you can find. I spoke with him personally before coming here."

Cheung swept the tumbler off the table; it shattered on the floor. "That's a lie. Kenzo knows where his son is. You could have just asked him. Why then did you come to me?"

Kiku calmly rose. "Takeo's location was not the real reason I came," she lied. "Kenzo wants to know who his true allies are. The war is spreading. Kenzo wants your sole allegiance. You are to have no further dealings with the Russians."

Cheung chewed his lip, his eyes darting back and forth like he was working out a puzzle in his mind. A leer parted his lips, revealing overly bright teeth. "Prove what you say. Where is Takeo?"

"Fumeiyo no ie." Kiku didn't hesitate to state her guess. Even if she was wrong, if she said it with enough conviction, Cheung would doubt his own intelligence. "But he is only there to mourn. Another reason why handing me over to the Russians would be a very bad idea."

Cheung glared at the glass shards on the floor. "Then tell me the poison."

Kiku turned and started walking for the stairs. "After I speak with Kenzo."

Something broke behind her, but she didn't glance back to see what it was. Jimmy was struggling against the two men holding him, and Cheung snapped, "Let him go."

A moment later Jimmy caught up to her, and he practically clung to her side as they climbed the stairs. Only the gargoyle accompanied them back up the three flights. Kiku's heart was pounding—not from fear but exhilaration. Like she'd just skydived through a canyon in a wingsuit and lived.

At the top of the stairs, the man unlocked the doors and glared at Kiku. His lips moved like he was making a practice run at some threat or sarcastic comment but had decided to keep his mouth shut.

She was going to let his earlier groping go—he did have to frisk her, after all, even if he had lingered and grabbed far too much. But now the man ogled her breasts again and winked.

"See you next time—"

Kiku's hand snapped out, catching the man's windpipe, then she pivoted and drove his face into the metal door. His legs were already wobbling, so she grabbed the back of his shirt with one hand and pitched him backward.

The troll flailed his arms in futility, wildly grabbing at the air in the hope of stopping his fall down the stairs. The sounds of bones snapping and his skull thumping echoed off the walls as he tumbled. The cement was as unforgiving as she was. Kiku was tempted to wait to hear Cheung's reaction, but she didn't have time.

If Takeo truly was at Fumeiyo no ie, he did not plan on returning.

He planned on dying there.

5

Kiku strolled out of the potter's shop and across the street to a jewelry store. Puzzled, Jimmy followed her inside, moving so close his thigh pressed against hers. As soon as he was in, he scurried over to the jewelry store's front window and gazed at the pottery shop they had just left, nervously watching the door.

"Are you seeing if we're being followed?" he asked.

Kiku grinned. "No." She made eye contact with the salesgirl, who hurried over. Kiku pointed at the display in the window. "I would like the chrysanthemum brooch and matching earrings, please."

Jimmy reacted as if he'd stepped on a bee. "We almost get our heads blown off, and you want to go shopping?"

"Lower your voice." Kiku strolled over to the register. "Of course we are being followed. Panicking will do nothing to stop it."

"But we could get a head start," Jimmy shot back.

"That is exactly what I do not want to do."

Kiku paid for her jewelry and took her time walking through the market—stopping in front of several shops, purchasing a pearl milk tea, haggling over a silk robe that caught her eye. By the time they reached the cab, Jimmy was bathed in sweat, and still following so closely he occasionally bumped her arm or hip.

"You should have gotten a cold drink when I offered you one," Kiku said as she snapped on her seat belt in the back seat.

"You're crazy. Jiro said you took risks, but you just poisoned the Rat King and killed or maimed one of his men, and you're not even worried about it?"

"I did not poison Cheung. It was simple almond extract." She held up the container for emphasis. "And as a thank you for the perverted pat-down and escorting me up the stairs, I merely ushered the deviant down them."

Jimmy shook his head in disbelief. "He's still going to want your head on a pike."

"Then he will need to get in line." Kiku sipped her bubble tea. "Besides, the Russians already want my head, so all the Rat King has to do is make a phone call. But I am certain he is on the way to the hospital as we speak." She pointed ahead. "Take this right. Are your men waiting at the car wash?"

"*Man*, not *men*," Jimmy said, his voice rising. "One guy. That's all you said we were going to need. I didn't know the whole Russian army was going to come after us."

"Do me a favor: stop talking until we get to the car wash. I would like to enjoy my drink."

The veins in the backs of Jimmy's hands stood out and he looked ready to rip the steering wheel off the column, but he closed his mouth. When they reached the car wash, he parked behind a large black Escalade.

"Nicely done," Kiku said. "That is the correct plate number." Remembering the Escalade's license plate had been a minor detail that she now hoped to turn into a masterstroke.

She thought Jimmy would be pleased to get the rare compliment, but he thrust his arms out toward the SUV and said nervously, "My guys faked it. If someone gets too close, they may be able to tell."

"It only has to work from a distance." Kiku tipped her head toward the guy in stained jeans and a dirty overcoat getting out of the Escalade. "Is he one of your men?"

"Yeah. One guy, remember? Me, you, and him. That's it. And I gotta tell you, there's no way the three of us are taking on the Russians.

They're born to fight. I heard when they were kids they didn't play 'pin the tail on the donkey,' they played 'shoot the head off the running guy' and used a real guy."

Kiku reached across the seat and handed him the remainder of her pearl milk tea. It was a little too sweet for her anyway. "Relax. Drink this and drive. Head toward the business district. Your *man* can leave." She opened her door.

Jimmy's eyebrows traveled in different directions. "Wait a second. You just want me to drive? What's my job in this?"

"You are the most important part." Kiku smiled, and Jimmy's chest puffed up as he took a sip of tea. "You are the bait."

Jimmy started coughing as Kiku walked away.

"No matter what happens, just continue to drive," she called back. "And keep under the speed limit."

The man standing outside the Escalade handed her a set of keys and a thick black fishing line that ran to the back of the car and the license plate.

"Have you tested it?" she asked.

The man nodded. "It's connected with pull-away magnets. Just give it a firm yank."

Kiku slipped the man an envelope and smiled. "Thank you."

Sliding behind the wheel, she spotted the ski mask on the front seat. Everything was in place. Now she just needed to move the bait into the trap.

She waved Jimmy forward. He scowled as he passed her and headed for the main road. Kiku waited for a few cars to move behind him, then followed. She was certain that Cheung had his people watching for the cab with its mismatched door, and it was only a matter of time before they would have company.

Jimmy did as he was ordered, driving slowly and carefully down the streets. After only ten minutes, the black Escalade that Kiku had been waiting for appeared.

She knew that getting vehicles in Hong Kong was a challenging task for the Russians, so she had been positive that they wouldn't abandon the Escalade they'd used to follow her from the airport—as long as the police hadn't seen the Escalade, just the motorcycles, why go to the trouble of switching vehicles?

Kiku let three more cars slip between her and the Escalade as it tailed Jimmy's cab. Jimmy was obeying her instructions and keeping to the speed limit. As they neared the business district, Kiku saw her opportunity and smiled. A security car had stopped in the left-hand-turn lane ahead. Big businesses frequently hired private security firms that consisted mostly of retired policemen, and the Hong Kong police treated them like their own. But there was one important difference: security officers did not carry guns.

She took out her pistol, laid it on the seat, and picked up the ski mask. Jimmy's cab passed the security car, and so did the Russians' Escalade. Kiku tugged the ski mask on over her head, veered across traffic, and pulled alongside the security car, unloading three shots into the hood of the car and one into each of the wheels on her side. For added effect, she shot out their back side window, before moving forward to give the security guards a clear view of her license plate.

Then, tires smoking, she jammed down the gas pedal and ran the red light. Behind her horns blared, pedestrians screamed, and sirens wailed.

Whisking off the ski mask, Kiku powered down the tinted windows and yanked the black cord. She heard the faint clang of metal as the fake license plate ripped free from the bumper.

Up ahead, she saw Jimmy turn right, and the Russians followed, clueless about the commotion in their wake. Kiku slowed down and took the turn. All around the block, sirens clicked on as the security guards' call for help was received by every police officer in Hong Kong.

Kiku pressed a switch on the dash for the pink and purple LED running lights underneath her Escalade. She turned the radio on, cranked up the volume, and began bouncing in her seat along with the pop tune. Flashing red and blue lights filled her rearview mirror as several cruisers raced onto the road behind her. When the first cruiser rocketed up alongside her, Kiku slowed and gave the scowling policeman a puzzled, ditzy wave.

The policeman in the passenger seat saw the Russians' Escalade up ahead, pointed, and shouted something to the cop driving. The line of police cruisers blasted past Kiku and fell in behind the other Escalade. The police loudspeaker boomed as the officers ordered the occupants to pull over. Kiku watched as the Russians cut the wheel and raced down a side street with the police in hot pursuit.

After three blocks she caught up with Jimmy, who was still driving straight down the road. She moved alongside the cab and motioned for him to pull over.

Jimmy pulled up against the curb, and she double-parked beside him.

"Get in."

Jimmy scrambled out of the cab, yanked open the Escalade's passenger door, and jumped in. His awkward smile—caught between admiration and terror—reminded her of Alex's face after she'd pulled off some maneuver that even she had doubted could be successful.

"That was amazing," he said. "How'd you get the police to go after the Russians like that?"

Kiku shrugged as she pulled back out. "The police are not your enemy unless you treat them as such."

"Did you see how many cruisers went after them?" Jimmy turned around in his seat, watching the still-growing line of police cars rushing to join the chase.

"I did." Kiku resisted the urge to point out that she was the reason the police were chasing them in the first place. "The Russians will not be leaving Hong Kong for a long time. Did you remember to bring your passport?"

Jimmy nodded. "Where are we going?"

"Japan."

6

Kiku drove the rental car along the winding road, headed for the mountains, with Jimmy stretched out in the passenger seat, snoring loudly. Tired herself, she took another sip of tea and checked her speed, making sure to keep well below the limit.

Fumeiyo no ie was located just outside a small town about halfway between Uda and Mount Kunimi. Set well inland, the estate and town were isolated, and any outsiders would raise immediate suspicion. Kiku pulled her hair into a high ponytail and wrapped a scarf around her head. She'd bought a pair of oversize glasses that enlarged her eyes and made her look younger and less sophisticated.

She wasn't at all worried about pulling off her part in the ruse. It was Jimmy's acting abilities that concerned her. She'd been over their cover story a hundred times, but he struggled with even the simple details.

Checking her GPS, she pulled onto a tiny mountainous road that forced her to slow considerably. As the road slowly turned back north, she sat up straighter, knowing that Fumeiyo no ie would soon appear on the hill opposite them. When it did, she felt uneasy for the first time about the difficulty and significance of the tasks she had set for herself.

Is Takeo there?

She pulled over at a spot that overlooked both the lake and the estate, then grabbed the easel, folding wooden chair, and painting supplies from the trunk. Even with all that noise, Jimmy remained asleep. Kiku made a mental note not to rely on him in any capacity for stakeout or guard duty. Unless she was using him as bait again.

She carried her supplies to the crest of the hill and set up the easel and chair. For appearances' sake, she'd had one of the cashiers in the art store outside Tokyo start the painting for her by preparing the canvas and roughing out trees common to Yoshino District. Now Kiku settled in, opened her art basket, and removed the camera hidden beneath the tubes of paint. Using the easel as an improvised sniper's nest, she clicked away, analyzing as she went.

In addition to the two-story mansion, the estate contained two guest houses, a boat house, and a small caretaker's cottage. All of the buildings were constructed with traditional black-tile roofs and dark-wood trim. A somberness seemed to seep from the main building and infect everything around it. Even in the wide garden that sloped down to the lake, all the trees drooped like mourners at a funeral.

She had heard the stories, of course. The house and the whole property were cursed, along with everyone who entered. She did not know if Takeo was here, but she felt a tightness around her heart and a strange sense of unease, which led her to believe he was within those walls.

Her teeth ground together. The thought of Takeo even pondering taking his own life filled her with fury.

Her hand shook, and she shut her eyes. Instead of the image of her former lover, one of the memories that haunted her frequent nightmares came to mind. Her sister's body was curled up on the floor; the gun used to kill her had been left behind beside her. Kiku remembered reaching for the gun and the way the skin at her temple recoiled from the touch of the cold metal as she pressed it against her head. She was only a child and she was all alone in the world.

Alone in Hell. All she'd wanted was a way out. She pulled the trigger. She knew there was a bullet in the chamber. But the hammer just clicked. Everything should have worked just fine, but the gun didn't go off.

The little girl she had been just moments before would have credited God, His divine grace, for the miracle that had spared her life. But she wasn't that girl anymore. That girl had died with her sister, along with the last of the goodness inside Kiku.

This new girl believed she'd been spared for a different reason. *So that she could avenge her sister.*

Kiku's eyes blazed open, and she glared at the gloomy mansion. Her heart was filled with hate and devoid of pity. Her revenge would have to wait, and the pain of that realization ripped at her, but she didn't care if a thousand demons haunted the cursed mansion. If they were there, she would deal with them, too.

Satisfied with her photographs, she uploaded the folder to the Cloud, deleted the folder from the camera, and took five innocuous photos of the lake and trees. She hid the camera beneath the tubes of paint and picked up her sketching pencils.

It wasn't long before the sound of engines came rolling up the road. She glanced at the rental car, where Jimmy was still sleeping. Two motorcycles crested the hill. One rider drove straight to her; the other went over to the rental car and rapped his knuckles against the window. Jimmy sat bolt upright, rubbing his eyes.

The man closest to Kiku skidded to a stop, sending dust from the tires wafting over her. She faked a cough as the man hopped down from the bike.

He addressed her in Japanese, filtered through a thick Australian accent, asking what she was doing. Kenzo's new head of security, Ryder, had brought several squad mates with him, so Kenzo's security force was now a completely different animal from the centuries-old system that Shin Uchihara and his family had upheld—until Kiku killed Shin. The other man, who had dismounted and was speaking to Jimmy, was Japanese. Kiku didn't recognize him.

"Sorry, I don't speak Japanese," Kiku replied in her best New Jersey accent. "I'm just painting."

The ruggedly handsome man grinned at her flirtatiously. "You're a New Yorker?"

"Jersey, actually. Trenton. You're English?" Kiku poked the bear.

"Australian." The man glowered as he stomped over beside her and glanced at the canvas. He flipped open the lid of her art basket and jammed his hand inside. "If you're just painting" —he pulled the camera out—"then what's this for?"

"Hey!" Kiku leapt to her feet and leveled a trembling finger at him. "Leave my stuff alone!"

Jimmy went to open his door, but the man standing next to the car shoved it closed. As the Australian turned on the camera, he tipped his head toward Jimmy. "Who's he?"

"My cousin. Who do you think you are? Give me my camera back." Kiku let her lower lip puff out as she made a mental list of the Australian's equipment. Sig Sauer P365 sidearm, tactical radio with earpiece, ankle holster, no vest, tactical knife on belt.

"We're private security, miss, and I want to know why ..." His voice trailed off as he looked at the five pictures of the lake and two trees on her camera.

Kiku tried to look close to tears. "If you don't give me back my camera and leave us alone, I'm going to—"

"Hold on." The Australian held the camera out to her. "Don't be getting your knickers in a twist."

Kiku inspected the camera, making sure her hands trembled as she did. "This is public property. I checked."

"It is." The Australian motioned to his partner at the car. The man grabbed the doorframe and began asking Jimmy questions. "So you're an artist?"

"Oil. Landscapes specifically." Kiku pushed her glasses further up her nose. "My grandparents used to live in town."

The man chuckled and shook his head. "I didn't mean to scare you, but we needed to check why you were up here. You weren't planning on painting for long, were you?"

"Well, I just started." She pointed at the canvas. "It may take me a couple of days."

He clicked his tongue and made a show of looking at the sky. "I don't think that's gonna happen. See, it looks like rain."

"There isn't a cloud in the sky."

"You're not from around here, so let me tell you something about Japan and rain." Smirking, he pointed upward. "The sky can look as blue as can be one minute, and the next it's like a typhoon. I'd hate for you and your cousin to get stuck up on this hill in a rainstorm. It could be dangerous."

Kiku nodded rapidly. She'd already gotten enough intel to begin planning. There was no point in pushing it now. "I didn't even think about checking the weather."

He relaxed, satisfied that he had humbled her. "That's one thing you always have to do out here."

"Well, thank you. It's a good thing I took the photos to paint from." Kiku put her camera in her basket and picked it up. The man turned to look at his partner. The Japanese man gave a nod and rolled his eyes.

The Australian turned back to Kiku. "No problem. Enjoy Japan. *Issho ni nenai.*" He bowed, and both men laughed. Kiku packed up her easel, pretending not to understand what he'd said—that he wanted to go to bed with her.

It would be so easy to kill both men on the spot. The Australian even turned his back on her. But they were insignificant, and their deaths would gain her nothing but unwanted attention.

Having gathered up her supplies, she headed for the car and opened the trunk while the motorcycles disappeared over the hill. Jimmy started to open his door, but Kiku ordered him to stay inside. He muttered something and slammed it shut.

Kiku walked over to the driver's side and stared across through the windswept pines to Fumeiyo no ie. It pained her to know that Takeo could be so near, yet inaccessible. In so many ways, the two of them were similar. Takeo—a man in control of his emotions—hid his true feelings. And Kiku ... she sometimes wondered if she had any.

In Japan, they call them *onryō*, vengeful spirits that haunt and harm the living. They look like people, but they are cold and empty inside. Hollow, like a shadow.

And if anyone tried to stop her from getting to Takeo, they would meet the wrath of a living *onryō* head-on.

7

From Fumeiyo no ie, Kiku had Jimmy drive south to Kumano, a coastal town she much preferred to Osaka in the north, and she checked them into a hotel.

Kiku spent the afternoon analyzing the photos she had taken at the estate and calculating the best way to reach Takeo. There were a number of things in her favor, and among them was the age of the buildings on the property. Due to the historic nature of the mansion in particular, security cameras were difficult to install and even harder to conceal. And from her analysis so far, they appeared to be nonexistent on the exterior.

Kiku suspected this was due at least in part to pride. Here in the heart of the Nakumora stronghold, Kenzo no doubt felt secure, beyond the reach of his enemies.

Pride makes one foolish.

Using satellite photographs and topographical maps, Kiku laid out the best path through the mountain forests to make an assault on the main house. Unlike in Western homes, rooms in Japanese structures were not assigned single-use functions, but she was certain that she knew which room Takeo would be staying in.

She was fortunate that she had visited the house once before, when she was nineteen. Daichi was paying a last visit to an old man suffering greatly in the final stages of cancer and about to die. Daichi referred to it as a "necessary errand." Kiku had stayed in the hallway, but she could still remember well what she had heard. Daichi was describing the garden to the old man. It was winter, but he spoke of its green grass and budding trees, and though it was close to midnight, with his words he painted a picture of the sun rising above the hills and soft, golden shafts of light dancing over the pond.

The old man thanked Daichi and told him that he loved him. The gunshot made Kiku jump. She hadn't expected it, but she was much more surprised by the look of tranquility on Daichi's face when he came out of the room.

It was only later that she discovered that the old man was Daichi and Kenzo's father.

Takeo would be in that room now—the large bedroom on the second floor that overlooked the ancient garden and the lake. If he was in there, finding him would not be a problem. Reaching him might be. But the real challenge was that she had no idea how Takeo would take her news—or even what she would tell him. Would he believe that Kenzo had ordered the murder of his own grandson? Or would he think she was lying to cover up her failure? Though she had not failed to protect Alex, and in fact Takeo's son would cheerfully rise in a few hours to help his great-uncle Daichi harvest the first strawberries and sweet peas on the faraway farm, Takeo thought that his only son, whom he had never had the chance to meet, had been killed on her watch.

She wanted to tell Takeo that Alex was alive, that he was bright and quick and looked just like him, but that would lead Takeo straight to Daichi and probably ignite all-out war among the Yakuza.

So much history, so much bloodshed.

Kiku stood and began to pace. It was almost evening, and she wanted to get moving. But first she needed to know for certain that Takeo was in the house. Jimmy had gone into town to see what he could find out; Kiku doubted it would amount to much, but maybe he'd surprise her. Jimmy was a street kid, and Jiro said he had a way with people. He'd even kept Jiro alive a time or two. Still, this wasn't networking with the petty thugs and thieves of Hong Kong. This was in a whole different league, high above his pay grade.

She strolled into the bedroom and put on black stretch pants and a long-sleeved black turtleneck. For appearances, she slipped a pair of tan khakis over the stretch pants. She'd yet to see a policeman in the small town, but walking through the lobby of the inn looking like a ninja would be more than a simple fashion faux pas.

From beneath the bed, she pulled out a heavy suitcase and flipped it open. She settled on a Springfield XD .45 ACP. It had more stopping power and less recoil than the nine-millimeter. She decided to go without a silencer. With the buildings clustered together and the echo effect in the surrounding hills, a silencer would be ineffective; someone was bound to hear the noise anyway. All she needed for offensive equipment was a tactical knife with a waist sheath and another one that attached at the ankle—plus her hairpin.

She was about to shut the case when she changed her mind and grabbed a set of brass knuckles. They were lightweight, slipped easily into her pocket, and were extremely effective because men never seemed to expect them.

The night-vision goggles and camera detection equipment contributed the most weight to her gear, but she considered them indispensable. Even though she had spotted no cameras, she wasn't taking any chances.

8

Takeo Nakumora stared across the garden to the dark waters of the lake below. The overcast night and drizzle matched his mood. Life for Takeo had never held more than brief, momentary flashes of happiness ... but this was his darkest day.

His father had ordered him to go to Fumeiyo no ie, and Takeo knew what that signified. He doubted his father intended for him to kill himself. This banishment was most likely meant only as a corrective tool for a wayward son.

But Takeo was long past feeling the lash of his father's *muchi* across his shoulders. He'd never been wild or rebellious, but he'd spent a lifetime trying to distance himself from his father. Takeo had been born to rule the Yakuza; his father had forged him to become his own replacement, insisting he go to the best American business school and then giving him control of the Yakuza's US interests. Jiro, too, had been groomed to take a role in the family business, and had taken over the money matters.

But Takeo had never wanted any of it. The dark side of the organization ate away at his soul. His father considered his reluctance a weakness; he tolerated it only because of Takeo's mother. Itsumi had died when he was just two, yet Takeo had inherited his mother's heart, as evidenced by his empathy for people. Kenzo insisted that Takeo, as a man, had to harden that heart.

Takeo had turned the American side of the Yakuza into a legitimate business entity. He abandoned drugs and prostitution in favor of investments and acquisitions that made the likes of Warren Buffett sit up and take notice. But instead of pleasing his father, this made Kenzo furious. It was not success, but defiance! He saw past the hundreds of millions Takeo had made to what he had cost the family in power and control.

And now this. Takeo's greatest failure. The death of his firstborn son.

Takeo had always wondered what fatherhood would be like for him —but he never dreamt that he would handle the role so poorly.

He hadn't known he'd gotten his American girlfriend pregnant back in college. Takeo had only become aware of Alex's existence a few months ago. Kenzo went ballistic when he found out. Not only had Takeo produced an heir, but that vulnerable, young heir was out in the world alone. Kenzo insisted Takeo call for Kiku to handle the situation. Takeo was hesitant to do so, viewing it as a babysitting assignment that didn't call for the Yakuza's best assassin.

He was wrong. But he believed that Kiku had protected his son. Until Shin went after her.

Takeo walked to the table and poured another drink. Empty decanters lined the bar. He couldn't seem to drink enough to drive the shame away. He knew he never could. Some things can't be drowned.

He pounded the double shot and poured another.

Shin Uchihara. Takeo shook his head, still unable to believe that Shin would plot against him, let alone kill his boy.

But that was exactly what had happened. Takeo's head of security, the middle son of the Uchihara, the family that had guarded his for centuries, his friend since elementary school, had betrayed him. Takeo's ignorance and blindness—the heart of his mother—had cost him the life of his son. It had *almost* cost him the life of the only woman he'd ever loved as well. Kenzo would be pleased that life was now turning Takeo's heart to steel, first by heating it to a temperature it had never known in the arms of Kiku, then by stoking the flames with the pride of fatherhood, only to cruelly quench them with his young son's murder.

So here, Fumeiyo no ie, was where he deserved to be. The house of disgrace. It was aptly named, and it was where he belonged. He had hoped to see Kiku one last time. But part of him was glad that she would be spared from seeing him in this mournful state. What could he say to her anyway? There was no way to apologize.

Takeo's time to grieve and reflect was limited. His father expected him to move on, marry, and produce another heir. That was the furthest thing from Takeo's mind. He had failed so spectacularly, there was only one way to atone for his sins.

He had already had all of the papers drawn up; his father would take over his business holdings. He doubted his father would let Jiro take over the responsibility—he was still too naive—but Jiro was Kenzo's son, and he would see that Jiro was well cared for.

It was Kiku whom Takeo worried about. Would she mourn him? Or curse his weakness? He'd once hoped ...

His vision was blurring. If he didn't do this now, he'd fall asleep, and that would be an even greater dishonor. He found the thought somewhat amusing as he poured himself one last shot. He stumbled to the balcony and toasted his father with mock solemnity and a deep bow. The spring rain was cool and refreshing, and he held his face up to let it fall on his cheeks. He finished the shot and set the glass on the railing, where it wobbled for a second, half on and half off, before tumbling down and shattering on the stone path.

Immediately, footsteps sounded from opposite directions, from inside the house and from below.

"It's just a glass," Takeo barked.

Two guards stopped in a pool of light, shielded their eyes, and looked up at him.

"I'm fine. You can go."

The guard on the left started walking, but the other man stayed where he was, back straight, feet splayed for stability. Ryder, his father's new lap dog and head of security. Takeo detested the man.

Even drunk, Takeo knew he could kill the ex-soldier, but from the set of his jaw, Ryder thought otherwise. Takeo's left hand tightened on the railing. He'd love one last fight.

Ryder gave him a curt nod, turned on his heel, and marched off into the darkness. Takeo glared after him, but his anger and thirst for violence faded quickly, the darkness of the house pressing down on him once again with its full weight of grief and despair.

It was unbearable. But not for long. Tonight would be his last spent in sorrow. Tomorrow he would sign the rest of the papers.

In the evening, he would do what he'd come here to do.

9

Kiku slipped like a shadow among the trees up the hill toward the estate. As usual for this time of year, a light rain was falling, and fog swirled around the twisted tree trunks. The rain and condensation weren't an issue for her night-vision goggles—other than forcing her to occasionally wipe the lenses—but she had concerns about how moisture might affect the camera detection equipment.

Stopping at the base of a thick old pine, she scanned the grounds. She'd made her way along the edge of the lake, past the croaks of mating bullfrogs and the boathouse, and past the caretaker's cottage. She was close enough to the main house now to hear the patter of rain on the tile roof, different from the sound of it trickling through the trees. The first guest house sat directly in front of her, and the second was directly across from it. Both were dark and appeared empty. The width of the main building, covered with blooming white wisteria, spanned the distance between the two guest houses.

When she was satisfied that no one was close by, she flicked up her goggles and took out the camera detector. Technology had made great strides, but it still had its limitations, such as distance and whether it would work in the rain. The detector was rated up to fifty yards. Kiku would stick to forty-five, maximum, given the conditions.

She swept the side and back of the nearest guest house. It was clear of surveillance devices. She wiped down the lens and slipped the detector back into her waterproof backpack.

She flicked down her goggles and studied the main house. Several windows glowed with soft light. The area surrounding the house looked clear, though it was hard to see between the spaces of the two rows of weeping cherry trees lining the path to the courtyard and garden. But the lights from the house created a corridor of shadow among the trees that she could use to get up next to it. Or she could skim under the long line of wisteria to the second guest house and check it for cameras—

On the second floor, a balcony door opened. Kiku pressed herself against the guest house, disappearing into the shadow, and flipped up her goggles, blinking rapidly as her eyes adjusted to the dark. When the man came into focus, her breath caught in her throat.

Takeo Nakumora.

Like a magnet, she had felt his pull ever since she set foot in Japan, and now she was close enough to hear his voice. Close enough to call out to him ...

He peered out into the rain. His shoulders were pulled back and he stood tall, but as he grabbed the railing, she thought she saw him sway. A glass fell from the railing and shattered on the walkway. Takeo barked that it was only a glass. It took all her self-control not to sprint across the grounds calling his name and waving her hands like a lovesick fool.

Within one second, the thick wooden door opened and two men ran out. The tall, stocky man asked Takeo if everything was all right. Kiku recognized Ryder, Kenzo's head of security. Takeo answered curtly in Japanese that he was fine and turned to someone inside and told them they could go. The first man started walking. Ryder hesitated, gave a nod, then turned on his heel and marched off into the darkness.

Kiku looked back up at Takeo. She needed to go to him. She needed to be at his side. Instead, she ground her teeth and pulled the camera detection unit out of her backpack. The house was at the outer edge of its range capabilities, but she had to be methodical.

She pounded her feelings into submission as she scanned the house. *Weakness gets you killed*, she reminded herself as she approached the side of the house. Ryder was on the grounds and there would be at least one other guard outside, plus probably two or three men inside.

The sensor did not go off until she reached Takeo's room. Sticking her elbow against her hip to steady her hand, she aimed at the open balcony doors. The detector softly pinged twice, and she zeroed in on both cameras. One was mounted under the roof, just to the right of the balcony, giving it a clear view of the balcony and anyone on it. The other was somewhere inside the room, but before she could get its precise location, Takeo went back inside and shut the door, blocking the signal.

Kiku's head jerked up. Just like that he was gone, and the overwhelming desire to rush to his side swept over her again. Footsteps sounded on the grass behind her, and she spun around.

Unzipping his fly, a man with a buzz cut and fully outfitted in tactical gear stepped around the corner of the building, mere feet from where Kiku crouched. At the sight of her, his eyes went wide, his mouth opened, and his hand moved from his pants to his gun, his fingers closing around the grip. But he was too late. Kiku's hairpin had already plunged through his eye and into his brain.

Kiku let the body slide against hers as it crumpled to the ground to soften the sound. Staring down at the corpse, she swore under her breath. She was not ready to extricate Takeo tonight, but now that she'd killed the guard, she had no choice. As soon as the guard was unaccounted for, Ryder would lock down the whole estate. And then what? Would they scramble to move Takeo to another location?

It wasn't a matter of simply hiding the body. If the guard did not turn up, the reaction to his disappearance would be the same as if she left him there riddled with bullets.

Cursing this unexpected development, she locked on an idea. It was a long shot, but it might work. She scanned the main house again through the goggles. A guard was smoking an e-cigarette at the far corner of the verandah, the chamber of the device glowing white with each puff. Kiku grabbed the guard she'd killed, lifting him slightly to get a feeling for how much he weighed. He was Japanese, slender and short, maybe a hundred and forty pounds. That was a lot for her to lug.

Kiku slipped her arms beneath him and through his armpits before wrapping her hands around his chest. Staying low, using her powerful legs, she walked backwards, dragging the body around the corner, and laid him on his back. She had avoided the porch and walkway, because they were so close to the house, but she now studied them closely. There was a gap beneath the porch—a small one, but she thought she'd be able to fit.

She slid her backpack underneath the porch, then returned to the body. She grasped the end of her hairpin and pushed it toward the man's chin, then turned it in a circle as if stirring a pot until she was satisfied with the size of the gaping hole in the man's eye socket. She quickly tucked the hairpin back in her hair, flicked her goggles down, and peered around the corner. The guard was still there, puffing away, but his attention was on the front of the house.

Kiku bent down and pressed the mic on the dead man's radio. After waiting a second, she did it again, and peeked around the corner.

The guard was now looking her way, and his voice came over the radio. "Reo?" The accent was Australian. Kiku held her breath. "Is that you, mate?" the voice asked.

Kiku clicked the mic once more and peered around the corner again. The guard was heading her way. She slid her goggles under the porch, unholstered Reo's gun, and pulled his body up against her. She dragged him backward until she reached the edge of the house.

The guard was slowly approaching. He reached the far corner of the guest house and called into his radio again. "Reo?"

"Cut the chatter." Ryder's voice boomed through the dead man's radio. The approaching guard stopped and drew his gun.

Kiku's arms shook from the strain of holding up Reo's body. She heard the guard's footsteps coming closer.

"Reo?" the guard whispered.

Kiku thrust her arm around the corner, pointing Reo's gun toward the approaching guard.

Three gunshots rang out as the guard opened fire.

Kiku shoved Reo's gun back in his holster and pushed his body forward. She dropped to the ground and scrambled beneath the porch. Praying that the ringing in the guard's ears from the gunshots would hide any sounds she made, she pressed herself against the dirt and wedged her body as far under the porch as it would go.

Shouting came from all over, and the area was flooded with light. The guard moved closer to the body and swore. "Oh, no … no, no, no!" Now that he was closer, Kiku recognized his voice. It was the man who had confronted her this afternoon.

"Nelson! Status!" Ryder snapped over the radio.

The guard—Nelson—couldn't seem to form words. "Ah …"

"Status!" Ryder bellowed. "How many?"

Nelson cleared his throat. A moment later, heavy footsteps rang off the wooden planks as someone strode across the porch.

"What the hell is wrong with you?" Ryder yelled, now standing directly above Kiku. A flashlight snapped on, illuminating the body. "Looks like they shot Reo through the eye. Sniper?"

"Ah … Ryder …" Nelson stammered.

Ryder marched off the porch and stopped in front of Nelson, next to Reo's body. "I heard three shots. How many did you fire?"

"I didn't know—"

A fist slammed into flesh.

Nelson crashed to the ground, holding his cheek. His head was now level with Kiku's. Fortunately, he was looking up at Ryder, pleading, "It wasn't my fault!" But even Nelson seemed to be struggling to believe that there could be any other explanation.

Another set of boots thundered across the porch, and a voice said, "Hold off, boss."

"Get your hands off me, Zane, or I'll put a bullet in your head," Ryder snapped. "Nelson killed Reo."

"He pointed his gun at me!" Nelson said.

"I think he was pointing something else at you," Zane said with a laugh. "Look at Reo's pants. He was taking a leak."

"I'm telling you. He—"

Ryder punched Nelson in the face again. "Shut up. Let me think."

"Look at the poor bloke's face." Zane chuckled. "You shot him right in the eye."

"I said knock it off." Ryder holstered his gun and swore. "Take the body down to the boathouse. Wrap it up, but don't get rid of it."

"Why don't we just pitch it?" Zane asked.

"Because I don't know if Reo was Kenzo's freaking favorite nephew or something." Ryder called Nelson a slew of expletives before promising to kill Nelson and everyone he loved if Kenzo held him responsible for this.

"What if you don't tell him?" Zane asked.

"Are you really that stupid?" Ryder said. "I just got off the phone with him, too, and he's *already* fuming. Just dump the body and come up to the main house. On top of everything, we're gonna have company tomorrow night. Now move."

Zane and Nelson grumbled as they picked up Reo's body and carried it away. Ryder remained standing almost directly above Kiku, forcing her to take short, silent breaths. For more than five minutes, he stood rooted to the spot, then finally he walked into the house.

Kiku waited an additional ten minutes before sliding out from beneath the porch. She pulled on the goggles and swept the yard. One guard was making his rounds. From the way he puffed on the e-cigarette, she guessed it was Nelson doing penance.

She cast one last glance at the second-floor bedroom, fighting the yearning to rescue Takeo right now. Her desire was a mind-altering drug; she fantasized about how easily she could take on all the guards. But she denied her heart's plea. Now wasn't the time.

Tomorrow.

Tomorrow she would save Takeo.

10

Kiku paced the floor of the hotel room, tapping her hairpin against the palm of her hand. Takeo was on the estate, but it was heavily guarded, and there was a security camera right inside his room. Nothing more or less than she'd expected. What bothered Kiku was what Ryder had said. *What "company" are they expecting?*

A key jingled as someone noisily attempted to open the door. Kiku drew her gun, crouched low, and moved against the wall. Humming a tune she couldn't place, Jimmy walked in and shut the door. Sliding a chair across the door, he muttered, "Stupid Kiku."

"Repeat that, please."

Jimmy shrieked and nearly tripped over his feet as he stumbled backward. Bashing his hip into a table, he swore as he kept a vase with a spray of orchids from crashing to the floor. "I didn't mean you were stupid. I—the chain!" He blurted out the words like they were an answer on a game show. "I mean you were stupid for not fastening the chain."

Kiku's eyes narrowed.

"Not *stupid* stupid ... I meant ... Will you stop pointing the gun at me?"

She holstered the gun. "How would you get into the room if I chained the door?"

"I couldn't—but that's the whole point of the chain." He smiled sheepishly and kept his hands up. "Neither could someone else."

"If the people who are looking for me discovered we are in this hotel room, that chain would not stop them or even slow them down." She glanced at the clock. It was almost two in the morning. "Where have you been?"

"I ran into this guy at the bar." Jimmy's eyes lit up. "He was playin' pachinko, but he stunk. We ran five-ten-twenty and—"

"Ran what?"

"Five-ten-twenty. We bet." Jimmy rubbed his hip again. "We started at five bucks and I got him up to twenty. Then he said a few of the local guys played five-card. So ... I got in the game."

"Does this story have a point?"

"I'm getting to it." Jimmy frowned, turned, and opened the little refrigerator. He opened a soda and drank half the can before continuing. "I found out a ton." His chest rose like he was about to belch, but a slight shake of Kiku's head cut him off. He looked like he was swallowing down pills as he turned his head and cleared his throat.

"Some Australian guys came into town. Two of them were in the place this afternoon, with a Japanese guy named Reo. He used to live here before he moved to Tokyo. Guy sounds like a real hard-ass. All the guys in town are afraid of him."

"You can tell them to stop worrying." Kiku crossed her arms. "We met, and we did not see eye to eye."

Jimmy looked nervously around the room and jerked his thumb toward the bathroom door. "Is there a body in the bathtub?"

"No. Reo is dead, but I left him where I found him. Continue your story."

Jimmy blinked rapidly, trying to process. "Okay ..." He finished off the can, turned back toward the refrigerator, and opened another one. "Before they came to the bar, they had gone to Usagi's."

Kiku was familiar with Usagi and her brothel, about twenty miles away in Katsuura. "Are you certain?"

Jimmy took a long sip. "One guy was there. Sorry, I've been eating peanuts all night." He wiped the back of his mouth with his sleeve. "And I didn't drink, so I could stay sharp to ask questions."

"How much did you lose?"

Jimmy frowned. "It turned out I was paying more attention to the questions than the game."

Kiku raised an eyebrow.

"About five hundred." He rubbed the back of his neck with one hand. "Is there any way you could count that as ... I don't know, a business expense or something?"

Kiku frowned. "Is that all the information you collected?"

Jimmy shook his head. "There's someone staying at Fumeiyo no ie. The guy didn't know who, but that's who the prostitutes are for, this bigwig who's staying there."

Kiku knew Takeo would never hire a prostitute. In cleaning up the American Yakuza, he had banned the practice. Then again ... *That was before I tossed a grenade into his life by letting him believe his son is dead.* Takeo's world had changed; perhaps his worldview had as well. She pushed her feelings for Takeo aside. This was an opportunity she needed to take advantage of.

"You did well," she said. She walked over to the table and picked up her jacket. "Do not wait up. We will have a hard day tomorrow and a longer night. Get some sleep. You can stay here tonight."

"Where are you going? Do you want me to come along?"

Kiku resisted sarcastically cutting down Jimmy's offer of help. It actually felt sincere. "No, thank you."

She stopped in the doorway, an impish smirk crossing her lips. "Be sure to fasten the chain so you can sleep soundly. When I come back, I will let myself in."

11

The burly man uncrossed his thick, tattoo-covered arms and held the door open as Kiku strolled into Usagi's brothel. Her casual posture and deadpan expression hid her revulsion. For her, it was as if she'd just entered Hell.

As a child, a life of forced sex with strange men had nearly been her fate, and her sister's—and the scars of that fact were both deep and easily reopened. Limited prostitution may have been legal in Japan, but Kiku abhorred it, and she despised any man who took part in it even more. She was well aware that some women claimed to have entered that life freely, but she had seen too many without a choice in the matter. Regardless of how they first became ensnared in that trap, most never escaped.

The town had seemed sleepy when she pulled in, and because of the hour, she half expected the house to be empty, but in the recesses of the large outer room, clusters of girls talked, like ghosts hovering at the edge of darkness, ready to vanish back into the shadows. The decor was a mixture of East and West—the low tables and reed mats were Japanese, while the plush leather armchairs were fashioned for the beefy hindquarters of tourists. The dozen or so women ignored Kiku. All were Japanese or Eurasian, and dressed in chiffons and silks, as if they'd been invited to a garden party at three in the morning.

At the sound of heels coming down the hallway, the women straightened up, went quiet, and smoothed their dresses. Kiku folded her hands in front of her and nodded when Usagi pushed open the screen. Usagi noticed her immediately and smiled.

"It has been far too long, Kiku. Please, join me."

Usagi was only a few years older than Kiku, but she looked significantly older. Her makeup was flawless, as always, but there was a lot of it, and it couldn't hide her sharply protruding collarbones or the lines around her neck. Running a brothel wasn't only brutal for the girls—for an owner, and a woman, who actually cared, there was also a price to pay.

Usagi was a unique woman. She and her younger sister, Shinju, had risen quickly in the Golden Blossom, as the brothel had been named back then. Soon the charming sisters maneuvered the old owner out and took over, providing the Yakuza with a generous cut. But life in the underworld was a dangerous gamble, and Usagi's little sister was collateral damage. A shamed father arrived one day and murdered his daughter with acid on the very spot where Kiku now stood. Shinju was disfigured in her attempt to protect the girl. Usagi blamed herself for her sister's fate and had her smuggled off in hopes of a better life. She had not seen Shinju since.

Kiku bowed her head slightly and fell into step beside Usagi as they moved down the hallway, grateful she did not have to venture farther into the brothel. Usagi opened the second door on the left, which led into a spacious office.

"May I offer you something to drink?" Usagi asked. "I just put on some tea."

"No, thank you." Kiku was sure the cups would have been thoroughly cleaned and the tea beautifully prepared, but it turned her stomach to think of even putting her lips to a vessel that had been touched by the revolting men who frequented this place.

Usagi took a seat at a small table in the corner and motioned to the chair beside her. Her smile fluttered briefly but rose again. "I know I sound childish," she said, "but I am disappointed. In the past, whenever you visited, you always brought a most thoughtful gift."

"My apologies." Kiku gave a slight bow. She did have a present for

Usagi, but giving it now would make her gesture appear to be a bribe, which would sully the gift. "I am under a time constraint."

"The world has sped up." Usagi picked up a delicate teacup and sipped. "I don't care for it." The blanket statement seemed to cast a wide net over life in general.

"An Australian man stopped by yesterday?" Kiku asked.

Usagi's teacup stopped halfway back to the table. The crow's-feet around her eyes pinched together. "Two of them. A solicitation on behalf of the Nakumoras."

The strain in Usagi's voice betrayed her fear. In their world, one had to make many assumptions; there were no uniforms or identification papers to confirm whose side someone was really on. If Usagi had been duped into completing a false request for Kenzo, the punishment would be quite severe.

"Rest easy, Usagi. Ryder speaks for the Nakumoras."

Usagi smiled, but her teacup rattled as she set it down.

"May I know what Ryder wanted?" Kiku asked this as delicately as possible, using an old Japanese expression to seem more sympathetic.

"Pardon my confusion." Usagi folded her hands and placed them in her lap. "But why is there a need for you to ask me what Kenzo desires?"

Kiku's heart sped up. She felt like she was walking across a frozen lake and the ice had just cracked. "Sometimes father and son do not communicate properly. Kenzo seems to be preparing a party for his son, but Takeo is not currently in the mood for festivities."

Usagi's head tilted slightly. "I do not mean to pry, but I heard a rumor that Takeo was in mourning, so I was surprised ... But not all men deal with loss in the same way. Please convey my condolences."

Kiku nodded, hoping that Usagi would believe grief was the reason for the communication disconnect and not realize the truth: that Kiku had gone rogue. "Thank you."

Usagi's lips pressed together. She reached for her tea but didn't lift the cup. "But if Kenzo wants to throw his son a party, who am I to argue? It's just ... a unique request." She sipped her tea. "And the fact that Kenzo's new man is such a pig does not help. Ryder wants me to provide ten girls, but he rejected almost all of them."

"Why?"

"He said they were homely. You know my girls and what a lie that is. They're all stunning. But now what can I do? It's too late to get anyone from Tokyo. I called in a favor and three girls are coming in the morning from Osaka, but they won't be enough."

"Was there anything unique about Ryder's request?"

"I am to provide ten women, but they will require the services of only one. And once the girl is finished, they want her to immediately place the used condom in this." Usagi rose, strolled over to her desk, and picked up what looked like a small silver thermos. "Then they are to give it to Ryder." She walked back to her chair and set the silver thermos on the table.

Kiku ground her teeth. "There is a way to solve your dilemma. It is a rather old-fashioned solution."

Usagi's eyebrows rose.

"Geisha. The makeup, kimono, and hair will cover any perceived flaws. Besides, Kenzo will more than approve of the idea."

Usagi bowed. "Once again, I'm indebted to you." Her smile widened. "That will work out quite nicely."

"I have an additional request." Kiku tried her best to sound casual. "I wish to surprise Takeo. I will arrive tomorrow afternoon and dress with the nine women."

Usagi nodded stiffly. "That is another unusual request."

Kiku smiled. "I would consider it a favor."

Usagi's eyes hardened, and she set the teacup down. "The other half of the rumor that I heard ... I didn't want to believe it. I was told it was you who had been protecting Takeo's son."

"It *was* me. That is correct."

Usagi crossed her arms. "You are up to something, Kiku. I may not know what it is, but I have been around too long not to realize something is going on. And not just with you."

"It is complicated." Kiku's heart pounded. She needed Usagi, and the brothel madam owed her. But could she be counted on? Kiku had never done well with trusting anyone. "It would be best if you did not know everything."

"Yet you come here?"

Kiku exhaled. "I have no choice. The only protection from retribution I can give you is deniability."

Usagi eyed her for several moments before she slowly shook her head. "Who am I betraying? Kenzo? Takeo?" She rolled her eyes and held up a hand. "Don't tell me. What do you need?"

"I need to go with your girls into Fumeiyo no ie tomorrow night. That is all. If I am discovered, play ignorant. If you want, hire ten girls and I will tie one up to make it look good."

"Why don't you just do that and leave me out of it?" Usagi set her elbow on the table and laid her head in her hand.

"Because I know you. You will accompany the girls to the house, and you would recognize me."

Usagi shook her head. "Come back tomorrow. Two o'clock. Use the back door. It takes forever to do the makeup and hair for a geisha."

Kiku took out a manila envelope and slid it across the table.

"I don't want your money, Kiku." Usagi's hand landed flat on the envelope, pinning it to the table. "I'll take it, but you don't need to give it. I can never repay you."

"It is not money and I did not help your sister for you. I helped Shinju because it was Shinju." Kiku stood up and bowed. "Please accept this gift and forgive me for lying earlier when I said I did not have one for you."

Usagi's hand shook as she opened the envelope. Several pictures of a woman tumbled out. Her face was badly disfigured, but she was smiling broadly.

"She is on a little island off Honduras called Utila. She opened a dive shop."

Usagi clutched the pictures and didn't look up. Her tears landed on the tablecloth, wetting the fabric.

"You should go see her someday." Kiku turned and walked to the door.

As she left the brothel and stepped out into the night, her head throbbed. She needed sleep but knew she wouldn't get any. She'd underestimated Kenzo's desire to continue the Nakumora dynasty. The man was ruthless. He had no intention of letting Takeo produce a suitable heir on his own terms; Kenzo was going to engineer one.

12

Kiku resisted the urge to touch her makeup-covered cheek. Her elaborate wig, decorated with birds and butterflies, was so heavy it was inadvisable to move her head anyway. Sitting in the chair beside her was Ami, a twenty-something-year-old who chatted on excitedly as if she was about to go to a prom instead of selling her body. Kiku could not help liking Ami. She was lovely, bright, and charming. Kiku wondered why Ami had such limited options that she would resort to this line of work. Or was it her own self-limiting beliefs that had led her here?

The two women applying the makeup stood back, grinning triumphantly. Ami got down from the chair and looked into the mirror. "What do you think, Mika?"

Kiku smiled. The real Mika had come into town two hours ago and was now downstairs tied up beneath the kitchen floor with the sweet potatoes, a tatami covering the hatch. Kiku had taken her name, just as she had taken her place. "You look spectacular."

Ami clapped her hands together. "We both do! He'll *definitely* pick one of us."

Kiku nodded. She had no doubt that Takeo would select her.

From somewhere down the hallway, a little bell rang, and like sheep to the slaughter, all the girls filed out and lined up. Usagi was waiting for them, with Ryder and Zane by her side. Zane grabbed his crotch as he muttered something to Ryder and laughed. Kiku could easily imagine the theme. And judging by the way both men were leering, Kiku's geisha plan was being well-received.

Ryder crossed his thick arms and nodded. His eyes traveled lustfully down the row of women, and Kiku silently swore at having missed an opportunity she only now recognized—asking Usagi to let the nine unselected girls ply their services with the guards. If Kiku needed to fight her way out, she would much prefer to fight a man with weak knees and tired arms from sexual exertion. Her pity for the girls had blinded her to the possibility.

And weakness gets you killed.

Usagi stepped forward and strolled down the line inspecting the girls, occasionally straightening a piece of fabric or whispering some instruction. When she reached Kiku, she said nothing. Their eyes locked briefly, and Kiku wished she had a moment to tell Usagi her thoughts.

Usagi walked back to Ryder and said something that made the Australian grin broadly. He gave an awkward bow, but even that had a slight mocking edge.

Usagi turned back to the girls. "I have explained everything to each of you individually." She held up an antique box that matched their period dresses; Kiku knew it contained the condoms and the silver cylinder. "If you are chosen, then once you are done, you will bring this directly to Ryder."

At the mention of his name, Ryder flexed his forearms, sending his dagger tattoos dancing, and tipped his chin up.

"There has been one change to the schedule," Usagi continued. "I am extending our special thanks to all of the gentlemen at Fumeiyo no ie. If you are not selected, you and the other girls will entertain Ryder and his men."

Kiku gave Usagi a small bow of acknowledgment. Usagi had given her the edge Kiku had failed to ask for. And Kiku had a feeling that she was going to need all the help she could get.

"I will see you when you get back," Usagi said. The words caused a slight ripple down the row of girls. Normally, any girls going off-site would be accompanied by Usagi and her guards, for their protection. "Ryder has given me his personal guarantee for your safety."

A girl next to Kiku muttered something. Kiku couldn't make out the words, but from the skeptical shift of everyone's expression, she guessed they all knew from experience that promises regarding men's behavior went out the window once the blinds came down. Prostitution was a dangerous profession, after all. The men who frequented prostitutes were questionable to begin with, and when you added in alcohol, drugs, and a disregard for women, the chances for violence escalated.

Usagi turned back to Ryder and whispered something else. Ryder shook his head. The vein in his left temple stood out. Usagi didn't back down. She whispered something else, and he nodded.

She turned back to the girls. "In appreciation for this change in protocol, everyone will receive an additional five hundred."

Zane leaned close to Ryder and Kiku clearly heard him say, "Don't worry about it, mate. It's not your money, and I'll make sure they earn it." He chuckled as he ogled the line of girls like they were steaks on a barbie.

Kiku had a sudden longing for her hairpin so that she could give Zane and Ryder the Reo eye treatment. But she took a deep breath and quelled the thought—regretfully.

Usagi started toward the doors, and the line of girls began to follow. But Ryder held up his hand and nodded to Zane. Zane's leer widened as he hurried toward the first girl and started patting her down. With the layers of fabric she wore, Kiku doubted he would have been able to feel a gun even if she had been foolish enough to bring one.

"Get on the bus," Zane ordered before moving to the next girl. By the time he reached Kiku, the novelty of feeling up the line of women must have worn off, as Zane took no more than a few seconds to roughly check her. She hoped his soldiering skills were as hurried and sloppy.

Once all of the girls were on the bus, Zane boarded and sat behind the driver. The bumpy fifty-minute ride went quickly and was uneventful. Most of the girls were quiet, but Ami, three rows ahead of Kiku, chatted away with the girl next to her as if there was nothing degrading about what they were about to do. Kiku didn't sit in judgement, as she lived in a glass house. She pondered whether or not it was self-preserving distraction behavior she was observing. Denial, maybe?

Ryder had followed them in a black pickup truck, and he pulled past the bus before it reached the estate.

"Wait here," Zane ordered as he got out to meet with Ryder. A minute later he stomped back onto the bus and whistled so loudly that many of the girls covered their ears. "Listen up. You will follow me inside. You go where I tell you to go and nowhere else. You are not to say anything to anyone. If you do ..." He squatted down in front of Ami and smiled coldly. "I didn't make any promises to anyone."

Ami's shoulders shook, and she nodded, even though he hadn't asked a question.

Zane stood and jerked his thumb toward the door. "Everyone out, and follow me." He pounded his fist into the arched ceiling of the bus as he walked down the aisle and jumped out.

Kiku and the other girls followed Zane into the main house and lined up, their geisha attire fitting in beautifully with the ornate décor of the centuries-old home. Two other men were already waiting inside. Kiku recognized them both: the Japanese man who had questioned Jimmy during their painting ruse, and Nelson from last night. She noted with pleasure the bruising along Nelson's jaw. Zane motioned to them, and they strutted forward and searched the girls again—far more thoroughly this time. Dresses were hoisted up, fifty-yard sashes were unwound, and each girl was examined.

"Too bad I didn't bring rubber gloves," Nelson cackled as he ran his hands up Ami's legs. She stared up at the ceiling, her eyes tightly closed, wincing.

The Japanese guard moved in front of Kiku. As he ran his hands across her arms, their eyes met briefly, but the man looked away.

Did he recognize me?

He was far less invasive than the others, and when he finished his search, he moved over to stand with Zane and Nelson. Zane spoke to Ryder on his wireless headset radio and told him they were ready.

Ryder strolled into the room and said, "All of you will accompany me into the main hall. Do not speak. Do not look directly at anyone. If you are chosen, you will come with me. Is that clear?"

They all nodded.

Nelson and the Japanese guard held the doors open, and the girls filed into the next room, where all the furniture had been pushed against the walls. Ryder strode across the room, opened another door, and stepped out. The silence grew into an oppressive presence as the girls waited.

The far door slid open once more, but the tall man who stepped through wasn't Ryder—it was Takeo Nakumora. His normal polished business look was gone. His crisp white shirt was opened three buttons down, and his suit pants appeared slept in—though judging by his wild eyes and pale complexion, Kiku couldn't guess the last time he had actually slept.

He looked down the row of women before turning to glare at Ryder, who had stepped in behind him. The sudden move made Takeo sway, but he quickly righted himself.

Ryder held his hand out toward the women. "They are a gift. Take your pick."

"If this is your idea ..." Takeo shoved Ryder so hard the Australian stumbled backward and had to grab a column to keep from falling down.

Kiku had to give the ex-soldier credit: Ryder's hand moved only slightly toward his pistol. If he had grabbed the weapon, Takeo would have called for his head.

But no one would have obeyed his order.

Nelson, Zane, and the Japanese guard's hands were resting on their firearms, but Kiku could see that their focus was on Takeo, not Ryder. Their allegiance to the Australian was clear. But perhaps not to Takeo—not in his current state.

Takeo turned to glare at the row of women. "Out!" he roared. "All of you! Get—" And then his eyes found Kiku. He froze, his lips twisted into something between a snarl and a puzzled smile.

Kiku held her breath and stared at the floor.

Blinking, Takeo stalked forward. He stopped seven feet away from her like he'd run into some invisible barrier and wiped his eyes with the back of his hand. He shook his head and stared again.

"They are a gift from your *father*," Ryder said, walking up beside Takeo—giving him a wide berth this time. "You can have them all if you want."

Takeo didn't look at the other women. His gaze was focused solely on Kiku. "Her," he said. "I want her."

13

Ryder grabbed Kiku by the arm to lead her away. "Looks like you're the lucky winner."

He took her up to the second floor and down the hallway to Takeo's door. But instead of opening it, Ryder opened the door directly across the hall. Inside sat a bored-looking middle-aged Japanese woman dressed in surgical scrubs and gazing at a laptop. On the table beside her was the antique box Usagi had shown the girls earlier.

"Explain it to her," Ryder said.

"There's nothing to it." The woman opened the antique box, lifted out the silver cylinder, and gave Kiku instructions on precisely how to use it. Then she returned the cylinder to the antique box.

"That covers the scientific part," Ryder said. "Now let me tell how you're gonna sell it to this guy. Carry the box in with you and bring it into the bathroom. If he asks, say it's feminine products or makeup. Once you're done banging him, go into the bathroom and follow Dr. Spock's instructions. Then bring the box straight back here."

"What if he wants me to stay?" Kiku spoke in a higher-than-normal tone and added a little dippiness to disguise her real voice. "Most guys don't want me to leave afterwards."

Ryder scowled. He obviously hadn't thought of that. He looked at the doctor. "How long before you have to get the cylinder back?"

"The sooner, the better. I need to freeze it right away."

"What if I ask for something?" Kiku suggested. "Like champagne. It gives me an excuse to leave. Then I can give you the box, and when I come back, he's none the wiser."

"That's good." Ryder smiled. "I'll make sure we have some champagne waiting. Do you have any other questions?"

Kiku resisted the urge to point out that not only had she not asked him anything but it was she who had solved the flaw in his plan. "Nope. I got it. I'm good to go."

"Let's do this."

Ryder patted her rear as they left the room. Kiku didn't know what offended her more, the fact that he'd touched her there or that he'd done so in the way a coach would smack the buttocks of a football player.

She carried the antique box to Takeo's door, took a deep breath, and knocked.

"Enter," Takeo called out.

Kiku slid the door open.

The room was dark, the only light coming from a table lamp in the corner to her left. Takeo sat in a low-backed chair near the balcony, facing inward. He didn't rise; he didn't even move.

She shut the door, daintily walked to the center of the room, and waited.

Takeo looked like a dying man. His face was pale and his cheeks unshaven and gaunt. His head was slumped slightly forward, as if even holding it up was now an effort. His hair looked as though it hadn't been washed in days and it hung down, hiding his eyes.

Kiku scanned the room. The king-size bed was made up, probably because he had not slept in it, since the rest of the room resembled a frat house on Monday morning. Used glasses and empty liquor bottles littered the bar. Clothes were strewn on the floor, along with uneaten food beginning to form mold. Kiku was truly shocked. She alternated between trying to see Takeo's eyes and looking around the room for the camera she knew was there somewhere.

Takeo raised his head, and Kiku inhaled and resisted the impulse to step back. His eyes were the darkest she'd ever seen them. Shiny and glazed. If she didn't know him, she would have believed him to be quite unstable. She wasn't completely sure he recognized her.

Off to the side, in a small nook, was a table with a single chair matching the one Takeo currently occupied. And there it was—the small statue on the table, a delicate bronze of a Japanese maple, its old roots grasping a rock.

Kiku was very familiar with this statue and the camera inside it; she had purchased an identical unit herself once before. She hadn't expected it to be so obvious. Well, it was obvious only to *her*, but still, Ryder should have taken into account the fact that she had consulted for Shin, the previous head of security. Ryder was foolish to have chosen this camera for this use, as its feed was video only.

Takeo motioned toward the chair at that very table. Kiku cursed the wooden geisha platforms that required her to take small, shuffling steps over to it. She set the antique box down on the table—taking care to position it directly in front of the camera—then sat down demurely and waited.

Takeo stared at her. Did he recognize her? She assumed he had downstairs, but now his face showed no recognition.

She should simply reveal herself to him. But, as with most things in her life, simplicity was not the easy choice. Surely he blamed her, at least in part, for Alex's death. She had disobeyed his direct order by not taking his son to Chicago and his protection. He had no way of knowing that if she had done that, both she and the boy would have been killed. And she had feared he would not give her time to explain. He had accepted his father's lie, that Shin was behind everything and that he was working for the Russians, so he would see her not realizing that as yet another failure. She was his personal security, after all.

But there was one more reason that Kiku sat still, waiting for the broken man to address her first. A petty reason. A shameful one.

If he didn't know who she was ... she wanted to know how far he would go.

She knew it was not fair to test him now. Not like this, broken and dishonored. Truly this had to be his weakest moment. But still, he had invited a prostitute back to his room. Would he follow through?

Kiku waited.

Takeo waited, too, staring at her with those dark eyes, his chest slowly rising and falling. Finally, with great effort, he placed his hands on the arms of the chair and rose. He lurched forward unsteadily and stopped two feet from her chair. As he looked down at her, a myriad of emotions swept across his drunken face. He clamped his eyes shut, reached into his pocket, took out a thick wad of cash, and dropped it on the table.

Kiku stared at the money. She had thought Takeo was at his lowest. But if he was paying for sex ... that proved he could sink lower than she ever believed possible. To say she was disappointed would be a gross understatement.

"Wait here twenty minutes and then leave." Takeo's voice was soft but clear. He turned and shuffled back toward the window, where he leaned against the frame and stared out into the night.

Kiku rose.

Takeo rested his head against the glass, his breath fogging the pane.

She started walking over to him, but he feebly waved her away.

"No!" His voice hardened. "No!" he repeated in Japanese.

What is he doing? Why would he pay a prostitute yet have her just sit there for twenty ...

Kiku's eyes opened in understanding. Takeo wasn't paying for sex. He was covering for the girl. If he simply sent a prostitute away, she would be beaten. Takeo was watching out for her.

"It is me, Takeo. Kiku." She bowed low and straightened up tall.

Takeo turned slowly to look at her fully. His dark eyes widened, and his breath came in puffs. His lips pulled back in a grin that she'd only seen before in an asylum.

"Demon!" he shouted. His crazed smile widened, and he attacked.

Completely taken off guard, Kiku blocked his first punch, but the rage-fueled blow knocked her sideways.

His left hand grabbed her throat and yanked her up off her feet. His momentum carried him forward, and they crashed together to the floor.

Kiku managed to slip her left hand underneath his fingers, but she lacked the strength to break his grip. Still, it gave her enough of a gap to breathe.

"Yōkai!" Spit flew from Takeo's mouth, and his right hand now circled her throat, too. "You took her from me!"

Kiku struggled to speak—and she knew there was no reasoning with Takeo anyway. Not now. He was mad, and believed this struggle was in fact with a demon.

He was close to being correct.

She slammed her fist into the side of his face.

His head jerked to the side, but he shrugged the blow off.

She hit him three more times. His lower lip split open. He ignored it, gave her a bloody smile, and squeezed harder.

Kiku brought up her legs and scissored them around Takeo's neck. She jerked back, but he was so strong she couldn't pull him off.

"You took everything from me," he hissed between clenched teeth.

Even with Kiku's left hand grabbing his fingers, her air supply was slowly being closed off. Her legs burned, and in his wild, hate-filled state, there was no stopping Takeo.

Her right hand fumbled for her belt.

"You drove her away." Blood dripped from Takeo's lip, and his smile grew as he leaned forward, adding his weight to his strength.

From her belt, Kiku ripped loose the monkey fist—a steel ball, wrapped in the same fabric as her dress, dangling from a long, embroidered cord. A lethal weapon.

The muscles in Takeo's forearms bulged. "You took my love."

Takeo had never admitted his feelings to her before. In spite of the pain, his words touched Kiku deeply.

She brought the monkey fist down hard on the side of his head.

Takeo grunted and fell sideways, his body rolling off hers.

Kiku lay on her back for a moment, trying to get control of her breathing without coughing. It was not as simple as it sounded. Gasping, she rolled onto her side and stared at Takeo. His eyes were closed, but he was breathing.

She smacked his face, but he didn't even groan. She pulled up an eyelid and swore. She hadn't intended to knock him out. But there was a fine line between the force it took to get someone off you and the force it took to kill them, and at least she'd ended up in the middle of those extremes; he was merely unconscious, not dead.

Groaning, she struggled to her feet and used a tissue box to block the camera in the statue as she opened the antique box and removed the condom. She needed time for them to make their escape, and there was only one way to get it.

Turning back to Takeo, she rolled him onto his back and gazed at his face. Now that he was out cold, he looked like the Takeo she knew. Handsome. Strong. Kind.

She unfastened his belt.

"Forgive me, Takeo," she whispered.

14

Kiku knocked on the door across the hall. It slid open immediately. Smiling, she handed the antique box to Ryder, who gave the doctor a thumbs-up.

The doctor hurried over and removed the cylinder.

"You two were making so much noise, I thought I was going to have to check on you." Ryder gave a lecherous grin. "There's a ..." he started to say. "On the table ..." His voice trailed off again.

Kiku faked a puzzled expression. Even a man like Ryder must have realized how vile it was to ask someone if they could move the box blocking their video camera so they could watch you having sex.

"Did he want the champagne?" Ryder asked.

Kiku nodded, and he grabbed a bottle off the table and handed it to her.

"Do you have glasses?" she asked. She sounded like a Japanese native speaking crude but serviceable English.

Ryder rolled his eyes. "I'm not getting those fancy little stemmed ones. There's plenty of them in the bar." He glanced over his shoulder at the doctor. "Did she get it?"

The doctor nodded. "She did. Now please, I'm concentrating."

Ryder huffed and turned back to Kiku. "Give it a couple of minutes before you go back in. You want to make it look good."

She nodded, and Ryder's focus shifted to her throat. Kiku had adjusted her makeup to hide the bruising on her neck, but she'd been rushed. Luckily, without the stupid wig, her hair covered most of her neck, but she wondered if he would notice.

Ryder glanced away to check his watch. Relieved he wasn't the most observant man, Kiku decided to press her luck. "He wanted ..." She exhaled. "Mr. Nakumora also requested ..."

"Spit it out." Ryder crossed his arms. "What's he want now?"

Kiku stared at the floor. "He asked me to get some rope."

"What would he need rope for?" Ryder asked incredulously. Even the diligent doctor turned to hear Kiku's answer.

"He wants to ..." Blushing, Kiku crossed her arms in front of herself, one wrist resting over the other in a submissive posture.

"Oh ..." The doctor flushed crimson and turned back to the table. Ryder chuckled. "Well, well, well, Mr. High-and-Mighty has a bit of a naughty side." He reached for his radio and pressed the button. "Anybody got any rope?"

"How much?" a man's voice asked.

"Just a length of it. Do you have any?"

"Yeah, there's some in the Jeep."

"Then move like you're on fire and get it up here." Ryder clicked the radio off and pointed a finger at Kiku. "You wait right here."

A few minutes later, a knock sounded at the door. Ryder slid it open to reveal an out-of-breath man holding a coil of black rope.

Ryder leered at Kiku. "Will that do?"

Blushing and bowing, she took the rope, pretending to clumsily fumble with the champagne bottle.

Ryder leaned closer to Kiku and whispered, "I use sheets, myself. They're softer, but they get the job done."

She bowed again, and both Ryder and the man who'd brought the rope grinned.

Standing at Takeo's door, Kiku glanced over her shoulder and waited for Ryder to slide his door closed. She then hurried into Takeo's room, set the champagne bottle aside, and dropped the rope on the floor. Takeo was still unconscious. She couldn't take him out onto the balcony because of the camera there, so she headed to the window on the left, slid it open, and took off her wooden geisha sandals.

She picked up a small table and set it down against the window. It was the perfect height; the top came to just above the windowsill. She moved back to Takeo and tied the rope around him, fashioning a harness. She rolled him onto his stomach, pulled him to his knees and then into a standing position, and slid her shoulder under his hip. Using this fireman's carry, she brought him over to the table and laid him down so his feet were sticking out the window.

She uncoiled the rest of the rope and tossed it over one of the thick beams near the ceiling. Kiku grabbed the free end of the rope, which now ran directly above her head, over the beam, and down to Takeo and wrapped it around her hand. She turned her rear end to the table and squatted down, making sure the rope ran underneath her right foot so she could use her weight to slow Takeo's descent. She took hold of the rope with both hands and pulled it taut.

Finally, she planted her feet, pushed her back against the edge of the table, and started to stand. The table tilted, Takeo slid down and through the window, and the rope jerked with tension.

Hand over hand, Kiku slowly lowered him, using her foot to hold the weight as she switched her grip. This ancient technique for moving heavy weights made it easy to lower Takeo all the way to the ground.

When he was safely deposited behind some azalea bushes, Kiku pulled the rope over the beam, careful not to let it drop. One would think rope wouldn't make that much noise, but if the whole length fell, it would get quite loud. She put the end of the rope between her teeth, climbed out the window, and dropped silently to the ground.

After coiling the rope—she didn't waste time untying the makeshift harness, and she hadn't wanted to use quick-release knots—she hoisted Takeo back into a fireman's carry and, keeping to the shadows, headed for the boathouse. She prayed that Jimmy was in position—and that she would have the strength to get Takeo to the rendezvous.

When she reached the guest house on the left, she was tempted to take a break, but Takeo's weight was quickly taking a toll on her muscles and it was best to keep moving before her body gave out. She was in top shape and had healed from all her recent injuries, but lugging dead weight was brutal.

After pausing only long enough to scan the open area between her and the boathouse, listening intently all the while, she hurried directly to the boats moored at the end of the dock. There were three boats in total, and all of them looked capable of high speed. They were probably used for water-skiing and recreation on the lake. She selected the farthest one because of its placement and because it was in shadow. After laying Takeo in the boat as gently as she could, she hopped in after him.

She smiled when she saw the key in the ignition. She had remembered that Kenzo liked to have all of his vehicles ready to go. Another security risk that she was grateful Ryder had not noticed.

Boats are notoriously loud to start, but she had no choice. The last thing she wanted was to push off from the dock and have the engine not turn over. The time for stealth was over.

As if to punctuate the point, lights suddenly blazed on at the main house and an alarm sounded. Kiku turned the key. The engine roared to life, sputtered ... and died. She swore.

Men were shouting now, flashlights clicking on.

Kiku crouched low and tried again. The engine started up, only to die another wheezing death. She considered trying another boat, but that option was taken away when a bullet shattered the side windshield—an impressive shot at such a distance.

She turned the key one last time. This time the engine started and kept humming, with an occasional cough as if it had a bad cold.

The sound of many different-caliber guns filled the air, then just as quickly went silent. Ryder had finally gotten control of his men. She pictured his panicked face as he screamed *"Cease fire!"* into the microphone, terrified that Kenzo's heir would be killed.

She cast off the tow line, ran back to the control panel, and gingerly eased up on the throttle. The boat started forward slowly, and soon a large wake churned behind it. Hoping the creaky engine just needed to blow the dust off, Kiku floored it. The boat shook as the engine coughed and sputtered. She eased back on the throttle and the sputtering stopped.

But she still cursed herself. Kiku's fist came down hard on the dashboard. She should have prepped her escape route in advance, leaving a gun in this boat and disabling the others at the dock. Her feelings for Takeo had blinded her.

A glance behind her showed four men already racing to the remaining two boats. If their engines were in working order, they might overtake her before she even reached Jimmy.

Kiku ripped open the dashboard storage compartment, rifled through it, and found what she needed: a rusty fishing knife. She ran back to Takeo and cut the rope off him. She then sliced two of the docking buoys from the side of the boat and took them and the rope forward to the steering wheel. The lake was smooth and there was no wind, but without her guiding it, the boat was steadily veering toward shore. Steering with one hand, she tied both ends of the rope to the buoys.

The first boat was closing on her now. Its engine was gunning at full throttle, and with four armed men aboard, she didn't like her odds.

She coiled the rope, grabbed one end in each hand, and dropped the rest of the coil at her feet. Turning so she faced the oncoming boat, she began to swing the right buoy around her head. Faster and faster she whipped it around. Then she released it, sending it far to the right. The coil of rope started to play out, and she quickly heaved the other buoy to the left.

Behind her, the lead boat zoomed closer, until she could almost make out the men's faces in the light of their dashboard. Then the boat's engine whined and shrieked, and the boat jerked to one side, sending its passengers lurching forward. A gun fired and everyone on board began swearing and shouting.

Kiku's makeshift spike strip had caught in the boat's propeller. She allowed herself a little smile and gave the engine more gas. When it started sputtering again, she had to ease back.

The second pursuing boat swerved, narrowly missing the now-drifting first craft. Kiku cast a quick glance at the far shore. It was almost dark, and she saw no sign of Jimmy or his truck. He was supposed to flash his headlights, but he wasn't the sharpest knife in the drawer and may have forgotten.

Or he wasn't there.

The possibilities spun through her mind. Something had gone wrong and he'd been caught. Or he'd decided that kidnapping the heir to the Yakuza was above his pay grade.

Either way, if Jimmy didn't make it, Kiku might not either.

The second boat was closing in fast. Kiku dug into the storage compartment once more, throwing things aside until she found a flashlight. She shined it on the water ahead. They were almost at the narrowest part of the lake, a thin channel only a hundred feet wide. Swearing, she clicked the light off.

Headlights flashed just ahead on her right.

Kiku ducked low.

A truck's engine roared, and a huge splash erupted behind her boat.

Kiku looked over her shoulder just in time to see the pursuing boat plow right into the cable now stretched across the water. The boat's windshield was sliced clean through, and the men inside screamed as they hit the cable going forty miles an hour. The boat jerked to the side and smashed into the bank as the truck pulling the cable was yanked sideways and dragged twenty feet before it finally stopped, its bumper ripped off.

The lake was once again quiet and serene, except for the inconsistent chugs and burps of the motor on Kiku's boat.

15

Kiku turned the boat toward the bend, where a little boat ramp hid behind willows and lush bamboo. She had only a few minutes before Jimmy was supposed to meet her there. But this time when she eased the throttle back, the temperamental engine sputtered and died. She turned the key to restart it and was rewarded with only an electric clicking noise.

There was no paddle; the boat was empty except for her, Takeo, and a tarp-covered bundle in the rear. She'd just started toward the tarp to see what lay under it when a spotlight illuminated the boat, followed by flashing red-and-white police lights.

Kiku, temporarily blinded, seethed as she lifted both her hands above her head, waved, and put on a smile.

The town's police force must be flush with cash to have patrolmen on the water, she thought. But then she noticed the police officer tucking away a fishing pole and realized it was just a case of wrong place, wrong time.

As the police boat came closer, the officer stood up. He was an older man, and his mouth dropped open when he saw Kiku. She had almost forgotten that she was in geisha garb.

"Hi!" she said, and added a cheerful wave. "I'm so glad to see you. I was out with my boyfriend and we ran out of gas."

The policeman snapped on his flashlight, illuminating Takeo. Kiku was relieved that she had cut the harness free—and even more relieved when Takeo groaned and rolled onto his side.

"He's had a teensy-tiny too much to drink. It's his birthday, so I dressed up and—"

"Does he need medical attention?" The officer deftly steered his boat next to hers and throttled back the engine to idle.

"He's fine," Kiku said, trying to sound reassuring.

The boats bumped, and Kiku grabbed the windshield to steady herself. The policeman climbed over the side into Kiku's boat, pulled the two boats close, and lashed them together.

"He just needs to sleep it off," Kiku continued. "If you could give us a tow to the dock right over there, my cousin is picking us up. I called him."

The officer knelt down beside Takeo and nudged him.

"Sleep," Takeo mumbled. "Let me sleep."

Kiku chuckled, and the policeman joined in. The officer rose. "Youth is wasted on the young," he said. "He should have drunk less and paid more attention to you."

Kiku smiled at the compliment.

The cop turned, and his flashlight shone off the tarp at the back of the boat. He lifted up one corner with his foot—then swore and stumbled back, dropping his flashlight. As the flashlight rolled along the deck of the boat, its beam illuminated the ghastly face of Reo's corpse.

16

Jimmy ran down the dock, but stopped abruptly when he saw that the approaching boat was a police boat. For a moment he looked like he was going to run back to the truck, until he spotted Kiku steering. His eyes widened, and he ran forward once more, the wood bouncing under his weight, to grab hold of the side of the boat.

"Do not tie it off," Kiku warned.

"Why not—" Jimmy's mouth dropped open when he saw the police officer bound and gagged in the stern of the boat next to Takeo.

"Is he dead? Tell me you didn't kill a cop!"

"If I had killed him, why would I tie him up and gag him?" Kiku set the engine to idle.

Jimmy pointed at Takeo. "He's not dead either, is he?"

Kiku shook her head. "Stop talking and help me get him out of the boat." She wrapped an arm around Takeo's waist and hoisted him up.

Jimmy swung one leg over the side of the boat. "Keep the boat against the dock!" Kiku snapped.

Jimmy hopped back out. "You said you wanted me to help you," he grumbled.

Kiku dragged Takeo to the side of the boat. "I said help me get him out of the boat, not get into the boat and let us all drift out onto the water."

"Right."

As Jimmy grabbed hold of Takeo, he saw the blood on the front of his shirt. "Did you shoot him?"

"No." Kiku scowled.

She picked up Takeo's legs while Jimmy grabbed him under the shoulders, and together they lifted him out of the boat, Takeo's head flopping.

"What are you going to do with him?" Jimmy asked, nodding toward the old cop. "Are you going to kill him?"

"The only person I am thinking about killing is *you*." Kiku ran back to the steering wheel and put the boat in a low-speed reverse. She held up a calming hand toward the policeman, who was shaking his head frantically. "I am going to push the boat back out onto the lake. Someone will find you in the morning. Understand?"

The cop stopped struggling and nodded. Kiku hopped onto the dock and gave the boat a hard shove. With the motor on low, the boat slowly disappeared into the darkness of the lake.

"Help me get him to the truck," she said to Jimmy.

She got on Takeo's left and looped her arm beneath his shoulder and around his back. Jimmy did the same on the right and they half-walked, half-dragged Takeo up the boat ramp.

"Did you bring my clothes?" Kiku asked.

"Of course. Did someone jump you guys? Who beat him up? Did you see the boat hit the cable? It was like—"

"That was nice work." Kiku looked ahead at Jimmy's truck. The rear bumper and tailgate were both missing. "It is damaged, though."

"Yeah." Jimmy pointed at his head, and Kiku noticed the bruise on the side of his face. "So am I. The boat hit that cable and the whole truck almost flipped over. I smashed my melon against the side of the truck and—"

"That is why I instructed you to steal a larger truck. The vehicle you selected is too small."

Jimmy's voice rose. "This is the only truck I could get."

"This truck has no working brake lights," Kiku said. "If the police see us, they will pull us over."

"I'm doing the best I can. I *did* stop the boat and the guys chasing you."

"Which will not matter if we are arrested driving away. We will need to get another vehicle. Did you pass any businesses or houses with cars parked outside on the way here?"

"I don't know," Jimmy said sullenly. Kiku glared, and he swallowed. "Maybe. Yeah. I think I saw a house. There was a pickup there."

They reached the truck. Kiku opened the door, and they stuffed Takeo in. He groaned like a sleeping man in the middle of a nightmare.

"You are driving," she said. "I need to change." She grabbed her bag out of the car and started to remove her kimono. Jimmy circled around the truck and stopped at the driver's door.

"If you try to so much as sneak a peek, I will put your eyes out," Kiku said without turning around.

Jimmy jumped into the cab, closed the door, and stared the other way.

It took Kiku less than forty-five seconds to get out of the outfit that had taken hours to get into and put on the change of clothes Jimmy had brought. She transferred the geisha costume to the bag and climbed into the cab beside Takeo, who was slumped over and snoring.

"Did you secure the hotel room?" she asked. She grabbed a water bottle and cloth and started scrubbing her makeup off.

"Yeah, but ..." Jimmy started the truck. "Shouldn't we just drive and keep going?"

"They will believe we will make a direct run for the airport. We are not going there."

Jimmy started down the winding road. It was deserted, but Kiku still wanted to put distance between them and the lake as quickly as possible.

"So where *are* we going?" Jimmy asked.

"There are several options," Kiku said. The truth was, she wasn't sure. She had no idea how Takeo would react to the news of his father's betrayal. She could plan all she wanted, but if Takeo wanted to go another way, she was a soldier and would follow.

"I still think we should just keep going," Jimmy said.

He pumped the brakes as they turned on a sharp curve. The tires screeched, and all three of them slid over in their seats. Takeo moaned.

"Concentrate on your driving. Besides ..." Kiku looked at Takeo wedged between them, his head leaning back against the seat and his eyes closed. She needed to talk to him, but not now, not in his state, and with Jimmy here. "Takeo is not ready—"

Takeo suddenly turned away from her. His chest heaved and he threw up all over the steering wheel, the floorboards, and Jimmy. The truck swerved violently as Jimmy started shrieking, swearing, and gagging.

"Calm down," said Kiku. "It is only vomit." She leaned Takeo slightly forward, but he appeared to be done throwing up. She wiped his mouth with the towel she had been using to remove her makeup. She powered down her window. "As I was about to say, he is not ready to travel."

"You think?" Jimmy grabbed the towel from Kiku and tried to wipe off the steering wheel. "If the cops pull us over now, we're definitely getting arrested, because this truck smells like puke and booze."

Kiku pointed at a house in the distance. "We will get another vehicle. Pull into the driveway."

Jimmy lowered his window and threw the dripping towel out. "Aren't we stealing their car?"

"Are you arguing with me, Jimmy?"

Jimmy leaned his head out the window to inhale. "All I'm saying is, that's not how it's done."

Kiku laughed. The thought of Jimmy telling her how to steal a car was so preposterous that she couldn't help it. In spite of her sore throat, she laughed so hard her sides hurt.

"What?" Jimmy kept his head out the window, trying not to gag.

Kiku wiped her eyes and studied the tidy little home coming into view on their right. "This is an older home that has been remodeled recently. Boat in the side yard and a truck beside it. Odds are it is a vacation home. That is what we want. If the owners live in the city, it could be a long time before the truck is reported stolen."

"Yeah ..." Jimmy slowed down. "But why pull into the driveway?"

"Because it is the simplest way to check if they are home. If I have no car, will that not arouse suspicion?"

Jimmy mumbled something and pulled into the driveway.

"If they are not home, you are covered in vomit and should hose yourself off. And yes, I am always correct," Kiku added as she got out of the car.

Jimmy's eyes widened like she'd suddenly developed psychic powers. She suppressed a smile as she walked up to the front door. She wasn't about to admit to Jimmy that she'd guessed that was what he'd been thinking.

Hesitating on the steps, she listened for dogs. With all the progress in technology, a good dog was still the best warning system a homeowner could have. But the night was silent, except for rustling pines. She stepped up to the door, rang the bell, and waited. After a minute, she rang the bell once more and waited another minute.

She strolled back down the steps. "There is no one here. Pull the truck up next to theirs."

Jimmy parked the truck, and Kiku walked over to the passenger door and pulled Takeo out. He was a bit more awake now; emptying his stomach had helped. She motioned to the new truck. "Get the door," she said to Jimmy.

"Do you want a hand?"

"You are covered in vomit. No."

She maneuvered Takeo into the passenger seat of the new truck. Then she climbed up onto the boat sitting on the trailer next to the truck.

"This might be another stupid question ..." Jimmy said, putting his hands on his hips and looking up at her. "But we *are* taking the truck, right?"

Kiku rummaged around in the back of the boat and triumphantly held up a T-shirt, a pair of men's swim trunks, and a beach towel. "Move the old truck behind the house. Then rinse yourself off and change into these. There is a hose at the side of the house." She tossed the clothes and towel to Jimmy and hopped down.

Jimmy started to jog toward the house.

"Move the truck first."

"I really want to get this puke off me," Jimmy whined.

Kiku sighed. "Go ahead. Wash the vomit off you, then go sit in more vomit while you move the truck." Kiku would have walked over and hit him on the head had he not smelled so foul.

Muttering, Jimmy got into the old truck and hid it behind the house. Reappearing a moment later, he jogged over to the house, turned on the hose, and stripped off his shirt. He looked over his shoulder at Kiku. "Don't you peek!" he yelled as he undid his belt.

Kiku laughed. "You flatter yourself."

Scowling, Jimmy stripped off his clothes and hosed himself down, while Kiku slipped over to the new truck. She had it started within a minute. She'd been stealing cars since she was a child and was quite proud of her hot-wiring abilities.

While she waited for Jimmy, she gazed over at Takeo, asleep again, with his head against the window. Her hand balled into a fist. She was well aware of how not normal she was. A normal woman could comfort him, stroke his hand, whisper soothing words in his ear. But the most comforting thing she could think of was to vow to slaughter his enemies and pile their corpses at his feet.

Jimmy waddled over. "Were there any other clothes in the boat?" The T-shirt was too small, and the swimsuit looked vacuum-sealed to his skin.

"No. Get in the back."

He pointed at Takeo. "Don't you want to have him lie down?"

Kiku reached out the window and smacked Jimmy in the back of the head. He swore and quickly got in the truck's narrow back seat.

The truth was, Takeo probably *would* be more comfortable in the back. But if something were to happen, she wanted to be right there to protect him.

She put the truck in reverse and got back out onto the road. She was breathing easier now.

"It is an hour to Kumano. Try to get some sleep." She glanced at the rearview mirror. Jimmy was pulling at the tight T-shirt collar and glaring out the window. "You did well, Jimmy. Thank you for following my instructions." She forced a smile.

Jimmy cleared his throat. "Well, I kind of did. I couldn't get everything you asked for. *Yet*."

Kiku glared. "Was I not specific enough?"

Jimmy held up his hands. "You were, but it's a long list, and it's going to take some time to get *everything*. I still have to rent the cars and find the clothes you wanted."

"You must learn to work more quickly, Jimmy. Time is a luxury we can ill afford."

"I promise I'll do it in Kumano."

Kiku opened the window. "Kenzo will waste no time hunting us down. His dogs are so close, I can hear them barking."

Jimmy's eyes flew open wide and he tilted his head to the side as if to listen.

Kiku tossed her head back and roared with laughter.

17

Once dawn arrived, Kiku knew it would be impossible to get any sleep. With her cup of tea brewed, she walked across the living room, past the long leather couch, sat at the desk, and pored over the map on the computer. A thousand different possibilities ran through her weary mind, but she had no idea what the man sleeping in the next room would decide—or whether she would even choose to listen to his decision.

Jimmy was late. It was almost nine o'clock in the morning, and she wanted to be on the road. But she had one more thing to do as well. If they were going to flee Japan, she needed to make sure everything was in place. She picked up her phone and dialed a number in the States. Hopefully, her friend was not asleep yet.

"Kiku?" Alice's voice was cheerful. "You won't believe how awesome everything came out!" As she often did, Alice spoke machine-gun fast. "It was a ton of work, but I got it all done. Facebook pages, fake concerts, YouTube. You two are all over social media. This artist friend of mine created at least fifty photos of you guys. You look amazing."

Kiku smiled. Alice had a way of making her do that. It was a gift Kiku cherished. "Thank you for helping me."

"What are friends for? Speaking of that, what is all this for? Is everything okay? Do you need me to come over there? Where is 'there,' the 'there' where you are?"

"I think you may have overdone it on the caffeine, Alice."

"Yeah ..." Kiku could picture Alice nodding rapidly, her ponytail bobbing. "I think you're right. Jack will be sorry he missed your call. He's out at his mom and dad's, picking up the wedding cake topper they got for us. It's getting close! I hope you'll be back in time, Kiku." Alice yawned. "Well, I better go. I haven't really slept since yesterday, but I'm psyched to have been able to help you for a change. Everything is all set. I'll send you the links."

The hotel room door beeped. Kiku drew her gun and pointed it at the door. "Thank you, Alice. I will speak with you soon."

The door handle slowly descended and the door opened a crack.

"It's just me," said Jimmy. "I know there's no chain on it because that's what you do, but I also don't want you to kill me. You probably have a gun aimed at my head."

He slipped into the room carrying a tray of coffees in one hand and three bags in the other, from the little noodle restaurant she had specified. She wanted a nice Japanese breakfast today, not sickly sweet hotel pastries. The coffee was a must, though.

Kiku holstered her gun. "Can you please not announce to the entire hallway that I have a firearm?"

"Sorry. I got breakfast."

"Did you get the cars?"

Jimmy nodded. "Why do we need two?"

"Appearances. And the clothing?"

"Yeah, I got them, and enough clothes and luggage to make Kim Kardashian feel inadequately packed." He set the coffees and food on the table near the couch. "I'm not telling you what to do, but how are you going to keep a low profile with all that stuff?"

Kiku ignored the question and picked up a coffee. "Thank you for breakfast."

Jimmy rolled his eyes and opened his bag. Each one contained a beautifully packed bento box; for Takeo she had ordered healing foods, and for herself, buckwheat noodles, seaweed salad, smoked octopus, and spicy pickles. Kiku's mouth was watering as she opened her box.

"Are you ever going to tell me the plan?" Jimmy mumbled through a mouthful of rice.

"When the time comes." Kiku tried not to make a face as she took one last sip of bitter coffee. It was disgusting, but like Alice, she needed the caffeine. She followed it with a sip of ginger tea and then took her first bite, closing her eyes with pleasure.

"Is he awake?" Jimmy asked.

"I have not checked. I will get him up shortly."

"He drank so much he probably shoulda gone to the hospital. Maybe I should just take a peek?"

"I would not do that," Kiku whispered. But he had already opened the door to the bedroom and taken a step in. Jimmy looked back, mouthed something unintelligible, pointed to his eyes, and smiled. The door swung shut behind him and clicked closed.

A second later, a solid thud was followed by splintering wood, the top hinge was ripped out of the frame, and the door burst open. Jimmy was thrown flat on his back, clutching his stomach, and he rolled out of the way a second before Takeo leapt over the wreckage into the room. His hair was standing on end, his mouth was twisted into a snarl, and his eyes were wild—but the pure insanity from the night before was gone.

"Good morning, Takeo." Kiku held up her cup of tea and gestured to the place she had set for him. "I ordered breakfast for you."

The fire left Takeo's eyes as he stared at Kiku. He shook his head like he was trying to clear the fog clouding his brain, and grimaced. "Who the hell is he?" He glared at Jimmy, who now stood stooped over, holding his stomach and coughing dramatically.

"A friend of your brother's. Jimmy, please pick up the door."

Grimacing, Jimmy lifted the door, the remaining screws on the bottom hinge pulling free, and set it against the wall. He quickly stepped away from the seething Takeo.

Like an old dog woken from a deep nap, Takeo growled low in his throat.

"Would you like to get dressed before breakfast?" Kiku asked.

Takeo's eyes widened when he realized he was still in his boxers. "Kiku, how—"

Someone pounded on the door.

"One moment." Kiku rose, pulled a few bills from her pocket, walked to the door, and looked through the peephole. Standing in the hallway was a very irate balding man with a potbelly.

"Open up!" he demanded. "This is the manager."

Kiku opened the door but blocked his way.

"What's going on in there?"

"My husband tripped. I'm very sorry for the disturbance." She bowed slightly and handed him six ten-thousand-yen notes. "There was some slight damage to a door. This should more than cover it, and please keep the rest for any inconvenience."

Kiku watched the manager's face, and she could practically see him calculating how much a door cost and how much profit he'd keep. When his eyes lit up, she knew he realized if he didn't say anything, he could have maintenance repair the door and pocket *all* the money.

"Is your husband all right?" he asked.

"He's fine. Thank you so much for asking." Kiku smiled. "It sounded much worse than it was."

The manager nodded and stuffed the money in his pocket. "Please let me know if you need anything."

Kiku stepped back into the room and shut the door.

Takeo came out of the bedroom, tying shut a bathrobe. "Out," he said as he passed by Jimmy.

Jimmy looked at Kiku, pointed to the bedroom, and mouthed, *Can I wait in there?* Kiku opened the door to the hallway, and with a scowl, Jimmy stalked out.

Takeo stood with his shoulders back and his eyes blazing. Kiku could see the questions swirling in his head, but she wanted him to stew a while longer. She sat down at the table, picked up her chopsticks, and resumed her breakfast.

For a long moment, he stood boring a hole in the floor with his eyes. Finally, he looked at her.

"Explain," he said.

She met his gaze. "How much do you remember about last night?"

"We'll get to that later. Tell me how my son died." His jaw flexed and his hands balled into fists.

"Please, sit down."

A rumble started deep within his chest like a volcano building pressure before an eruption. "Kiku …" he said through clenched teeth.

She waited, trying to think what she should do right now. Comfort him? Defend herself? If Kiku wanted to kill him, she could think of nine different ways to do it—but when it came to affairs of the heart … she had nothing.

"Why did you disobey my order to come to Chicago?" Takeo snapped. From the corded muscles in his neck, she knew he was struggling to contain himself. She doubted he would get physical with her, but he could easily destroy the room if he became angry and violent. "If you suspected Shin, you should have warned me."

"I did not suspect Shin then."

"Then why did you ignore my order?"

"Because at that time, I suspected *you*."

Takeo winced. She might as well have just cut out his heart. The fire faded from his eyes, but he said nothing and remained standing. She decided to hold off telling him about Jiro's warning until she had finished explaining. "Someone inside the Yakuza was tipping off the Russians. That much I knew. Circumstances pointed to you."

"I had no idea." Takeo scowled as if his admission caused him physical pain. "Shin was working for the Russians. It was a coup."

Kiku sipped her tea, set the cup down, and shook her head. "Shin was feeding information to the Russians, but he was not working for them; nor was he starting a coup. Shin was Uchihara. He would never betray his responsibilities to your family."

Takeo slammed his hand on the table so hard the wood cracked, sending her teacup sailing. Kiku made a mental note to leave more money for the hotel manager.

"Do you really expect me to believe that Shin did not betray me?" Takeo stepped close, glaring down at her.

"Shin did betray you, but he remained loyal to your family until death. The Uchiharas serve the head of the Yakuza."

"*I* am the head of the Yakuza."

"No. You are the head of the *American* Yakuza."

Kiku watched as her words sank in. Takeo's bloodshot eyes rounded slightly in confusion before slamming shut. He stood like that for a long moment, then turned his head toward the window and opened his eyes again—slowly. Kiku had expected to see many emotions when he realized that his own father had ordered the murder of his son, but not the profound sadness that marred his face and haunted his eyes.

Several minutes passed as Takeo stood there, staring out the window, his thoughts lost to her.

"What town are we in?" he asked at last.

"We are in a little town just north of Fumeiyo no ie. Kumano."

Takeo turned back to her, his face strangely relaxed considering all he'd just discovered. He bowed deeply. "Thank you for telling me this." He started for the bedroom. "Leave me enough money to get to Tokyo."

He stopped in the doorway, his hand grabbing the empty frame, and looked back over his shoulder. He seemed to want to say so much more to her, but gave her only a slight nod of his head.

"You cannot go after your father, Takeo. In Japan, he is king. You will not get within one hundred yards of him."

"Then I will kill him from a hundred and ten."

"Takeo ..."

"He murdered my son, Kiku. Do you expect me to do nothing?"

"No. But you need the correct facts in order to take the right course of action."

"What do you mean?"

Kiku inhaled deeply. She realized that if she did not tell Takeo the whole truth, there would be no stopping him from going to Tokyo to avenge his son.

"Takeo ... Alex is not dead."

18

Takeo sat staring at his shaking hands. "What did you say? My son ... he's ..." He grabbed the table, shoved it aside like it was nothing, and grabbed Kiku's shoulders, crouching down in front of her so their eyes were level. "Do not deceive me. Not about this. Are you lying to get me to come with you? Is this some kind of trick so I won't go after my father?"

His hands trembled so much he was shaking her. Kiku knew it wasn't a conscious act; if it had been, he'd be picking himself up off the floor. She resisted the urge to break free; even with Takeo, she found it difficult to be touched.

"Your son *is* alive."

Takeo broke away. Squeezing his hands into fists, he began to pace and mutter. "But the body ... yes, you could have faked that, one of Shin's men ... Shin?" He spun around.

Kiku nodded.

"But the San Francisco medical examiner said ... there was a finger, teeth ... She confirmed it was Alex."

Kiku crossed her arms. "You checked my story."

Takeo's eyes narrowed. "Get that look off your face. You lied to me."

"It was necessary."

"I prayed you were mistaken. But the medical examiner said with that evidence, she was positive."

"She was well paid."

"Where is Alex?"

"Safe."

Takeo stopped pacing. "*Where?*" he bellowed.

Kiku closed her mouth as Takeo stalked across the floor. The wild look had returned to his eyes, and his mouth twitched into a snarl. Kiku let him walk right up to her.

"Be careful of your next actions," she warned.

"I want to know where my son is."

"He is with a friend of mine. He is safe."

"A friend ... Stratton? I *knew* something happened between you two."

Kiku smirked. She didn't intend to fan the flames of Takeo's jealousy, but at that moment she pictured Jack Stratton's crooked grin and it had a contagious effect. "Alex is not with Jack."

Takeo's eyes flashed. She hadn't denied his accusation. Nothing physical had ever transpired between her and the young police officer, but Jack was a hard man not to love, and in truth, part of her *had* fallen for the detective. However, she would never kindle that flame, because of Alice. And because of Jack himself. He was a deeply moral man, fiercely in love with Alice, and she would not be able to keep him as a friend if she did not respect those boundaries.

"Then where is he? I have a right to know." Takeo glared at her.

"No, you don't." Kiku stepped forward. "I give you my word that your son is safe. I cannot say the same for you. If you attack your father now—"

"I have no choice."

"Everything is a choice." Kiku pointed at the chair. "You need to listen. Sit."

Takeo's hands balled into fists and she watched the storm roll across his face. He was a man of deep emotions, and when a tempest stirred those waters of the deep, nothing would stop the tsunami.

"If you attack Kenzo now," Kiku said, "you will throw your life away and mine along with it."

"I will not allow you to come," he snapped.

Kiku laughed—real laughter, from the belly—until she needed to wipe tears from her eyes.

Emotions boiled across Takeo's face—humiliation, anger, puzzlement, disbelief. Then his scowl softened and his shoulders trembled and he laughed, too; not as hard or as long, but for a short time his deep baritone blended with hers in much-needed emotional release.

When silence fell in the room once again, Kiku pointed to the chair and Takeo sat down, shaking his head.

"If you were anyone else ..." His smile faded as he looked up at her. "What's your plan?"

"First I need to tell you the whole story." She sat down opposite him and detailed everything that had happened since Takeo first gave her the order to determine whether Alex was his son or not. As she recounted the harrowing ordeal, she watched his handsome face carefully. He hung on her every word, especially when it came to Alex. In his dark eyes, she could see his love for a boy he had yet to meet. And when she told him of Karen Harris and her betrayal of their son, she saw the steely flash of anger. She told him everything—except the details concerning Daichi.

For several minutes, Takeo sat drawing in one long, deep breath after another. Kiku recognized this as his method of readying himself for battle.

"*Osoreirimasu*, Kiku ... There are no words to adequately express my gratitude." Takeo looked off to the side, but not fast enough to hide his eyes, rimmed with tears that were forbidden to roll freely down his chiseled face.

Kiku closed her eyes to honor his show of vulnerability.

"So, the mighty Kenzo made a deal with the Russians," Takeo said after clearing his throat.

"He tried. Cade will not be satisfied with anything other than an eye for an eye. He wants a son for a son."

"And to my father, Alex wasn't considered a loss, because he is half American?"

Kiku nodded. "But now that your father is aware that you know what he did ..."

Takeo got up and went into the kitchen. He poured a large glass of water, downed it, and poured another. "How many men do I have in Japan who are loyal to me?"

"Not enough." Kiku crossed her arms. "Kenzo reigns supreme. Even the men who said they were on your side, I would be suspicious of."

"What about Jiro's men?"

Kiku chuckled. "Jiro's *man*. Jimmy is loyal to Jiro, but that is all. Your brother's heart is in the right place, but the only things he ever did in Tokyo were dance and drink."

Takeo frowned. "I can hold Kenzo off in America. I've turned most of our investments legitimate. We have the men to defend ourselves, but not enough to bring Kenzo down." He set the glass down on the counter. "That gives us nothing."

"You are wrong."

Takeo smiled ruefully. "And why is that?"

"Our position with Kenzo will now be no different than with the Russians or any gang. It is like America's cold war: we can ensure each other's mutual destruction."

"And you think that will stop Kenzo?"

"First we need to get you out of Japan. Once we are in the US, we can dictate our terms from a position of strength. We can make Kenzo realize that a truce is mutually beneficial."

Takeo shook his head. "My father will never honor an arrangement like that."

"I am aware. And when he moves to break it, that is when I will kill him."

Takeo pushed away from the counter and slowly walked over to her. Kiku stayed seated, her hands folded over her crossed legs. He squatted down in front of her, placing one hand on top of hers and the other close to her cheek. His eyes locked with hers, searching, seeking permission to touch her. Ever so subtly, she tilted her head toward his hand. His fingers gently stroked her hair. There was a longing in his eyes that she easily recognized. She felt it, too. But now was not the time to satisfy that hunger.

Kiku stood and surveyed the wreckage of the overturned table. "You need to get ready, and you need your strength. I will have Jimmy get you another breakfast. We must leave as soon as possible. Your father is no doubt looking for us already."

19

With the sound of the shower in the background, Kiku stood by the window, a burner phone in her hand.

Daichi sounded winded when he answered. "Your timing is horrible." Kiku heard Lilly, his wife, giggling in the background. It was after midnight and they were obviously in bed.

"I have him. We are preparing to leave."

Daichi snapped to attention. "I've got to hand it to you, Ōkami. I never thought you'd make it."

"You are a bad liar." Kiku played with a string on the curtain. He'd called her "Wolf," a sure sign of respect. "If you believed that, you would have come here yourself."

"I don't come where I'm not asked."

"You are full of lies, Daichi. How is Alex?"

"I've never seen a happier kid. Between helping around the farm and growing like a weed, I'd have thought he'd be utterly exhausted at the end of the day, but Alex still ends up playing video games with Hwan till late." Daichi chuckled. "Oh, to be young."

"Thank you for watching him."

"I'd be better at watching out for you." There was a long pause. "Is it because of the hand?"

"What?" The question puzzled Kiku.

"You saw me in action. I can still do the job lefty. Wait, you're not thinking because I'm hitting sixty that I'm too old? Because that's—"

Kiku laughed. She pictured Daichi's face twisting in frustration and would have laughed louder, but she did not want to be overheard. "You men are so ... vain. It has nothing to do with your age or your missing hand. Kenzo will not kill Takeo. But if he found out that *you* still draw breath, he would burn the planet down to ensure you were dead."

Daichi exhaled. "That's what I thought."

Kiku wiped her eyes and chuckled. "Sure it is. Now that you've been reassured of your competence and vitality, I need a favor."

"Sure. I'm really in the mood to help you out after you've been laughing at me."

"I need you to meet us in Alaska in a few days. We will be coming into Dutch Harbor. I'm not sure exactly when."

"Are you flying in?"

"No."

Daichi whistled low. "I know you like playing with fire, but is there a reason that you're strolling straight into Hell?"

"Because neither Kenzo nor Novikov thinks I will take the risk. As you just demonstrated, men have an issue with pride."

"So do women. But you've got a different problem, Kiku—you like to fight. And if you get into enough fights, you're going to lose. Those who live by the sword die by it."

"You are quoting Scripture to me now?"

"I'm stating facts."

"Here are the facts." Kiku hurriedly ran down the details of her plan, then said, "Give me an alternate plan to extract Takeo from Japan with a greater chance for success, and I will take it." She wasn't taunting him; if Daichi did have a better idea, she would be a fool not to listen.

Daichi chuckled. "It's crazy, but it's definitely not what they're expecting. And I have to admit, the website you sent me looks legit."

"My friend is quite competent. Green light?"

There was a long pause and a faint tapping on the other end of the line. Daichi used to have a habit of tapping his trigger finger against things when he thought. She wondered what he did now that the finger was gone.

"Green light," Daichi whispered. "But if something happens in Russia, there's nothing I can do for you. It's a black hole. I have zero contacts."

"I know. And thank you again for taking care of Alex."

"He wears me down, but it has been a pleasure. Are you heading here after Alaska?"

Kiku heard the strain in his voice. "No. I've told Takeo Alex is alive, but I haven't said anything about you, and I plan on keeping it that way. I have to go now. I'll call you soon."

The shower shut off.

"Take care, Daichi."

"I'll have Lilly pray for you."

Kiku hung up and closed her eyes. His last words bothered her. She knew Lilly was taking Daichi to church regularly now. She'd laughed when she first heard about it and joked about the roof falling on his head and bolts of lightning raining down from the heavens. But if hard-boiled Daichi could shake off his past ...

She thought of the missionaries she knew as a little girl. The couple who took her and her sister in for a while, the Petersons, were always smiling. Every time they saw her, they made her feel like they'd missed her terribly since the last time, even if she had done something wrong. The woman said it was *unconditional love*, the kind of love that exists no matter what and would never turn you away. She said that was how God loves us—unconditionally.

Kiku glared at herself in the window. A tree cast half of the glass in shadow, splitting her reflection at an odd angle. She closed her eyes.

Daichi was going to ask Lilly to pray for Kiku—because he felt he couldn't do it himself. Of course he hadn't said that, but she was certain that was what he'd meant. Kiku felt the same way. How could God listen to someone like her after all she'd done?

She opened her eyes and smiled. Daichi said she'd be walking into Hell. If that was the case, she'd feel right at home.

20

Takeo was towel-drying his hair as he walked out of the bathroom, a second towel wrapped around his toned waist. "So what's this plan of yours?"

Kiku smiled. "Jimmy's due back any minute. He's bringing part of it with him."

Right on cue, the door swung open and Jimmy staggered in, loaded down with bags. A petite Korean woman walked in behind him, rolling a small suitcase.

"Morning!" Her voice was bright and cheerful.

Kiku pointed to the bathroom, and the woman rolled her suitcase in.

"Who is she?" Takeo asked.

"I've got no clue. Kiku told me to get her, and when I pulled up, she just jumped in and didn't say a word."

"She only speaks Korean," Kiku explained. "Her name is not necessary. She is assisting us with our cover. Takeo, keep your towel on. You and I will go first. Jimmy, did you get the van?"

"It's outside."

"And the Stingray?"

"It's reserved, but I need someone to give me a ride to the rental place." He looked back and forth between Takeo and Kiku. "It's too far for me to walk."

Kiku rolled her eyes. "It is ten minutes away. Go. We are busy."

Jimmy grumbled something but was careful not to slam the door when he left.

Takeo crossed his arms. "What is this plan?"

Kiku smiled. She didn't mind it when Takeo struck his "I'm in control" power pose. While he did have final say over the plan, it was only because she willingly yielded that right. Besides, he always followed her plans. Her eyes wandered over his broad chest and the muscles rippling in his forearms. Even though his face was a neutral mask, the reddening at the tips of his ears gave away his embarrassment at the way she was undressing him with her eyes.

Kiku liked confident men—men whose power came from somewhere within, was not put on like a costume. Power that came from money or position was easily lost, but inner resolve could never be taken away.

And Takeo was a strong man. Every man could be broken, as she had just seen, but men like Takeo rose from the mat after they were knocked down. And it was Kiku's job to help him to his feet. She was his protector, his confidante, and, most importantly now, his adviser.

It was easy to picture Takeo as a daimyo, ruling over his kingdom in feudal Japan. Kiku had grown up loving those stories; her sister had made the tales come alive. But it was fortunate for both of them that they were not born in that era. The daimyo were known for taking many wives, and Kiku, who would have been Takeo's *chakusai*—his first wife—would never have let him live if he'd taken a second wife or a concubine.

Kiku's smile ticked up impishly. Of course, he'd never have had the need to desire one anyway.

"We are going to America via Alaska," she said. "We'll end up in Dutch Harbor."

Takeo shook his head. "The airports will be too well watched."

"That is why we are taking a cruise. The ports will have minimum coverage."

Takeo's neutral mask cracked as his thick brows knit together. "No. It's too risky."

"It is faster and cleaner. We only have one stop in port."

"The Russians have put ten million on your head. If I'm caught, Kenzo will negotiate for my release. But if they catch you, you're dead."

Kiku nodded. "True. But that does not negate the fact that going through Russia is our best chance."

"It's not worth the risk." From the look on Takeo's face, it was going to be a hard sell.

Kiku shook her head and took out her phone. "You need to look at our cover story before you reach that conclusion."

As Takeo scrolled through the various pictures and articles on the web page, his eyes widened. He stopped and pointed at a photograph of himself with his hair dyed white and spiked up.

"How did you do all this?"

Kiku took back the phone, opened another web page, and showed him the bios for Takeo and herself. "I have a very talented friend."

Takeo studied the phone in bewilderment. "We're members of a band?"

"A duo. Classical Warfare. You play piano, I sing. Our music is a fusion of classical music and alternative punk."

"But I look nothing like that picture."

Kiku pointed to the woman who had reappeared in the bathroom doorway and was waiting patiently, a smile on her face. "That is why she is here."

"So you plan to sneak off to America by trying to attract attention?"

"Exactly. Let's get started."

While the Korean woman dyed Takeo's hair, Kiku explained the rest of the backstory that she and Alice had come up with. They'd kept it as simple as possible, using many details from Takeo's real life. Takeo listened intently.

"You also wear these." Kiku handed him a pair of dark sunglasses. "Always."

"Like Roy Orbison."

"Exactly. 'Pretty Woman' is my favorite song. Did you know Roy Orbison's children wanted him to go to Disneyland, but he said that it was impossible because of how many people would recognize him? So, his son convinced him to remove his sunglasses, and no one recognized who he was. The same effect works in reverse."

Half an hour into their transformation, Jimmy returned, out of breath. Kiku, her hair wrapped in plastic, strolled out of the bedroom to greet him.

"Is this all for the disguise?" Jimmy asked as he set down more bags. "My suit's in there. What's my cover?" His eyes brightened.

"There is more to your disguise than just the suit." Kiku handed him a pair of glasses with round frames. "You are our manager."

Jimmy grinned as he put on the glasses. "Is she going to do something with my hair, too?" He ran a nervous hand over his thick mane.

"Not exactly."

Jimmy relaxed—until Kiku held up the items in her hands.

"You need a completely different look." She handed him some electric hair clippers, a can of shaving cream, and a razor. "Use the kitchen sink. Try not to make a mess."

Jimmy stared down at the equipment, his expression one of horror. "No. No. You want me to shave my head?"

Kiku handed him a fake passport. In the photograph he was completely bald. Even his soul patch had been cleaved off.

"That ain't gonna happen."

"I'll park the Stingray in long-term parking. When you return to Japan, you can keep it."

Jimmy frowned thoughtfully, then nodded. "Deal." He hurried into the kitchen.

Kiku smiled. "We leave in an hour," she announced.

As she returned to the bathroom, she felt a pang of guilt for what she had said to Jimmy. She did intend to keep her word and give Jimmy the car. But she hadn't mentioned one important caveat.

If you live that long.

21

The drive to the northern tip of Japan was a delicate dance. Normally, Kiku would have stayed within a few miles per hour over the speed limit to avoid attracting the attention of the police. But when sitting behind the wheel of a cherry-blossom-red Stingray, driving like a typical person was what would bring scrutiny. Or at least, that was how she justified driving fast.

They flew down the road, the wind streaming their hair back. Even Takeo was smiling now. Kiku had to admit that she loved their outlandish dye jobs. The silver was so bright it was close to white, and it made them appear so exotic that everyone passing by craned their necks to look. Some passing motorists even drove alongside them snapping pictures.

"I'm not sure this is such a good idea," Takeo grumbled when a busful of schoolchildren smiled and waved as the Stingray sped past. A highway patrol car pulled around the school bus and started to follow them. Kiku checked her speed. She was a little over ten miles an hour above the speed limit. She eased off the gas and moved over to the left to let the policeman by. As the patrol car passed them, the two officers inside smiled and waved to Kiku.

Kiku smirked as she waved back. "Maybe you should reassess that opinion."

Takeo laughed.

Jimmy was still behind them in the van, looking as cross as ever. He hadn't stopped scowling since he'd shaved his head. Kiku thought he looked good bald, but he clearly didn't agree.

"It's twenty-one hours to Sapporo," Takeo said. "Are you planning on stopping?"

"And give you a chance to drive? Not on your life." Kiku instantly regretted her word choice, but Takeo only laughed again.

"Are you getting superstitious on me?" He leaned against the doorframe, his silver hair dancing in the wind. She couldn't see his eyes because of the sunglasses, but his head was angled her way.

"No." She wasn't superstitious, but she was unnaturally worried about Takeo. Even now, it felt like he'd suddenly be snatched away from her. "I will get you to America. Breathing," she added with a chuckle.

Takeo's right eyebrow rose above the rim of his glasses.

"It is an inside joke," Kiku explained. "I did a favor for a friend. He wanted me to bring someone from Thailand back to the United States. I sent the man back in two boxes. My friend was quite disturbed. Now, when he asks me for a favor, he always specifies that the person has to come back breathing."

Takeo laughed. "You should tell Jack Stratton that he should also specify in one piece."

She'd never told him about her work for Jack; Takeo had been checking up on her. She'd thought he'd be upset, and now that she'd given him those stupid sunglasses, she couldn't read his eyes.

"I was saving that surprise in case the next person he asked me to find proved to be difficult."

"Are you going to his wedding?"

"It is four weeks away. A lot can happen between now and then."

An awkward silence filled the car, which Takeo finally broke, tapping his finger against the doorframe. "If we make it back, I will accompany you."

Kiku found herself involuntarily speeding up. She'd accompanied Takeo to numerous functions, under the guise of business and typically for the purpose of stealing something or killing someone. What would this be? A date?

Takeo folded his arms across his chest and leaned his head against the window. "Besides, I have a couple of questions that I'd like to ask Mr. Stratton."

Kiku settled back into her seat, a smile slowly spreading across her lips. Now she had even more motivation to survive. A meeting between Takeo Nakumora and Jack Stratton was one encounter she didn't want to miss.

But they had a lot of ground to cover before they got to the States. Kenzo would have everyone watching all exit routes out of Japan. She was sure someone must have chosen before to escape via the cruise ships that sailed from Japan, touched down in Russia, and finished up in Alaska, although not a single case came to mind. She hoped that was because the ones who chose to flee that way made it out.

She wasn't entirely happy with her own plan. She preferred the simple-is-better approach, but that wouldn't work here. They would never make it through an airport in any disguise, and even on a boat, Kenzo would expect her to disguise their age or ethnicity. Choosing to leave from the cruise's second stop, Sapporo, rather than Tokyo helped them avoid Kenzo's stronghold and the madness of the city. Once they got out of Japan, she would feel much better. Passing through Russia wasn't of great concern to her; it was one port, and they would stay on the boat, gambling.

After that ... things would get dangerous again. Very dangerous. The thought of the icy stretch across the Bering Sea and the Aleutians chilled her blood. No escape routes there, that she knew of. She was working on that conundrum, and so was Takeo.

Her thoughts drifted instead to another painful topic: her life's mission, to repay the debt she owed her sister. Vengeance for Akari. She was closer: she had two names now, Gary Dunn and his boss, Jeff Klein. She had yet to meet Klein; he would know the men responsible for her sister's death.

The van beeped behind, and she glanced in the rearview mirror. Jimmy was frantically moving his hand up and down. She glanced at her speedometer and saw she was driving at well over a hundred miles per hour. Easing off the gas pedal, she swore under her breath.

She couldn't send Jack to talk to Klein. Jack was too noble and too law-abiding for what she needed him to do. And she couldn't send Daichi, because she needed him to watch Alex. Once again, vengeance would have to wait.

Still, as they sped northward through the afternoon and evening, and Takeo took over driving so she could rest, Kiku's thoughts would not leave her sister. Today would have been Akari's birthday. The pain of losing her beautiful, wise sister sank its fangs into her and she allowed the poison to spread—encouraged it. It was natural to try to avoid pain: people paid their therapists to help them forget it; addicts paid their suppliers for whatever worked to numb it—but not Kiku. As a child, she had been unable to prevent her sister's murder and had run from the horror. Kiku the woman did not run from pain; she drew power from it.

Unable to sleep, she closed her eyes and let memories of her sister run freely through her mind, each one slicing off a piece of her heart. With each cut, Kiku became colder, more focused.

She'd make it through Russia. She'd ensure that Takeo was safe. And then she'd find the men who had taken Akari from her.

22

Sapporo in June was as rainy and cool as Kiku had remembered, but now she had a cherry-red Stingray to brighten her arrival. Clad in a black silk chiffon evening dress with a thigh-high slit and with Takeo in a black tuxedo at her side, it struck her that the fact that they were on the lam was comical. The people in the crowd gathered to board the ship jostled with each other to catch a glimpse of the handsome celebrity couple who had arrived in their midst. As Kiku, her dress fluttering in the sea breeze, strolled around to the front of the Stingray, and Takeo moved to stand next to her, they looked like models on a photo shoot, as they'd intended, and they played it to the hilt, surveying the enormous cruise ship from behind mirrored sunglasses.

Jimmy unpacked the suitcases and instrument cases from the van and pushed the overloaded luggage cart toward the boarding line. Alice's homemade logo for the band had been a genius touch, and it was stenciled all over their suitcases: *Classical Warfare*, and underneath, a samurai sword crossed over a blossoming branch of cherry.

The name rippled through the crowd, and the questions and excited speculation began:

"Is that a band?"

"I think I've heard of them; didn't they just get back from a tour?"

"They're big in Europe."

"I love them!"

Phones were ripped out of pockets and people started snapping away. Takeo remained stoic, but Kiku waved and smiled, showing her white teeth.

"My father doesn't know what a computer is," Takeo whispered. "But who else will see these photos?"

Kiku maintained her smile, even as she realized she had underestimated the impact their appearance would have. The band was entirely fictional, yet these people were behaving as if they already knew of them. Did people really blindly follow celebrities like this?

A teenage girl thrust a notebook and pen at Takeo and breathlessly asked, "Can I please have your autograph?"

Kiku wondered if her plan was working a little too well.

At the entrance to the gangplank, another phase of the scheme was under way. Jimmy was arguing with two members of the boat's crew—a man and a woman, both in crisp white uniforms.

"This is completely unacceptable," Jimmy snapped. "We were supposed to be upgraded to a suite! Do you know who I am?"

"No, sir, I do not." The ship's officer was patient but businesslike, arms crossed in front of him. Behind him, the woman pecked away at a computer tablet.

"I insist on speaking with the captain," Jimmy demanded.

The officer was politely indignant. "Since the captain is busy getting the ship ready to set sail, that will not—"

The woman tapped the man's shoulder and handed him the tablet. The man attempted to brush it away, but she was persistent. He glared at her before roughly pulling it from her hands. As he scanned it, his eyes widened. Then he looked up and bowed his head.

"My deepest apologies, Mr. Sano."

Jimmy pushed his glasses up his nose haughtily. The man scurried over to the female officer and whispered instructions into her ear. As he handed the tablet back to her, Kiku saw the Facebook banner and smiled. Alice had posted fake details of their recent cruise aboard this ship's sister craft registered in the Bahamas. Alice had also come up with the idea of mentioning, with vague details that were impossible to corroborate, that Classical Warfare were on the cruise because they were the personal friends of one of the cruise line's owners. But who would care about corroborating details when Alice's dazzling slideshow of doctored photos and made-up trivia was dancing by? The website was a masterpiece.

The man stepped aside. "Please follow Kim, who will expedite you through security and boarding, and I will make sure your luggage is taken up to your suite."

Jimmy accompanied their luggage, while Takeo and Kiku followed Kim to security. The security officer barely gave their passports a second glance as people continued to photograph the couple. Kiku noted that the more men snapped pictures of her, the closer Takeo stood to her. She smiled at his unconscious drive to show the other men whom she belonged to.

Once they cleared security, two Japanese men in business suits stood waiting for them. Kiku touched Takeo's hand and pointed them out with her eyes. He nodded slightly.

The men walked forward and stopped in front of Kiku, blocking their path. She felt Takeo's muscles tense, and Kim stopped in her tracks and stood off to the side, where she could intervene if necessary. Kiku shifted one foot back. Takeo did the same.

"Excuse me." The shorter man bowed. His brow was sweaty and he licked his lips nervously. "May I please get a picture with Asami?" He had already learned her cover name.

He started to wrap his arm around Kiku's waist as the other man took out his phone, but Takeo swatted the man's hand away and pulled Kiku two more steps back. "Do not touch her." He spoke with the intensity of a general ordering an execution, and Kiku could feel his voice rumbling through his back.

The man skittered sideways like a frightened horse. "Sorry. Please forgive me." He gave another bow.

Kiku raised an eyebrow at Takeo and motioned the man over. Grinning from ear to ear, he stood close to Kiku but made sure not to touch her. Then the two men swapped places, took another photo, and thanked Kiku and Takeo profusely.

"You need to relax," Kiku whispered as they returned to following

Kim, who was waiting for them by the elevator. "This is all part of our cover."

"I am relaxed." Takeo scowled. "I thought I was supposed to be a temperamental artist."

Kiku grinned at him. He was right; everyone was playing their parts perfectly—even the walk-ons who didn't know they were playing a part. As they waited for the elevator, a group of five teenage girls surrounded them. In between flipping their hair, giggling, and swooning, they managed to ask Kim if she would take a picture of them with Classical Warfare.

Kiku made a mental note to invest in social media. In the short walk from the car to the ship, all of these people had learned their fake names and swallowed the lie that they were an actual band without hearing a single note played.

Takeo stretched his arms out like a mother hen, and the little ducklings scampered to his side, wiggling as close to him as they could get. Kiku reluctantly stepped out of the shot, trying not to let her displeasure show on her face. As Takeo's smile widened, she realized she must be doing a lousy job of it.

Kim snapped several pictures and handed the camera back to one of the girls. Kiku motioned for Takeo to move to the elevator. Instead, Takeo smiled wickedly and suggested, "How about a selfie!" The girls squealed, clapped, and pressed even closer to him.

Kiku was ready to force the elevator door open and push the lot of them down the shaft, but the elevator dinged, and she, Takeo, and Kim stepped inside, and Kim herself blocked the girls from getting on with an outstretched hand.

"You're in the Imperial Suite," Kim said, "on Deck Twelve."

Kiku nodded and leaned closer to Takeo. "You'll have to be careful, dear. If you took a selfie on that balcony, it would be so easy to fall right over, and it's unlikely you would survive from that height."

"You don't have to worry about falling over the rail," Kim said reassuringly. "Most reported falls from cruise ships are people intentionally jumping over the side."

Kiku smiled at Takeo. "I'm certain a few were pushed."

Takeo chuckled nervously. "She's kidding."

Kim nodded, but the look on her face suggested she wasn't so sure.

Kiku tipped her generously when they reached their suite—which was magnificent. It was an oval, with one of the long sides leading out to a crest-shaped balcony that offered a magnificent view of the ship and sea beyond. The ceiling was made of mirror-like material, reflecting the room's opulent décor, and the walls were covered in a pewter-and-silver textured wallpaper dappled with the ambient light. Kiku kicked off her heels and let her feet sink into the plush carpeting that blanketed the floor. Takeo walked over to the piano next to the sliding glass door leading out to the balcony.

"Let's hope no one requests a private concert, Asami."

Kiku laughed. "We should avoid that at all costs."

She collapsed onto the white leather sofa. It was modern and sleek, set in a chrome frame. She pulled her knees up to her chest to make room for Takeo. There was plenty of seating in the spacious living quarters, but she wanted him close. He joined her, still wearing his sunglasses. They took a moment to rest, exhausted from the stress and relieved that their story had held up so far.

A minute later, however, someone knocked on the door.

"It's me," Jimmy huffed.

Kiku opened the door. Their great collection of baggage had been transferred onto three smaller carts to navigate the corridors on the cruise ship. Jimmy and two porters pushed the carts into the room, then Jimmy tipped the porters and closed the door behind them.

He looked around and whistled. "Do you have any idea how much this suite costs?" He hurried over to a bottle of champagne on ice. "They give you a free rental car and a guide at every port, a study, a private dining room, a personal butler, and a fully stocked bar." He headed straight to it, grabbed a glass, and took out a whiskey. "Do you guys want one?"

"After you unpack the bags," Kiku said as she strolled around the room staring at the light fixtures.

"Can I ask the butler to unpack?"

"Certainly not." Kiku swept through each room.

"What's she doing?" Jimmy asked Takeo as she reappeared from the bathroom, staring at a wall sconce.

"Looking for cameras and microphones," Takeo said curtly. He walked over to the bar, poured himself a drink, and sat down in a leather chair.

Jimmy wiped his mouth with the back of his hand, then rubbed the top of his head and made a disgusted face. "I swear I sweat more now that I don't have hair. How do bald guys do it?"

Kiku continued to sweep the room. "Where is your cabin, Jimmy?"

"My cabin?" Jimmy repeated, clearly confused. He poured another drink.

Kiku frowned at his glass. "Two drinks is your limit."

"We're on a cruise," Jimmy whined, then held up a hand. "Okay, two, I get it."

"Where is your cabin?" Kiku repeated.

Jimmy shrugged. "Here. There are two bedrooms, one for me and ..." His words trailed off as he stared at Kiku's narrowing eyes.

Takeo chuckled and smiled at Kiku as he sipped his drink. "Looks like we're bunkmates." He swirled the liquid in his glass, the ice clinking against the side. "There's nothing you can do to change it now; we have to keep our cover after all."

The two men exchanged frat-boy grins that Kiku was tempted to slap off their faces. She strolled toward the bedroom, her chiffon dress trailing out behind her. She stopped in the doorway, revealing a length of gleaming thigh.

"I would never think of changing our sleeping arrangements." Her almost-black eyes sparkled beneath her long lashes. "I did not think you would be comfortable sleeping next to me."

Takeo raised a puzzled brow.

"I always sleep naked."

Takeo's ice clinked against the side of his glass, and despite his sunglasses, she knew his eyes had widened. She could tell from the flush of his ears.

"I am going to take a nap before dinner," she said. "You may join me if you like."

23

They were obliged to accept the captain's invitation to dinner that evening; it was all part of their cover. But despite the danger, in some ways it felt like a game. Kiku exchanged her black evening gown for a red one, while Takeo continued his man-in-black look.

As for Jimmy, Kiku didn't know if he was just getting into the role or if he was destined to wear a bow tie and glasses, but he was rocking the look and performing the hip manager act to perfection. And, from the attention he was receiving from some of the women in the dining room and his obvious enjoyment, it appeared he was rethinking his original negative assessment of his makeover.

The captain started the dinner by asking a lot of questions about Classical Warfare, but Kiku deftly steered the subject to a nautical discussion; she knew people preferred to talk about themselves. Soon everyone at the table was busy chatting away about their own lives—everyone except the honored guests.

After dinner, Kiku was about to excuse herself and return to the cabin when the captain made a not entirely unexpected request.

"If I may be so presumptuous, we'd love to hear you both perform," he said.

Before Kiku could politely decline the invitation, Takeo announced,

"Love to." He finished his third whiskey sour and set the glass down on the table with a loud click.

Kiku's face remained a neutral mask as she stared at Takeo. *What happened to avoiding this at all costs?* She cursed herself once again for giving Takeo the Roy Orbison sunglasses. She couldn't see his eyes, and therefore had no clue what he was thinking.

Grinning roguishly and reminding her of his uncle Daichi, Takeo rose from his chair.

The captain smiled broadly. "Wonderful."

Jimmy kicked Kiku's foot under the table, leaned over, and whispered into her ear, "Do something."

All the options for stopping Takeo—including punching him in the nose—raced through her mind, but they were derailed by an overriding question: *What is he up to?* Like a spectator watching a race car crash, she was transfixed, wanting to see the outcome and unable to look away.

"I am sorry, but I have a bit of a sore throat, Rin," she said, smiling thinly. "You know how I get when I don't drink enough water. Let's go back to our suite and sip something warm, out on the balcony." She added the last part as a not-so-veiled threat.

"I'm sorry to hear that," the captain said with a frown. Kiku picked up on the suspicion in his eyes.

"No worries!" Takeo bowed politely to the table. "It looks like this will have to be a solo performance."

Jimmy kicked Kiku again, and she pinned his foot to the floor with her high heel. Jimmy ground his teeth and let out a stifled whimper.

"Are you okay, Mr. Sano?" asked the waiter filling Kiku's water glass.

"Fine." Jimmy cleared his throat. "I'm just wishing I'd thought to sell tickets. I could have made a bundle."

A chuckle flittered around the table as Takeo strolled over to the grand piano, where a man sat playing soft background music. As Takeo approached, the piano player looked over to the captain, who nodded. The musician rose from the bench and stepped away.

Jimmy leaned in close and whispered, "Get ready to abandon ship. This is going to be as successful as the *Titanic*." Kiku gave him a withering glare.

Takeo sat on the piano bench and turned to look at Kiku. All eyes in the room traveled back and forth between the pair as if watching a tennis match, and the moment seemed to stretch into minutes. An uncomfortable murmur rolled through the room as people began to wonder what the man seated at the piano was doing and why he was just staring at the beautiful woman in the red dress.

Kiku was wondering the same thing. Why was he doing this? And then it dawned on her. Takeo was silently asking her a question: *Do you trust me?*

She felt like she was about to leap off a cliff. She saw no way out of this mess other than embarrassment and a blown cover. But ... she did trust Takeo.

He needed to know that. She raised her head, smiled, and gave a slight nod.

Takeo turned to the piano. He raised his hands, flexed his fingers, balled them into fists, and repeated the action twice. Then he began to play.

There was a little gasp of surprise among the crowd as he began a teasing remixed introduction to a classical piece, and then a hush fell like a velvet curtain. It took Kiku a moment to place the melody, but once she did, her smile grew. Chopin's "A Maiden's Wish." He was playing it for her, and it was impossible for her not to swoon as the notes danced through the elegant hall.

She'd known him since he was a boy, and she knew he could play some traditional Japanese music, but she hadn't realized ... A puzzle piece from the past fell into place in her mind. Kiku and Takeo used to spar often as children, daily sometimes. All of their sessions ended the same way—with Takeo saying he had to go practice. He never mentioned *what* he practiced, and Kiku never asked, because she thought he was embarrassed. She knew he only practiced because his harsh father forced him to. She had, incorrectly, guessed the violin.

As the song built in intensity, it increased in tempo and morphed into a wild mix of classical, jazz, and rock with a relentless, pounding bass line. Takeo transformed as well. A huge grin was plastered across his face as his fingers flew across the keys, his hands a blur, his silver hair like a spear dancing above his forehead.

He finished the composition. When he took his hands off the keys, the stunned silence that had settled over the diners suddenly erupted in applause and whistles and chairs scraping back as everyone stood, and Takeo took bows, grinning from ear to ear.

Kiku stood, too, amazed at his talent ... but not completely shocked. She was a good judge of people—she'd had to be, in order to stay alive as long as she had—and she'd always known that Takeo had greatness inside him.

He pulled his glasses down for just a second to give Kiku a wink. When she felt herself breathing faster than normal, her eyes scanned the room, searching for anything amiss, but everything seemed fine. Her heart was beating faster too—usually a warning sign of danger. And then her eyes met Takeo's once again, and she understood. *He* was the reason for her body's response.

The crowd quieted as Takeo held up a hand, gave a quick bow, and sat back down. The hushed room eagerly waited for what would come next. Takeo swung the microphone stand so the mic was closer to his mouth.

Jimmy's eyes widened. *He sings?* he mouthed to Kiku. She shrugged. At this point, nothing Takeo did would surprise her.

"This song is for the woman in red. It's her favorite."

Kiku kept her eyes on Takeo as he started to not only play but sing her favorite song: "Pretty Woman." Something inside her soared, but she also felt like a terrified rider on a roller coaster, clinging to the bar. All eyes in the room were on her, and she felt vulnerable and awkward. She wanted to lash out and make everyone look away. But as Takeo continued to sing, she stopped thinking of the other people in the room. She saw only Takeo. And he peered over the rim of his sunglasses, never taking his eyes from her.

When he finished, everyone in the room was once again on their feet and clapping. Two girls rushed to the piano with pen and paper in hand, and a dozen more people followed.

Kiku leaned over to Jimmy and raised her voice above the din of the crowd. "The casino is open until three a.m. You can charge up to five thousand dollars to the room. Do not come back to the suite before the casino closes."

"What? That's awesome, but ... Oh ..." Jimmy's face and bald head turned crimson.

Kiku looked back at Takeo. Even surrounded by people and signing autographs, his gaze was still fixed on her.

She rose. "Please excuse me, Captain. Thank you for your company this evening."

The men at the table rose as Kiku stood. She strode toward Takeo, eager to extract him from the crowd and take him back to the suite.

Takeo had wanted her to trust him. She had. Now she would return the favor.

24

The sun was just starting to lighten the horizon when Kiku opened her eyes. The ship wasn't moving, which meant they had passed into Russian waters while they slept. Most of the passengers would be getting ready to disembark and take a bus for a tour of Petropavlovsk-Kamchatka and some of the peninsula's many volcanoes. Of course she, Takeo, and Jimmy would stay aboard the ship.

She rolled over to study Takeo beside her. He was sleeping peacefully, a contented smile on his face. She imagined he'd be asleep for quite a while.

She felt tempted to wake him for another round of lovemaking, but pushed the idea aside. She didn't know what the morning, or the future, held for them. Though a sexual tension had always run through their relationship, and this was now the third time they'd been intimate, Takeo was still her employer, and she had a job to perform. Afterward, would they return to the previous status quo?

She slipped softly out of bed, pulled a clean shirt over her head, grabbed a pair of comfortable pants, and laced on a pair of sneakers. Then, unable to resist, she darted back to the bed and hovered over Takeo's handsome face before stealing a tender kiss. She watched for his reaction and Takeo stirred slightly, then rolled over. If he had sneaked up on her like that, she probably would have stabbed him to death before even opening her eyes to see who it was. If there ever was another tête-à-tête, she'd have to warn him.

The door to the suite clicked loudly as she darted into the hallway, but she doubted it would wake either of the men. Jimmy hadn't gotten back to the room until after three, as instructed, and judging by the way he had crashed into tables and cursed on his way to his room, he must have gone well over his two-drink limit. She and Takeo had behaved like teenagers surprised by parents—they huddled beneath the covers, giggling but not stopping what they were doing.

Now Kiku took the elevator down to the main deck, where she scanned the crowd. She was surprised by the number of people bustling around—crew and passengers alike. On the dock, she spotted a small contingent of police getting ready to scan disembarking tourists, but it was no larger than normal.

She strolled to the end of the deck to watch the rising sun, wishing she'd brought a jacket. Spring was kind of a relative term in this part of the world. She looked back over her shoulder at the bars of bronze light shining off the windows of the upper decks, and saw something that made her catch her breath.

There, forming up in the very room where Takeo had serenaded her the night before, were a dozen men in combat gear, carrying weapons—she was guessing Stechkin automatic pistols—and wearing the black berets of OMON, the Russian national guard. Getting caught by the Black Berets was slightly better than being apprehended by the army, but not by much.

Kiku turned and started rapidly back toward the stairs. She had left the room without her phone, and now there was no way of warning Takeo that they were coming for him.

No. There *was* one way. Instead of going up the stairs, she darted back into the hallway and yanked the nearest fire alarm. Within two seconds, sirens wailed and lights flashed.

Kiku bolted for the staircase, taking the steps three at a time. Beneath her, doors opened and passengers began streaming out into the stairwell in a panicked frenzy. When Kiku reached the level of the suite, she cracked open the door and peered down the hall.

She was too late; it was already packed with police. And over their shoulders she saw Takeo's silver hair as he was led out of the room in handcuffs and Jimmy's bald head behind him. There was no way the team she had seen in the dining hall had gotten here that fast. They must have split up earlier.

She let the door close and started back down the stairs. With this many police swarming around, there was no way she could free Takeo and Jimmy. She needed to keep herself from being captured. It was time to get away.

Cruise passengers moved shoulder to shoulder down the stairs. Even though they were in port, many of them had donned life preservers. When they reached the lowest deck, Kiku headed away from the crowd. She had to find an alternate exit; the police would be looking for a woman with silver-white hair. Her disguise was now her biggest liability.

As she hurried down the hallway, an elderly woman in a wheelchair came from the opposite direction, pushed by a younger woman. Attached oxygen tanks clattered as the chair jostled over a seam in the deck. Kiku pressed herself against the wall to let them pass.

"Is it a real fire?" the old woman asked nervously.

"I do not think so," Kiku said comfortingly, a plan clicking into place in her mind. She turned to the younger woman. "You'll want to turn left before the end of the hall and make your way back out on deck. There is a bottleneck down there." As she spoke, she lifted a small emergency oxygen tank from the side of the wheelchair.

The young woman thanked her and continued on her way. Kiku palmed the oxygen tank at her side as she ran down the corridor.

Two Black Berets opened the door at the end of the hallway, took one look at her, and shouted, "You there! Stop!"

Kiku stepped into the nearest room; its door had been left open in spite of the warning over the loudspeaker not to. She slipped into the bathroom near the entrance and waited.

When the first guard's head appeared through the doorway, she slammed the oxygen tank against his temple. He crumpled to the floor. The second guard, a large man with glasses, reached for his gun, but in the confined space of the cabin entranceway, his elbows bumped the walls, slowing him down. Before he could get a shot off, Kiku's fist came down on the bridge of his glasses, breaking his nose, then she brought the oxygen tank down on the crown of his head. The man dropped to his knees and slumped down next to his fellow guard.

Kiku considered striking him again, but one look at his eyes rolling back in his head told her he was unconscious; it was only his bullet-proof vest catching against the wall that was keeping him somewhat upright.

She took his gun, stepped out of the room, closed the door, and sprinted toward the door at the end of the hall. She had to make it to the main deck.

She was ten feet from the door when it opened again, revealing yet another Russian guard. She flung the oxygen tank like a hatchet. It tumbled three times before striking the man in the forehead and bouncing high into the air. She grabbed it by its metal top before it hit the deck, stepped over the fallen policeman, and slowed to a deliberate walk as she headed for the side of the ship facing away from the port.

She gulped in air, trying to prep her lungs for what she was about to do. It was crazy, but not impossible. Navy SEALs accomplished this same feat, and many others, too, had jumped from the decks of cruise ships and lived. Granted, most of them were attempting suicide—which this most likely was. But it was her best chance.

She didn't break stride as she grabbed the railing and vaulted over.

25

Kiku plummeted off the side of the cruise ship toward the water below, her arms crossed in front of her, tightly gripping the oxygen tank against her chest. She let the gun fall from her hands. She might be able to hold on to the oxygen tank, but not while holding the gun. Pressing her feet tightly together, she took one last deep breath and mentally prepared for hitting the water. She knew that most people drowned because they gulped water in—if they survived the brutal physical impact at all.

Kiku expected it to be bad, but the shocking violence of it could only be compared to an explosion. A brilliant flash filled her vision, followed by crushing pain. Momentum shot her in so deep she wondered if she should brace herself against striking the harbor floor. But then she slowed, and for a moment she hung in place.

She'd somehow managed to hang on to the oxygen tank, although the metal valve had cut into her hand. She waited for the oxygen to start flowing before she exhaled and breathed in from the tank.

Trying to calm her pounding heart, she gave herself a few moments to drift up slowly. As the waves of pain faded, they were replaced by a different, much worse, sensation—the icy cold already numbing her body.

She started to swim, floating upward as she went, careful not to get too close to the surface. It was exhausting swimming in sneakers, and her wet clothes made her feel like she was wearing a weight vest, but she would need her shoes and clothes when she got to shore. Thinking ahead to those actions kept her mind from shifting into panic over her current situation.

Slow. Steady. Conserve your energy.

A pylon rose before her, rearing up out of the murky water. She'd reached the main dock. She was tempted to grab hold until she saw the barnacles. Bracing herself with her sneakers instead, she clamped her burning eyes shut. The cold was jabbing into her now, but she shifted her focus by picturing the dock and where she needed to go.

She swam the length of the dock, working her way down the pylons, and kept going. The current was pulling her closer to shore now. She should be nearing the marina and the row upon row of pleasure boats moored there. That was her goal. If she could just reach one of the boats, she'd be safe.

She was trying to swim faster now, but for some reason, the harder she kicked her legs, the slower she went. Her whole body burned. She exhaled and put her mouth to the oxygen tank, but there was no air coming out. She twisted the valve further, but it was empty.

Letting go of the tank, she kicked for the surface with all her might, her hands clawing at the water as the pressure built in her chest. Her head broke the surface, and she gasped for air.

The water around her was quiet. The dock was still clearly visible, and no one was lingering at this end. Her plummet over the railing of the cruise ship seemed to have gone unnoticed in the chaos of the fire alarm.

Coughing and sputtering, she searched for the closest boat, but she'd grossly underestimate the distance she'd covered. The marina was still a hundred yards away. She thought about rolling onto her back and floating, but she knew if she stopped now, she'd die. She'd drift along, close her eyes, and wash up on shore a week later.

She embraced that image of her crab-eaten face. Was that how she wanted to go? She kicked her legs and kept swimming.

Takeo would be dead in a week, too. She forced herself to imagine him strapped to a chair, the hands that had created such beautiful music broken and twisted, his face battered and bloody as some stupid thug lifted a crowbar over his head.

Her arms reached out and her hands cupped the frigid water as she pulled herself forward. She couldn't feel her fingers anymore, but still she kicked and grabbed at the water; each movement felt as if fighting against an unseen beast beneath her that was pulling her down.

She was growling now, and she struggled not to start screaming. She hurt so much ... she'd never known a body could hurt so badly. Were her muscles pulling away from her bones? Had she shattered something when she hit the water and didn't realize it?

She reminded herself of the stakes. Kenzo would find out that his youngest son had helped them, and he'd kill Jiro, too. And what would happen to Alex? Would he seek revenge for his father? Would Daichi go with him? They'd both die. And then Kenzo would slaughter Hwan, Baba, and Lilly.

Lilly ... Kiku could almost hear Daichi's voice: *"I'll have her say a prayer for you."*

This would be the answer to a prayer made on her behalf. Maybe she'd already died, and this was her hell. Kiku bit the water like a mad dog, unable to control herself. Salt water splashed into her mouth as she swore. Her left arm stopped working, just shut down completely. Her right arm arched again, but she choked as water washed over her head and filled her mouth.

Fury raged inside her, a burning anger at a God Who continued to mock her. She lifted her head one last time to glare at the sky and tell Him what she thought—and she saw the last boat in the marina was less than ten yards away. Kiku laughed. It wasn't a chuckle, but a full-blown, insane guffaw. Choking, coughing, and crying, she forced her body to keep swimming. She was *so* close. Five more strokes.

Another little wave washed over her, and she sank under the surface. The water wasn't so cold anymore. She was almost there. Could she float to it?

She blinked, and her blurry eyes burned. The boat was a black, fuzzy outline. The sun made the water above her head sparkle. It looked beautiful.

Why is the water gold in the morning, Akari?

Kiku was walking around the pond with her sister while her mother painted up on a little hill. Kiku looked around for her father, suddenly worried for him, but there he was, asleep in his little rowboat, his fishing rod dangling over the back. Kiku leaned over the metal railing above the pond and watched the water swirl into the fish run. The gold sparkles danced across the surface, so close that she could almost touch them. She stretched way out ... and her fingers slipped off the railing.

She tumbled end over end and landed hard on her stomach in the water. Sputtering, she broke the surface and started to swim, but she wasn't going anywhere. The swirling water of the fish run was pulling her back.

Akari was screaming. Her mother was running. Kiku panicked. What would happen if she was pulled into the whirlpool? The water came out across the road, but was there a grate underneath the road? Could she hold her breath that long?

Kiku was flailing her arms now, crying and terrified, but one voice rose above all the others, her father's.

"Swim! Swim!" He dove into the water.

Kiku's eyes snapped open. The beast was dragging her to the deep, but she wasn't going to die without a fight. Her hands clawed the water and she kicked hard, her father's voice urging her on.

She surfaced right behind the boat's ladder. Her right hand grabbed the rung, but her left hand wouldn't open. Groaning, she used her left elbow instead. Rung by rung, she pulled herself up and over the side, and flopped into the back of the boat.

But she didn't stop. If she stopped there, she'd die.

She crawled to the boat's main cabin and fumbled with the door. It was unlocked, but her motor skills were gone and even her right hand was not responding correctly now. Still, with effort, she somehow managed to pull it open. She dragged herself inside, and toward a messy bed with a thick blanket.

She was so cold, she just wanted to curl up in that bed and drift into oblivion. But she had to get her wet clothes off.

She had no idea how long it took her to remove her frigid clothes, but it felt like eternity. Her eyes weren't focusing anymore; her mind wasn't thinking properly. But at last, she crawled up into the bed and wrapped the blanket tightly around herself.

As she closed her eyes, she pictured her father, dripping wet and proudly carrying his frightened little girl out of the pond.

If he hadn't encouraged her—here, today—she'd be dead.

That was three times she owed him her life.

She smiled at the thought, just before she passed out.

26

Kiku's eyes snapped open, and she gasped. Her whole body throbbed, and it was far worse even than after the time she had been tortured and caned from head to toe. She started to close her eyes again, but the haunting melody of Chopin's "A Maiden's Wish" played through her mind.

Takeo needed her.

Keeping the blanket wrapped around her shoulders, she rolled off the bed, grateful there was no one nearby to hear her moans. From the position of the sun, she guessed it was late afternoon. She winced as she picked up her shirt. It was still soaked, and so were her pants, underwear, socks, and sneakers. Her first task was clear: drying her clothes.

She started rooting through the cabinets. She set aside a med kit, a large fishing knife, three coffee cans, and a dozen cans of stew. Her eyes lit up when she found a portable stove. It was small—only big enough to heat the stew or boil a pot of coffee—but that was all she needed.

She warmed a can of stew and scarfed it down. She then spent the next half hour trying to get the feeling back into her hands by wringing out her clothes and arranging them to dry over the stove. Next, she searched the rest of the boat and found fishing tackle, a wrench, a screwdriver, reading glasses, and a thick wool sweater. In the bathroom she found an old toothbrush, a comb, and half a bottle of aspirin. She took six, even though she felt like downing the entire bottle.

When her clothes were mostly dry, she dressed in everything but her socks and shoes, putting on the heavy sweater as well. Her body still ached, but she needed to focus on moving forward. Which meant doing something about her bright silver-white hair.

She tried wrapping a rag around her head, but that only made it look like she was trying to hide something. That oddity alone would probably get her pulled over for questioning. With the blanket wrapped tightly around her, she crept out the cabin door and across the exposed deck to the engine compartment. She flipped up the cover, grabbed a handful of grease, and snuck back to the cabin and into the bathroom. The grease was disgusting, but just a small amount stained her white hair dark black.

She laid the rag on the counter and folded it into a triangle, then fashioned it into a hairband. She slicked her hair back into a traditional low bun to hide any white hair she might have missed with the grease, wrapped the band around her head, and tied it beneath the bun. She put the reading glasses on low on her nose to make herself look older, and checked herself in the mirror.

She had to admit, if she wanted to look like a broken-down Japanese woman living in Russia, her outfit was impressive.

It was wonderful to slip into her warm, comfy socks, but the feeling was short-lived. Her sneakers were still damp, and when she put them on, her socks were quickly soaked once more.

She grabbed the screwdriver and left the fishing knife behind. If she was stopped by the police, it would be easier to explain a screwdriver than a knife, and she could kill someone effortlessly with the tool anyway.

Every muscle in her body protested as she stepped off the boat and onto the dock. Walking was a bit of a challenge still, and she found it more comfortable to walk a little hunched over. The few men standing on the pier gave her a pitiful glance as she limped past.

She started toward the park at the end of the pier, then noticed a sign for ferry parking and changed direction. The theft of a car at the ferry would probably not be reported as quickly as one at the park. To her relief, the lot was pre-pay, so she could drive right out without having to steal a wallet first.

She approached a plain sedan and with a quick pop from the screwdriver shattered the driver's-side window. She had the door open and the car started in under a minute, the longest part of which was spent sweeping the tiny glass pieces off the seat before getting in. She raided the glove compartment, removing a half-full pack of thick Russian cigarettes and some loose change, then drove toward the guard booth, where a bored-looking man sat with his feet up.

"Excuse me?" Kiku said in Russian, leaning out the window as she drove up. "I need to fill out work papers at the police station. Can you give me directions?"

The man hardly glanced up as he rattled off directions to the station. Kiku thanked him and pulled out of the lot. Her hands shook as she cranked up the heater, regretting that she'd had to break the window. She drove at the speed limit as she crossed toward the center of the city. Traffic was busy, and the tourists blended with locals heading home. The business district thinned out, and soon she was turning down the street toward the police station.

Kiku was surprised there was no fence around the drab, boxy building, and none even around the police vehicles, consisting of a half dozen police cars and a huge, six-wheeled armored personnel carrier that looked as if it could transport a small army.

Kiku kept driving and pulled into the parking lot of the building next door, which was almost identical and had a sign that read LOCAL HISTORY MUSEUM. There were only three cars in the lot; she parked behind one, making sure she had a good view of the police station. The concrete building was three stories tall, with a small green space out back. The chief's office would be in that corner—it had the best view. Takeo and Jimmy were most likely being held downstairs in the holding cells.

She didn't have time to wait to rescue them. The police had descended in force on the cruise ship—far too many police for just a routine pickup. Takeo and Jimmy would be interrogated—if Jimmy was even still alive. And Cade Novikov's men would not be far behind. The local Russian police force, while still grafted with the military and beholden to the state, had come a long way from the corruption of the Soviet Union. But the Russian underworld had enough money and power to corrupt and coerce almost anyone.

Kiku rubbed her hands together, trying to warm them up.

A corrugated metal door on the side of the police station rattled and rolled up slowly. A thin woman in coveralls appeared, pushing a deep, yellow fabric cart loaded up with laundry bags. Kiku grabbed the cigarettes off the seat and got out of the car.

Part of her screamed, *Stop! You don't have a plan!* But she kept her battered legs moving forward. A sliver of an opportunity had presented itself, and like it or not, now was the best time to strike.

"Hey!" Kiku called out gruffly.

The Russian woman raised her head. She wore dark coveralls and a yellow and green headscarf that held her hair back. She scowled at Kiku with weary eyes. "What?"

"Do you have a light?" Kiku tossed a cigarette into her mouth.

"Do you have a spare?" the woman shot back as she pushed the cart over to a rusty van and opened the van's rear doors.

Kiku held out the pack—but dropped it just before the woman took it.

"I'm so stupid," Kiku muttered. She bent down to pick up the pack, and came back up with the screwdriver in her hand. She stepped close to the Russian woman and pressed it against her throat. "Get inside."

"I have no money." The woman glared.

Kiku resisted the urge to smile. Angry hostages were often the best behaved, because they listened and didn't fall apart. She hoped this would be the case now.

"Get in," she repeated, and the woman complied. Kiku followed her, clicked on the overhead light, and closed the van's rear doors. "I need your clothes and your badge."

The woman's expression changed from puzzlement to understanding. "You're crazy. You'll never get those guys out of there. There are too many police."

Kiku kept the screwdriver against the woman's throat. "Take off the coveralls." The woman did, letting them fall to her feet. "Hands behind your back." Kiku pulled a drawstring out of a laundry bag and used it to tie her hands. "Sit down."

The woman glared at Kiku. "Are you going to let me live?"

"How did you know I was after those men?"

"You're Japanese and so are they. I heard a woman with them got away. I never thought you'd come after them. I doubt the Russians did either."

Kiku raised an eyebrow as she tied the woman's ankles.

The woman picked up on it. "I'm not Russian." She spat to the side scornfully. "Chechen," she announced proudly.

"So you have no love for the Russians?"

"None."

"Yet you work at their police station."

"My daughter and I need to eat."

Kiku grabbed a cloth to gag the woman, but the Chechen shook her head. "That cloth is soiled. If you are gagging me, can you please use a clean one?" She nudged another bag with her elbow.

Kiku dropped the cloth and got out another. As she twisted the towel, she eyed the woman. "Have you seen the men?"

"Will you kill me after I tell you?"

"No."

The woman nodded. "One is beneath the cells in the lower basement."

"How many levels does the basement have?"

"Two. The cells are on the first. Beneath the cells, there is another level. You never want to go to that level."

"Do you have access?"

"Yes, but I have never been there."

"Did you see the police take the man there?"

"No. A secretary told me."

"What about the other man?"

The woman shrugged. "I cleaned all three floors and didn't see him. He is some big shot. The men were bragging and preening like roosters that they'd caught him."

"Where would they normally keep the high-profile prisoners?"

"The lower level. I'm sorry, but one of your friends may already be dead."

Kiku swallowed the bile rising in her throat. "What kind of security do they have?" She held up the badge on the front of the woman's coveralls.

"The sensors on the doors read my badge. It opens all the doors. I can get anywhere. There is a service elevator just beyond the door I exited. It will take you to the lower level."

Kiku stared at the woman. Her brown eyes stared unflinchingly back.

"Thank you," Kiku whispered before tying the gag in place. She considered knocking the woman out, but didn't think it was necessary.

She put on the woman's coveralls—badge attached—then hopped out, transferred half the bags from the laundry cart into the van, and started pushing the cart toward the police station.

There was a saying in the Yakuza: *You never want to get caught by the Russian police, because going into the station house is like getting dragged into a snake hole.*

Kiku shook her head. *And now I'm breaking into a snake hole.* She just hoped she'd be able to break back out.

27

After pushing the cart inside the building, Kiku hit the switch to lower the metal door behind her. Feeling a claustrophobic wave of fear wash over her, she started to hum, both for cover and to calm her beating heart. Practicing her Russian accent with "Pretty Woman" brought a little smirk to her face as she pushed the cart over to the service elevator.

The button lit up with a jaundiced glow, and a deep vibration echoed in the hallway. She could hear people walking around, but no one was in sight. The elevator dinged, and the doors opened. Kiku pushed the cart inside.

"Halt!" someone called out in Russian, and Kiku heard running footsteps.

The doors were almost closed when a hand was thrust through the opening and blocked them. A uniformed officer shoved the door open. He scowled at Kiku as he got on, making his bushy eyebrows knit together like an enormous caterpillar.

He pressed the button for one floor down. Kiku had already pressed the button for the lowest level. His gaze traveled from the elevator buttons to Kiku and back again. The muscles in his forearms flexed as he read her name badge. His eyes widened, and he turned his head to look back at the doors, his right hand moving toward his baton.

Kiku's hand shot out for the man's temple, but he moved too quickly, his arm pivoting up and blocking her strike. He countered, swinging fast and hard, putting everything into his punch and pushing off his rear foot. Kiku dodged it, and the policeman's hand bashed into the metal door. She heard a bone in his hand snap. The man's mouth opened for only a second before Kiku's uppercut slammed it closed again.

He rocked back into the elevator wall, but as his back struck the metal, he shoved Kiku. It was a glancing blow, but it flung her across the small space. Wiping his bloody mouth with the back of his hand, the policeman smiled grimly and once more reached for his baton.

The smile vanished when he realized that Kiku had pulled his baton out of his police belt. She brought it down in an arc against the side of the man's head, and he began to crumple to the floor. She caught him and steered him toward the cleaning cart; it caught him at the hips, and momentum carried him forward and in. She pulled a laundry bag over him just before the elevator shuddered to a stop, then pivoted to face the opening doors.

Two policemen stood on guard just outside. They eyed her quizzically.

She held up an apologetic hand and shoved the cart against the back of the elevator, causing a loud bang. "Sorry for the noise. I hate this part of my job." She let fly a long stream of colorful Russian curses and added "lice outbreak" at the end.

It was a good story. They were housing men in rat-like conditions, and whenever that was the case, lice were quick to follow. The policemen stopped dead in their tracks.

"I've been cleaning all day. I'm covered." She scratched her neck and her armpit for emphasis.

The doors started to close. The policemen exchanged a glance and stepped away from the doors. "That sucks," the younger officer called out just before the doors closed all the way. Kiku guessed that was his way of offering sympathy.

She'd kept the baton hidden behind her leg, and now she tucked it against the inside of the cart. Reaching under the laundry bags, she removed the unconscious officer's gun, checked the magazine, made sure a round was chambered, and stuffed it into her pocket.

The elevator continued to thunder downward. Kiku rolled her shoulder. The last thing she wanted was a fight. She hoped when the doors opened, there would be a single policewoman stationed there, preferably one who was about to retire.

The elevator rumbled to a stop. The doors opened. Three policemen stood at a desk eating pizza. None of them was under six feet tall.

Kiku groaned silently. She pulled the cart out of the elevator into the hallway. Muttering and swearing, she turned to the men and snapped, "I'm collecting all bedding, clothing, sheets, and towels." She scratched her cheek hard enough to leave red streaks. "This new lice outbreak is worse than the last."

The man at the desk closed the pizza box and made a face. "All the units are empty. You can clean Unit Two. It's the only one with bedding." The three exchanged some inside joke and grinned.

Scratching her backside, Kiku started pushing the cart toward the metal door at the end of the hall. She held her badge up to a scanner, and the lock clicked. Awkwardly, she held the door open while pushing the heavy cart through.

The stinging odor of urine hung in the next hallway. Three doors on the left were labeled *One*, *Two*, and *Three*. Another door with a security reader stood at the end. There were no cameras, although upstairs she had noticed several. She guessed the Russians were more concerned with keeping a lid on what they were doing down here than with security.

As Kiku pushed the cart past Unit One, she glanced inside. It was empty, not a stick of furniture. Just a hole in the floor in one corner, presumably for waste. She continued to Unit Two. This one was also unfurnished but not completely empty; there was a blanket on the floor, covered with blood. Kiku's anger started to rise as she remembered the policemen laughing at their inside joke. Judging by the amount of blood splattered all over the room, whoever had been held here was now dead.

Cell Three was empty as well. At the end of the hallway, Kiku pressed her security card against the reader. She got a yellow light, but nothing else happened. The door remained locked. She tried again, with the same result.

Kiku leaned over the cart, shoved a laundry bag aside, and pulled the security badge off the unconscious police officer and pressed it to the reader. This time the light turned green and the lock clicked. She yanked the door open.

This hallway was identical to the one she'd just passed through, except for the cell numbers. Again, the first cell in this area was empty, as was the second.

The last one wasn't. In the middle of the boxy concrete room, a man was strapped to a chair with a hood pulled over his head. The seat was like something out of an old black-and-white movie used to electrocute prisoners. Leather straps secured the man's wrists and ankles. From the tweed suit, Kiku knew it was Jimmy.

She opened the door, pulled the cleaning cart into the doorway to block it open, and rushed over to the chair. Jimmy shook uncontrollably and muffled cries came from beneath the hood as she struggled with the restraints. She pulled them off. A gag with a plastic bit had been wedged into his mouth, and she removed that as well.

At the sight of her, Jimmy's eyes widened and he tried to smile. His left eye was black and blue, his lip was swollen, and blood ran from his nose.

"I'm dead, right? There's no way Kiku would come in here for me." He rubbed his wrists. "You're an angel, right? You just look like her for some screwed-up reason. Or this is a trick. You're some Russian lookalike with greasy hair and—"

"Shut up and get undressed."

Jimmy's head rocked to one side. "Okay. Now I know you're the real deal." He kicked his shoes off and started taking off his pants, awkwardly and obviously in pain.

"How often do they check on you?"

"I don't—" He stopped, closed his eyes, and grimaced. "Like, every half hour. It's screwed-up. The last four times they didn't even ask me anything. They just came in, smacked me around, and left."

"They're trying to break you down."

"Well, it worked the first time; they didn't have to keep doing it. But I didn't know anything to begin with, so it's not like they got anything they didn't already know." Jimmy stripped down to his underwear.

"When was the last time they came?"

"About five minutes ago. I think it was only one guy."

"Where are they holding Takeo?"

"I don't know. They split us up when they brought us here. I haven't seen him since."

"But Takeo did come with you to this building?"

Jimmy nodded.

"Help me." Kiku turned to the cart and lifted the laundry bags off the unconscious cop.

"Where'd you get him?"

"Later," Kiku snapped. "We need to take your clothes and put them on him."

"You brought your own decoy. You're like a super ninja."

"Shut up, Jimmy. I did not know I would be using him as a decoy. I just could not leave him in the elevator."

Together, they lifted the policeman out of the cart and removed his clothes. Kiku dressed him in Jimmy's clothes while Jimmy put on the policeman's uniform. It was a little large for him, but not too obviously so. They then strapped the officer into the chair, gagged him, and pulled the hood over his head just as his eyes fluttered open.

Jimmy grabbed the policeman's hat out of the cart and put it on. "I think I can make this work."

"Get in the cart, Jimmy."

"What? Why? I can do this."

Kiku narrowed her eyes, and Jimmy obediently climbed into the cart. She covered him up with laundry bags.

"Did they keep your hood on the last time they beat you?"

"Yeah. Why?"

She looked back at the man in the chair. A taste of his own medicine would be kinder than what Kiku wanted to do to him.

"Where are we going?" Jimmy whispered.

"We are going to get Takeo."

If Takeo was being held in this police station, he was likely being interrogated by the chief in his office. From the bowels of the station to its heart—she would go anywhere to find Takeo.

28

Kiku pushed the heavy cart through the door and back into the first section of cells. The hallway was empty. After closing the door quietly behind her, she passed by Unit Two, and fought back her fear that the blood was Takeo's.

Jimmy was alive—and if the Russians had let Jimmy live, then surely they would not have killed Takeo ...

Unless they had confused the two. Kiku's mouth went dry as she remembered what the cleaning woman had said. Her heart sped back up and she started to hum, once again picking "Pretty Woman."

The three policemen were still standing at the desk by the elevator, but the pizza box was now empty. As she approached, one of the men picked up the box and started toward her cart.

"Unit Two was loaded with lice," Kiku announced, pointing down at her cart. "They're probably going to have to burn all this. The fumigator is coming tomorrow."

The man stopped where he was and flicked the pizza box into her cart.

Kiku scratched her armpit and pressed the elevator button, praying the old elevator wouldn't take too long—*ding*.

The doors opened, and Kiku pushed the cart inside.

God does have a sense of humor.

The elevator rumbled and shook as it carried them up. Her fingernails dug into the palm of her hand. She was guessing that Takeo was in the chief's office, because considering who Takeo was and who was looking for him, it wasn't a job to leave to subordinates; and she was guessing where the chief's office was based on the building's layout and views. Guessing was all she could do, and these were the odds she was forced to take.

It was after hours, and the top floor was practically empty. A few staff members scurried out of doorways, only to disappear a moment later into other ones, like groundhogs.

Kiku rounded a corner and stared down a long hall. The good news was that she'd guessed correctly—the sign on the corner office indicated that it was the chief's office. The bad news was there was a muscular guard in front of the door.

Kiku stopped her cart in front of what appeared to be a conference room, retrieved the trash can, and dumped its contents into her cart. She repeated the process at the next room. If she covered the laundry with enough trash, the guard would assume it was all trash.

But she had to hurry; time was not on her side. There was no way of knowing if her decoy downstairs would hold up under close inspection. Or if someone would notice the policeman was missing; there was always that chance. But one thing was clear: she had to get rid of the guard in front of the chief's door.

She stopped her cart in front of the office two down from the chief's. She walked in, scanned the room, and took note of the name on a brass plaque on the desk. Then she pushed the cart in front of the door at an angle, making sure to leave enough room for the guard to get by, and leaned out.

"Excuse me?" she called over to the guard. "Officer Alexeev's gun is on his chair. Should I move it?"

The guard swore and stalked forward. "What a fool," he muttered.

Kiku stepped aside and pointed to the chair. As soon as the man passed her, she shoved the door closed and brought the baton down on the back of his head. He pitched forward, bounced off the chair, and slumped down next to the desk.

Kiku grabbed his legs and stuffed him under the desk. She didn't bother tying him up; it would take too long. She turned the light off and closed the door behind her as she left.

She pushed the cart to the chief's office and knocked.

"Not now," a voice bellowed in Russian.

Kiku knocked again and cracked open the door. "I'm sorry to disturb you," she said sheepishly as she peeked in.

Takeo sat opposite the chief at a round table in the corner of the office. He was once again dressed in his tuxedo, and she saw no bruises or blood. Both men had drinks in their hands. A tall window beside them overlooked the park and, in the distance, the harbor. If Kiku hadn't known differently, she would have assumed they were just two friends discussing the weather.

The police chief was a broad-shouldered man with the face of a pug. When he looked at Kiku's face, his little eyes rounded. He was bright. He knew she was the woman they were searching for.

Kiku drew the gun, stepped into the office, and closed the door behind her. Takeo grinned.

Surprisingly, the police chief did, too. "So, this is the infamous Kiku. You are correct: she is most impressive. Beautiful, too."

Kiku stepped closer, keeping her gun aimed at the chief's chest. "Thank you. Using two fingers, remove your sidearm and place it on the table."

The chief cheerfully complied, holding the grip with only his index finger and thumb. "Would you care to join us for a drink?"

Takeo grabbed the gun and stood. "It's good to see you," he said to Kiku with a smile.

Kiku dragged the table away from the chief. The glasses on it rattled and spilled.

"With your outfit," the chief said in a mocking voice, "I hope you're planning on cleaning that up before you go." He chuckled.

Kiku reached under the table and yanked out the sawed-off combat shotgun mounted beneath it. "You looked a little too comfortable sitting there. You still do. Your ankle gun, please. Again, two fingers."

Takeo aimed the chief's own gun at him. The chief, now frowning, reached down for the pistol attached to his leg and handed it to Kiku.

"Stand up." Kiku moved behind him and removed a third gun from the holster at his back. She patted him down and took the cuffs off his belt. "Hands behind your back."

While Kiku cuffed him, the chief eyed Takeo. "Before you run off, that proposition I offered is still open."

Takeo shook his head. "There's no need to get into a bidding war with the Russians for my release now, is there?"

"This is my city. You won't make it out. Pay me a toll and I will let you go."

Kiku smiled. "You are not our toll collector. You are our ticket to ride." She grabbed a Russian flag off the wall and twisted it up by quickly spinning her wrist. "Open your mouth."

The chief's little eyes narrowed into slits. "If you—"

Kiku boxed his ear with the butt of her gun. "Open. Your. Mouth."

Glowering, the chief complied. Kiku gagged him.

"I don't know where they took Jimmy," Takeo said.

"I have him. Can you do me a favor? Move to the other side of the cart and keep it from tipping." Kiku pushed the chief toward the door and opened it. Takeo walked to the other side of the cart and held it down while Kiku pulled out four laundry bags. Jimmy's bald head appeared, and he gazed up at them, blinking like a possum discovered in the trash.

"Slide over," Kiku ordered.

"What? Why?" Jimmy whispered.

Kiku elbowed the police chief as hard as she could just below the solar plexus. He doubled up and she yanked him forward, flipping him up and into the cart.

"That's why," Kiku said.

Jimmy swore, and he and the police chief glared at each other like two dogs in a cage.

Kiku gestured to the cart. "My apologies, Takeo."

Takeo frowned.

Kiku did her best not to grin, but she was unsuccessful.

Takeo climbed on top of the chief, whose face turned bright red with indignation. With the three men in the laundry cart, Kiku could fit only three of the four bags back inside. She set her sore back against the cart, and her thighs screamed in protest as she shoved the lumbering cart down the hall. Once she got it going, it wasn't that bad, but she was already dreading trying to get it on and off the service elevator.

Two office workers passed close to her as she made her way down the hall and didn't give her a second glance. But when Kiku hit the elevator button, the whole cart suddenly started shaking.

"Stop moving or I will shoot you, Chief," Takeo's muffled voice threatened. The chief mumbled something, but Kiku couldn't make out the words through his gag.

"Sorry," Jimmy whispered. "It was me. So itchy ... the lice are all over me." The cart shook again.

Kiku was tempted to hit Jimmy with the baton.

She pretended to adjust the bags as she glanced up and down the deserted hallway. "There are no lice, you idiot. I lied."

"Oh ..."

The cart stopped moving. The elevator doors opened, and Kiku used her anger to push the cart inside. If Jimmy's stupidity had gotten them discovered, the Russians would have been the least of his worries.

She pressed the button for the ground floor. The elevator shook and rumbled and moved at a maddeningly slow speed. Kiku held down the door close button the whole way; she was unsure if that trick actually worked, but the last thing she wanted was someone else getting into the elevator, leaving her to add another body to the cart.

The elevator made it all the way down to the loading dock and the doors opened. Kiku grunted as she strained to get the heavy cart moving once more. She rolled up the door and pushed the cart outside—just as three cars were skidding to a stop in the rear parking lot.

Kiku's heart sped up.

The Russians had arrived.

29

Six cars had now stopped halfway across the lot. An old man sitting in the back seat of the lead car glared at Kiku.

Kiku swore under her breath. He'd recognized her. *Patrov.* She was amazed the old creep was still alive, considering his daily intake of vodka and cigarettes. The cigarette he currently had in his mouth bobbed up and down as he yelled at his driver. The men in the cars behind Patrov's started yelling too, no doubt wondering why they had stopped.

The passenger door of Patrov's car burst open. Kiku grabbed one side of the cart and pulled down as hard as she could.

"Roll toward me!" she shouted in Japanese, knowing Takeo and Jimmy would respond.

The laundry cart turned on its side, and Takeo rolled out, the sawed-off shotgun ready his hands.

Kiku dragged the chief out by his hair. Yanking his gag down, she pressed the gun to the back of his head. "Order them to hold fire."

"Stop!" the chief bellowed. "Hold your fire!"

Jimmy wiggled out from beneath the laundry bags and held up the chief's pistol, aiming behind Kiku. "We've got problems."

Kiku glanced over her shoulder. Several armed policemen were taking up strategic positions in the doorway.

The chief glared at Takeo. "You are trapped. You should have taken my offer."

Patrov got out of his car. "It looks like you don't have the situation under control after all!" he shouted.

At least eighteen men in total had gotten out as well, and all had taken up firing positions, using the cars for protection. Their array of weapons ranged from pistols to machine guns.

"My men have everything under control," the chief bellowed back. "Tell your men to stand down."

Kiku pressed the gun against the back of his head. "Give your men the same order."

She scanned the parking lot. With the amount of firepower on both sides, there was really only one option for getting out of here. The military APC. The armored vehicle was their only cover from the Russians. She wasn't too concerned about the police, not while she had a gun pointed at the back of their chief's head, but Patrov was a vicious man, still wanted for war crimes; he would just as soon kill the chief and every policeman present if that was what it took.

"Give us Nakumora and the woman," Patrov said. "Then we'll go."

"Send over my money!" the chief shouted back.

"Shut up, you fool," Kiku ordered. She pulled the chief toward the APC's door.

Patrov smiled.

"Cover!" was all Kiku could blurt out before Patrov's men opened fire at both Kiku and the police.

The police returned fire, but the tactical superiority definitely lay with Patrov's men.

"Inside!" Kiku dragged the chief backward.

Takeo yanked open the large rear door, and all four of them dove in. Even inside the vehicle, the sounds from the war zone outside were deafening. Each bullet that struck the armor plating rang like a giant bell—and they were inside the bell.

Kiku used hand signals to motion to Takeo to keep his gun on the chief.

"DO YOU HAVE THE KEYS?!" Jimmy shouted directly in the chief's ear.

The chief's face flushed so red that Kiku thought something in his head might actually rupture. She was tempted to let Jimmy know that he was screaming in Japanese, and from the look on the chief's face, he didn't speak the language. Either way, she doubted he kept the keys to a military vehicle in his pocket, and she didn't need them anyway. The main difference between hot-wiring a car and hot-wiring a military vehicle was that the latter was much easier because there was more room to move around. She had the engine started in less than thirty seconds.

"You better get us moving!" Jimmy shouted, now directly in *her* ear. Kiku was about to punch him in the mouth when she noticed where he was pointing. One of the Russians had taken a rocket launcher out of the trunk of a car.

"Get on the gun!" she ordered as she put the APC into drive.

The chief saw Jimmy grabbing the fifty-cal and shook his head. "No ammo!" he bellowed above the din.

Kiku circled her hand above her head to signal to Jimmy to keep moving. Jimmy's face twisted in puzzlement, but he swung the gun around and pointed it at the Russians.

The bullets hitting the APC stopped as the Russians dove for cover. Kiku smiled. The Russians had no way of knowing there was no ammo in the gun.

The APC bumped over the curb. When it turned onto the road, a rocket streaked by the little side window in the cab, traveled halfway down the block, and slammed into a tree, completely obliterating it.

Jamming down the gears, Kiku steered past the bark, smoke, and debris of the exploded tree, toward the middle of the street. Patrov's men were firing at the APC again, the shots pounding the vehicle like hammers.

Takeo motioned for Jimmy to watch the chief and moved up to the front beside Kiku. "What can I do?"

Kiku smiled. She could think of several flirty answers that would make him blush, but as far as the current dilemma went, she had no need for him. "Sit back and enjoy the ride."

The steering wheel spun in her hand as she rounded a corner. The

Russians' cars, as well as several police cars, were now giving chase along the desolate road.

"Heads up!" Takeo warned.

Two police cars appeared ahead of them, entering the street from opposite sides, and stopped bumper to bumper, blocking the road.

Kiku accelerated. The APC smashed into the police cars so hard they twisted around in almost a full circle, but she hadn't counted on the dangers from inside the vehicle: Jimmy had been thrown against the side and his gun fired. The bullet ricocheted twice inside the enclosed space. Everyone began screaming and swearing. It took Kiku a moment to calm them down and determine that no one had been hit.

"It's got a hair trigger!" Jimmy shouted at the scowling chief. "And my fingers are sore from your goons working me over!"

Kiku was about to cut into him, but when she rounded the next turn, she saw she had bigger worries. Coming down the street straight at them were two APCs identical to the one she was driving. And she was willing to bet that these APCs were equipped with ammo.

"Hang on!" she shouted as she prepared to take the next turn.

"Where are you going?" Takeo asked.

"We need to lose them."

"You can't," the chief yelled. "This is my—"

One of the APC's fifty-cals opened fire, and the rest of the chief's bragging was drowned out as a stream of lead punched into the rear of their APC. Kiku barreled into the turn, taking out three cars parked against the curb, and gunned it. A moment later, more bullets slammed into the back of their APC. A large hole appeared in the corner near the roof.

"Looks like you just lost your command," Takeo said with a laugh.

The chief stumbled toward the front. "Give me the radio!"

Takeo turned the radio on, clicked the receiver, and held it up to the chief's mouth.

"Cease fire! This is your chief! Cease fire! I *command* you!"

Though the chief was shrieking, Kiku doubted anyone could hear him over the hail of bullets. And even if they did, she doubted they cared that their chief was inside.

Welcome to Russia, where they will go to any lengths to prove who's in charge—even slaughtering hostages along with their kidnappers.

The right rear of the APC suddenly dropped, and the vehicle sagged and shimmied. The sound of dragging metal filled the confined space.

"I think we just lost something vital to the whole driving process!" Jimmy shouted.

A tunnel was just ahead—a narrow, old one, carved through the mountain when the czars were in control, marking the edge of the city. It was their only way out of here. In the barren isolation of Russia's vast expanses, there was nowhere to hide and you had to go miles in either direction to the next road or town.

Kiku jammed down the gas.

The chief stopped his shrieking into the radio, his eyes filling with horror. "The tunnel is too small! You won't fit!"

Kiku said nothing. That was exactly why she was speeding up.

"Kiku? I think he's right." Takeo's voice was calm even as he grabbed his seat belt and pulled it on.

Kiku did the same. "Hang on to something."

She slammed on the brakes. Jimmy screamed as he grabbed a strap dangling from the ceiling. The remaining tires skidded along the tar, smoke and dirt billowing up beneath the wheels. They were still traveling quite fast when the APC smashed into the tunnel like a ramrod into a musket.

Kiku groaned as she smacked into her seat belt. Her ribs hurt, but it was the pain in her hips that was most excruciating. She shook her head and raised an eyebrow, confused. It sounded like they were still braking, and—

"Brace!" she shouted.

She pressed herself back into the seat a moment before the nearest pursuing APC plowed into them. The chief shot forward, his body slammed into the console, and he dropped to the floor, unconscious. Jimmy somehow clung to his strap even as he was thrown to the floor. Takeo appeared dazed, and Kiku's hand shook as she unbuckled her seat belt, but the three of them were uninjured.

Concrete and rebar had cracked a hole in the windshield, but it wasn't large enough for a person to fit through.

"Cover your ears," Kiku said, picking up the sawed-off shotgun. She aimed at the windshield and unloaded. It took six shells to blast the hole wide enough for them to wiggle out. The chief would stay where he lay.

Kiku climbed out onto the hood, then dropped down to the road. The two APCs had completely jammed up one entrance to the tunnel.

Takeo jumped down beside her, followed by Jimmy.

"What do we do now?" Jimmy asked.

"We run!"

30

Though they couldn't see the end of the tunnel because it curved, Kiku knew they were close. She ordered the others to stop. Her lungs burned and her legs throbbed. Takeo stood with his back stiff, ready to fight. Jimmy was nearly doubled over, panting for breath. The wail of emergency sirens filled the tunnel from up ahead.

"There's no oncoming traffic," Kiku said. "The police must have blocked off the tunnel."

"We're trapped?" Jimmy swore.

"Takeo, follow me," Kiku ordered. She hurried to the side of the tunnel, sat down, and patted the ground next to her.

Takeo raised an eyebrow but sat next to her. "I can't wait to hear your plan."

Kiku ripped off her greasy headscarf and tried in vain to smudge Takeo's hair, doing her best to slick it back a bit, then handed it to him. "Hold this against your head like you are injured, and put your head on my shoulder to hide your hair. Jimmy, come over here and kneel beside him."

They both did as she asked.

"Jimmy, repeat after me. *Помо́чь им*. *Po-MOYCH im.* Do it."

Jimmy repeated the Russian phrase.

"Again."

Jimmy repeated it again.

Takeo laughed and smiled at Kiku. "You're brilliant."

The sirens grew louder now, echoing off the walls of the tunnel, and a police cruiser, its lights blazing, came around the bend in the tunnel toward them, an ambulance close behind it.

"Jimmy, when they pull up, say those words and point down the tunnel. Then wave the ambulance over."

"But why would the police listen to me— Oh." Jimmy looked down at his stolen police uniform.

The police cruiser skidded to a halt.

Holding the side of his bruised face with one hand, Jimmy frantically pointed down the tunnel with the other. *"Помóчь им! Помóчь им!"*

The policeman jerked his thumb at the ambulance behind him and hit the gas. As the cruiser pulled away, the ambulance slowed down.

"Say *Помогúте* to them," Kiku whispered. *"Poma-GEET-yeh."*

"Помогúте!" Jimmy shouted, waving frantically to the ambulance crew. The ambulance skidded to a stop. Two men jumped out of the cab and yanked open the doors to the back. They froze when Kiku placed her gun against the back of the shorter man's head.

"Both of you, listen to me," she said in Russian. "If you do exactly what I say, you will live. If you do not, I will kill you both. I promise you that." She read the taller man's name off the badge on his shirt. "Lebedev. How many policemen are at the end of the tunnel?"

"Three," Lebedev stammered.

"You drive. If a policeman stops you, tell him you are taking three victims to the hospital. Then head north with your lights on." She checked the shorter man's badge as well. "Bobrik—you get in the back."

Bobrik did as ordered, with Takeo and Jimmy climbing up behind him.

Kiku grabbed Lebedev. The man was shaking as she pulled him close. She lowered her voice. "Listen, I'm trying to get them to back off, but the little guy, the one in the police uniform, he's crazy. I can convince him to let you go, but you've got to listen to me. Just get us out of town, and we'll tie you up and get a different ride. Understand?" Lebedev nodded. His lower lip trembled. "Calm down. Just stick to the story and you live. Got it?"

Lebedev nodded again. "I tell the officer that I'm taking three people to the hospital. And I drive north."

"Perfect. Get in."

Kiku waited until Lebedev had gotten back into the cab before she joined the others in the back. She smiled when she saw that Takeo had wrapped a length of gauze around his head to conceal his silver hair.

"Please get on the stretcher and hold on. Bobrik, put two straps on him and pretend to be working on him."

Takeo lay on the stretcher and grabbed the sides. "Make sure the straps are loose," he said.

Bobrik's hands shook as he pulled a strap across Takeo's legs and another across his chest.

"Tuck that strap beneath me, but don't fasten it," Takeo ordered. Bobrik did as he was told.

Kiku told Jimmy to watch the door, then she took up a spot just behind the driver. There was a little window between the back of the ambulance and the cab, and she opened it.

"Just stay calm, Lebedev."

Lebedev nodded as he turned the ambulance around to face the way it had come. With lights flashing and sirens blaring, they rushed toward two police cars blocking the entrance to the tunnel. Three officers were busy directing traffic.

The ambulance came to a stop, and Lebedev powered down his window.

"Careful," Kiku whispered.

One of the policemen walked up to the driver's-side window and placed his hand on the side mirror as if he was holding it in place.

"I've got three injured," Lebedev said. "I'm taking them to Regional."

The policeman nodded, but as he lifted his hand off the mirror, a second officer rapped on the back door. "Open up."

Bobrik started shaking.

"Stay calm and open the door," Kiku said. She put her gun under the hem of her sweater, making sure that Bobrik saw it was still aimed at him, and studied her companions to see if they were ready for their roles. Jimmy held a huge cold pack against the side of his head, obscuring his face. Kiku couldn't imagine Takeo panicking, but his feet were practically vibrating, his hands had balled into fists, his eyes were tightly closed, and his lips were pulled back into a grimace. For a moment, she wondered if he was really hurt. He'd been wearing his seat belt when the APC crashed, but he might have hit his head.

She was about to ask him if he was all right when the policeman pounded on the door again. "Open up!" he bellowed, and Bobrik opened the door. Kiku's fingers tightened around the gun.

The policeman grabbed the door with one hand, his other resting on his gun. "We're looking for—"

Takeo convulsed, his head pressing against the stretcher and his back arching in spasms. A strangled moan escaped his lips and the veins in his neck protruded.

Bobrik rushed back to Takeo's side, shouting at the policeman, "What? What do you need?"

Takeo let out another strangled cry. The policeman's eyes quickly scanned the scene, then he nodded and shouted, "Go! Go! Good luck!" He slammed the doors shut.

The policeman at the driver's window stepped back, and Lebedev hit the gas and the siren at the same time.

Kiku nodded to Bobrik. "Good job. Now sit down on your hands." She turned her head and called into the cab, "Lebedev, drive north, fast, but keep it under eighty. You did very well speaking to the police."

"What about me?" Takeo sat up, the strap across his chest falling into his lap. "I should be nominated for an Academy Award." He grinned like a Cheshire cat as he took the strap off his legs.

"Your talents never cease to amaze me," Kiku said.

Jimmy repeated the line she had given him earlier: "*Помóчь им*! And I covered my face!"

"You all did a good job," Kiku said. *Men and their fragile egos.* She looked at Bobrik. "You, too. Keep it up and we will let you go soon."

The man was doing everything she had instructed him to do, sitting on his hands and keeping his mouth closed. His eyes searched her face, and he nodded.

He believed her.

He shouldn't have.

31

Kiku kept her gun trained on Bobrik as Lebedev drove them across the city. When they neared Petropavlovsk Regional Medical Center, she called to Lebedev, “Swing two blocks east. I do not want you passing right by in front of the hospital.”

“Sorry,” Lebedev said. “I’m sorry.”

“You are doing fine.”

Bobrik shifted uncomfortably. Kiku raised an eyebrow, and he hung his head and stared at his feet.

Jimmy began rooting through the cabinets like a squirrel looking for a nut.

“What are you looking for?” Takeo asked.

“Aspirin,” Jimmy said in English. “Some kind of painkiller.”

He turned back around, and Kiku winced at the sight of him. She had not had much time to really look at his condition before now, but clearly he’d taken quite a beating at the hands of the Russian police. His right eye was so black and blue it was nearly closed, and his lower lip was split with a nasty gash.

“Left cabinet.” Bobrik pointed by raising his chin. “In the pouch with the yellow label.”

Jimmy held it up.

“That’s it.” Bobrik nodded.

Smiling, Jimmy ripped it open.

“Wait,” Kiku said. “Bring it here.” She read the label, then nodded.

Jimmy took two pills. “It’s like OxyContin or morphine or something?”

“Aspirin,” Kiku said.

Jimmy pointed at his swollen eye. “I need something stronger than that.”

“I’m not carrying your unconscious body around.” Takeo gave Jimmy a withering look as he adjusted the sleeves of his tuxedo.

Kiku rose and moved to Takeo’s side. She put her mouth so close to his ear, her lips brushed his skin. “We need to head east.”

Takeo shuddered and she felt his arm trembling through his suit.

“Vladivostok,” she said, louder. “We can get help there.”

Bobrik raised his head slightly. He’d overheard. As she’d intended him to.

Kiku started to turn, but Takeo grabbed her arm. Their faces were so close, Kiku’s instinct was to pull back, but she held her ground. Takeo’s eyes searched hers. She watched the storm of emotions play across them, but she could not read a thing; it was like staring into the ocean and trying to unravel the mysteries of the deep.

Finally, he nodded and let her go. Flustered, Kiku returned to her seat and peered out the little window toward the front. The ambulance had passed the hospital now and was heading out of town.

“Stay on this road, Lebedev.”

Soon the buildings got smaller and homes dotted both sides of the road. Kiku didn’t want to get too far out in the country before switching to a different vehicle.

“Slow down and shut your sirens off,” she ordered.

They passed a gas station and an apartment complex. Neither offered what she was looking for: a nondescript car that would go unnoticed for at least five hours if it was stolen. A garden center with a pickup parked at the side caught her attention.

“Lebedev, turn into that garden center.”

The ambulance slowed, and Bobrik began breathing heavily. Kiku turned to him and forced a smile to comfort him, but judging by the terrified look on the young man’s face, it had the opposite effect.

"Bobrik," she said brightly, "please do not worry, but we are going to gag you and tie you up." His chest heaved as he gulped in air. "Calm down. We will leave you both in the ambulance out back."

Bobrik nodded.

"Pull up behind that large shed," Kiku ordered Lebedev. Then she turned to Jimmy and pointed at Bobrik. "Strap him down on the stretcher."

The second the ambulance stopped, she threw the doors open and covered the driver's door with her pistol. The last thing she wanted was for the driver to run off screaming.

"Come out slowly, Lebedev. With your hands up."

Lebedev stepped out of the ambulance. His hands were shaking and his arms kept going weak and starting to lower before he shot them back up again. He looked like he was dancing.

Kiku pointed to the rear of the ambulance. "Get in."

She stepped back and kept Lebedev covered. When Jimmy and Takeo finished strapping Bobrik down, Kiku pointed at the backboard. "Now strap Lebedev to that."

Takeo and Jimmy strapped him down, leaned the backboard against the rear wall, and gagged both men. Kiku tilted her head to the doors, and both Jimmy and Takeo got out. Kiku, still inside the rear of the ambulance, shut the doors behind them.

Bobrik started crying. Both men were shaking their heads and pleading with her. Because of the gags, Kiku couldn't understand what they said, but their meaning was clear. Kiku's index finger tapped the gun.

Minimize exposure.

Daichi's instruction still echoed in her head. It wasn't murder. She was maximizing the chances of the job's success by minimizing exposure. Then again, she'd made sure Bobrik believed they were heading east. If he lived to tell the police that false story, it would draw pursuit in the wrong direction. That was better than killing him, right?

Indecision gets you killed. This sort of debate with herself was a new and reoccurring phenomenon, and she hated it. Who were these men to her? She didn't know them. She didn't owe them anything.

She glared at the wall of the ambulance, where a photo had been taped up. Bobrik, the young paramedic, with a woman and a little girl with blond curls. Probably his wife and daughter. She pictured the girl sitting in her mother's lap, crying and asking one question over and over: *Why? Why would someone kill Daddy? He helps people.*

There was only one answer Kiku could imagine the mother giving, the only correct answer: *Some people are just evil.*

32

Kiku hopped down from the ambulance and shut the doors behind her, the slam echoing across the field behind the garden center. Takeo and Jimmy eyed her suspiciously.

"Is there a problem?" Kiku asked.

Takeo stared at the ambulance and raised an eyebrow. "Well ..."

Jimmy looked puzzled. "I didn't hear any shots. Did you stab them?"

Kiku scowled. "I am using Bobrik to throw off the police. I want them to be searching for us going east, to get a ferry to Vladivostok." She started walking toward the pickup truck parked at the side of the building.

Jimmy moved alongside Takeo. "Wait a second ..." He was whispering, but Kiku still heard him. "Does that mean she let them live?"

Her expression darkened even more. Her reputation was built on ferocity and ruthlessness, and her notoriety was a weapon that she wielded with precision. When people fear you, it keeps them in line ...

When they don't ...

Stupid Jack Stratton. He was the cause of these foolish emotions swirling around in her brain. Ever since she met Jack and Alice, she'd been off her game. When she saw the photograph of Bobrik and his family, she couldn't help but think of Alice and the incredible pain she'd suffered as a child, when her parents were murdered. Kiku had experienced similar pain, and she could not, *would* not, inflict a lifetime of it on that little girl.

Her thoughts returned to Jack Stratton. *Mr. Protector of the Innocent.* She'd live to make it to his wedding just to cause him some sort of grief in return for all this angst.

She peered into the back of the pickup. It looked like a work truck for the garden center and had black tarps piled in the back. She yanked open the door and got to work. It took her longer than normal to hot-wire the vehicle because of her aggravation. She broke the panel on the steering wheel column as she pulled the ignition wires out. But at last, the wires sparked and the old engine turned over. Better yet, when she unrolled the paper bag on the passenger seat and looked inside, she almost fainted at the beautiful smell of four buttered rye rolls. She let out a soft moan before sinking her canines into one of the soft rolls.

Kiku slid out of the cab, broke one of the rolls in half, and silently handed Takeo and Jimmy each one and a half rolls. She waited a moment while they all enjoyed their unexpected blessing, then turned to Takeo, seductively licking butter off her fingers.

Takeo gave a smoldering smile.

Kiku returned one of her own. "We will head north. I need you and Jimmy to get into the truck bed and hide under those tarps."

"I can grab a couple of plants and put them in for appearances before we go," Jimmy offered.

"No." Kiku smiled. "Thank you. It is a good plan, but we need to leave now."

Jimmy jumped into the back of the truck, but Takeo stood watching Kiku. He reached into his jacket and pulled out a wallet. "You'll need to stop for gas." He tossed it to her.

There was so much Kiku wanted to say to him. They hadn't yet had a chance to speak after the night they'd spent together. But now was not the time.

Takeo grabbed the side of the truck and climbed in. As if he could read her mind, he said, "We'll talk about what happened on the ship later."

Kiku did not like to be bossed and the lines between them were now blurred. The man was infuriating.

Takeo climbed underneath the tarp, and Kiku tied it down. She grabbed two rakes leaning against the side of the truck and placed them down over the lump in the tarp—roughly. Takeo groaned, and a satisfied grin crossed her lips. She lifted up a rake and let it fall once more before climbing into the cab.

The truck rumbled down the road. Takeo having his wallet was a game-changer: now she didn't have to worry about stealing cash. Clearly, he'd gotten VIP treatment at the police station if they'd let him put on his tuxedo and bring his wallet. She couldn't wait to wash the grease out of her hair and change her clothes. She fantasized about her next bath as she stayed on back roads, avoiding the interstate. It had been almost ten years since she'd last traveled the route, but she knew the way. The real challenge of Russia was its enormity, its vast expanses. It was so much easier to disappear into a crowd of people than into a Soviet-controlled field of wheat. For someone who had grown up in Japan's dense cities, Russia's cold, empty spaces were terrifying, and she had almost six hundred miles to cover for their best shot out of it.

Just before dawn, with the truck well hidden, Kiku took a short nap. Sleep deprivation and Russia were a dangerous combination, she'd found in the past. They gassed up in Klyuchi, bought some strange Russian candy bars, and munched them in a field of wildflowers surrounded by snow-capped mountains. In Ossora—the tiniest, grayest town she had ever seen—she made a small stop to steal some fruit off a grocery truck.

She had been driving for just over four hours without having seen a single light except for the stars, when a loud bang sounded at the front passenger side, the steering wheel jerked in her hand, and the truck pulled toward the side of the road. Cursing, she hit the hazard lights, pulled over, and stormed around to the front of the truck to see the right front tire was shredded.

Takeo's head appeared from beneath the tarp. "Need a hand?"

Kiku understood that Takeo was just being noble, but after driving all this way without a break, her anger flared. And judging by the expression on his face, he'd picked up on that.

"Or not ..." he said.

Kiku exhaled and kicked the tire. "I would appreciate the company," she lied. Despite her feelings for Takeo, he was still her boss.

Jimmy's head popped up, too. "Can I stretch my legs? They're killing me. I can change the tire for you if you want."

Kiku nodded. Her legs felt like they'd been beaten with baseball bats. Jimmy and Takeo both groaned as they climbed out of the truck. The wind and the darkness felt like something alive, blowing the sea air through the pines and biting sharply at their skin.

"Where are we going anyway?" Jimmy asked as he dug around in the truck for tools to change the tire.

"There is a boat to Dutch Harbor we can take from Tilichiki. I have a contact there who can get us on a cargo ship." Kiku was shaking with cold. She retied her improvised hairband so it covered more of her head. *Now I know why Russian women wear babushkas*. The only good news was that Jimmy knew how to change a tire and they only had a couple more hours to go.

"When we get there, can we do something about my hair?" Takeo rubbed his silver locks. "The easiest fix would probably be a razor."

"No!" Kiku blurted out—a little too loudly, she realized, but she loved Takeo's hair. Shaving his head would be like taking a lion's mane. The thought sickened her.

"Oh, when it's *his* hair, suddenly you're concerned," Jimmy grumbled as he strained to push down on the lug wrench. The wrench slipped off the nut and bounced off the tar. "These lug nuts must be welded on."

"You need to pull on one end of the wrench and push the other," Takeo said.

"I did."

Takeo smirked and held out his hand. Jimmy handed him the lug wrench and stepped back. Takeo strutted arrogantly over to the car, put the lug wrench on the tire, and threw his weight into it.

It didn't budge.

Jimmy grinned. "See!"

"I'm just warming up." The seam in Takeo's tuxedo suit strained as he put his all into getting the rusty nut to come loose. But after almost a full minute of effort, he stopped and stood up.

"I'm telling ya," said Jimmy, "they put it on with an air wrench. There's no way we're getting it off."

Kiku put her hands on the hood of the car and stepped up onto the wrench. She gently bounced up and down on the handle until the nut turned. Trying not to smile, she held her hand out to Jimmy.

"Show-off," Jimmy muttered.

Takeo's laugh trailed off as headlights appeared up ahead. Kiku swore. She'd been so preoccupied with the tire that she'd stopped watching the road. Jimmy started to leap back into the truck.

"Stop," Kiku ordered. "Too late."

"My gun's in the back," Jimmy whispered.

"So is mine," Takeo said.

Kiku shook her head. She hadn't left hers behind. It would be enough to handle any threat.

Emergency lights clicked on atop the approaching vehicle, sending Kiku's heart racing. But when the blinding headlights passed, she could see it was only an old pickup truck modified with a tow winch and lights.

The truck pulled over behind them, turning the area around them almost as bright as day, and a young, blond Russian man hopped down from the cab. "Just a flat?" he asked in Russian.

"Yes, we're fixing it now," Kiku replied. She had to shield her eyes from the light to look at him.

"How's the spare?" The man walked forward a few steps. His eyes traveled from Takeo to Jimmy to Kiku. His eyebrows arched high and his face twisted up like he had bitten a lemon.

Inside, Kiku groaned. Takeo was in his tuxedo, Jimmy was in a police uniform, and Kiku, in her bulky sweater, still looked like a cleaning woman. Talk about raising suspicion.

Jimmy picked up on it. "First our luggage gets mixed up and we have to wear weird clothes"—he tugged on his shirt for emphasis—"and now *this* happens!" He gave the flat tire a kick.

The tow truck driver seemed satisfied with the explanation.

Kiku reached for her wallet. "Our luck has been terrible until you came along. I bet you could change this tire much faster than we can?"

She held out some cash and cast a quick look at Takeo to cut off any further explanations.

The man nodded rapidly as he grabbed the money. "Sure can."

The young man worked with the speed of a NASCAR pit crew. In less than three minutes he had the truck back on the ground and all the tools put away. Kiku thanked him profusely. Takeo and Jimmy got into the cab with her, and they drove away.

"You did a fine job with the tow truck driver, Jimmy," Kiku said.

"Thanks. Thanks a lot," Jimmy said, grinning from ear to ear.

With the tow truck now out of sight, Kiku pulled over. "Back under the tarp."

"There's the Kiku I'm used to. The air was nice while it lasted," Jimmy grumbled as he hopped out.

Takeo didn't move. "Even you can't go forever. Can I take a turn driving?"

Kiku shook her head. "No, thank you. Not until we get you a suitable disguise."

Takeo nodded and got out of the cab.

Kiku looked up at the night sky. It was going to be a very long night.

33

As the truck made its way down the winding road, the cloak of darkness made it all the more startling when three sets of headlights appeared in Kiku's rearview, gaining on her rapidly. She powered down her window, slapped her hand against the side of the truck, and called back, "We may have a problem." Then she jammed the gas pedal to the floor.

But the old truck began shaking when it hit sixty miles an hour. Kiku swore. There was no way they'd outrun anybody in this thing. She pulled her gun from behind her back and drove with one hand.

The three vehicles rapidly closed the distance and were only two hundred yards behind her when they reached a straightaway. The closest vehicle was a tow truck; it flipped on its emergency lights and started flashing its high beams.

Kiku held the gun in her lap—pointed at the door—and called back, "It's that same tow truck again." And she understood why it was following. The tow truck driver thought they were three Japanese tourists out at night on a deserted stretch of road—in other words, easy prey. Despite the fact that they were driving cars, not boats, these men were basically pirates.

Kiku's rage kicked into a low simmer. The tow truck raced up beside her, a second man now in the passenger seat. The driver waved, and the man next to him leaned his head out the window. He looked like the driver's older brother—early thirties, also blond, but with a hard edge to him. He grinned and waved, too.

"I need to ask you something. Pull over!" he shouted in Russian.

His brother was pulling on his arm now. The passenger tried to shake him off, but the driver was insistent. The two men spoke for a moment, then the passenger's head whipped back around to Kiku. "Where are your friends?"

"I have none," Kiku shouted back. "Go home."

The other two vehicles now caught up as well. A sedan pulled in behind the tow truck, and a pickup truck pulled right up to Kiku's bumper, its high beams on. Kiku flipped up her rearview mirror.

The passenger's face twisted into a snarl. "Pull over," he demanded, pointing at the side of the road.

But the passenger had made the mistake of keeping his weapon at his feet. He lifted it up by the barrel, and the driver reached for something, too. They were both far too slow.

Kiku shot the passenger in the head, then waited a heartbeat for the driver to react. The tow truck was four times the weight of her vehicle, and if he cut the wheel her way, he'd crash into her and kill them all. But the driver reacted the same way all sane humans would: he leaned away from the horror. And when he did, his hands still on the wheel, the truck turned away from Kiku.

She shot the driver in the head, too, as Takeo and Jimmy began firing. Takeo put three quick blasts into the windshield of the truck behind them and Jimmy unloaded his pistol.

When the pursuing truck swerved off the road, Kiku jammed her foot down on the brake pedal. The driver of the sedan did, too, but again too late—confirming her impression that these were just Russian country bumpkins and not an insurmountable threat. As the sedan came up beside Kiku, she saw the horrified expressions on the two men's faces. And she saw the passenger's pistol coming up and aiming for her.

She fired three shots center mass. The passenger's gun tumbled from his hand and clattered onto the road. The driver got off one wild shot before Kiku took him out as well, being careful to strike only the man and not the car itself. She then jammed on the gas, pulled in front of the still-rolling sedan, and slammed on the brakes once more, bringing both vehicles to a stop.

All the braking and accelerating had thrown Takeo and Jimmy all over the truck bed, and both were swearing at her now. She jumped out of the truck and strode over to the driver's side of the sedan, keeping her gun trained on it. But it was clear both men were dead.

Takeo and Jimmy jumped out of the truck, and Kiku pointed at the pirates' pickup truck, which had stopped just off the road, some distance behind them now. The three of them walked back to it cautiously, guns raised, Takeo going left, Kiku right, Jimmy moving up the middle. The driver and two passengers were dead.

Kiku pointed at Jimmy. "Get their guns and any money. Pick and choose from their clothes for the least bloody. The outerwear is spattered, but the clothing beneath may be all right. You both need to change, quickly. Takeo, come with me. We will check the other truck."

She and Takeo ran to the tow truck. These men were dead, too. Kiku shut off the lights and rummaged in the rear seat while Takeo checked the front. From the pants pocket of the passenger, Takeo removed a wad of cash.

Kiku found a watch cap under the seat and tossed it to Takeo. For herself, she took a work jacket from behind the seat and put it on. It smelled terrible, but she instantly felt warmer.

They ran back to Jimmy, who was decked out in a warm jacket and pulling on some gloves. "This guy was loaded." He held up a thick wallet. "This hat is good—you want it?" Jimmy pulled it down on top of Kiku's head, bending her ears out like a woodland elf.

Takeo chuckled. "You should see yourself in that hat! I *loved* you in the red dress, but this look may be my favorite yet!"

Jimmy stood, frozen in sheer terror at the realization of what he had done.

Kiku snatched the wallet from Jimmy. "Move."

The three of them ran back to the sedan and dragged the two dead men out. It was time to switch vehicles, and luckily this one had a bit more speed. Kiku popped the trunk and pulled out an old blanket as Jimmy and Takeo wiped the blood off the front seat. She used the blanket to cover the seat, and they were back on the road in under three minutes.

Jimmy grumbled from the back seat, "Just our luck to run into those guys. I guarantee they were going to rob us, shoot us in the back of the head, and bury us in a ditch."

"I would have preferred to keep one alive," Takeo said. "Then he'd have warned the other locals to leave the 'Japanese tourists' alone."

Kiku glared into the darkness. Monsters bred monsters. It was the way of this fallen world. The Yakuza was started because monsters took advantage of the outcasts, and the Mafia began the same way.

It was also in the story of her rebirth as Kiku. She could hardly remember hearing her given name anymore, but she would never forget the day she earned the name Kiku—*Chrysanthemum*.

She was only twelve, dressed in a beautiful white silk dress with embroidered swirls and lace trim, when three men came to kill Daichi. He was drunk and she knew he hadn't seen them as they strode through the kitchen of the restaurant. So she killed them all with an eight-inch chef knife. Her beautiful dress was splattered with their blood ... and Daichi said she looked like a chrysanthemum.

Kiku.

She leaned back in her seat and let the night air whip around her. She felt at peace at night. That was only natural, right?

Monsters love the dark.

34

When they reached Tilichiki, a new challenge awaited them: Kiku's friend was nowhere to be found and had left no message for her. Tilichiki had an airport, as well as cargo ships leaving for Alaska every couple of days, but it still felt like literally the end of the world, the end of everything. And she couldn't help but worry about her contact's mysterious silence—unless he was telling her to get out of there.

Still thinking about a way out, Kiku directed them to a pharmacy. By the time she walked out of the store, she had what she needed to carry out the next phase of a new plan.

Russia had forced her hand, but it would not beat her. She found Takeo waiting in the driver's seat and Jimmy in the front passenger seat. She was about to order Jimmy to get in the back when she noticed the police cruiser parked across the street with two officers inside. Takeo quickly popped the trunk, and Kiku stuffed her purchases in and climbed into the back seat.

"Who's the wheelchair for?" Jimmy asked, puzzled.

Kiku ignored the question. "Dutch Harbor is off. I have a new plan. Head to that gas station down the road." She kept her eyes on the police as Takeo pulled out of the parking lot. They were chatting away and didn't even look in their direction.

"We've got a half tank of gas," Takeo said.

"We need to get your hair dyed. Mine, too."

Jimmy rubbed his stubbled head. "I'm good."

"Actually, I have a different idea for you"—Kiku held up her hand to cut off Jimmy's questions—"but let's get Takeo squared away first."

Takeo drove down to the busy gas station.

"Head over to the pumps," Kiku said. "Jimmy, take your time filling up, wash all the windows, and then park on the side of the building near the men's room."

Takeo started to reach for the trunk release, but Kiku shook her head and held up a shopping bag. "I have everything we need in here. Follow me." She got out of the car and shut the door with both men still inside.

Jimmy whispered, but she still heard him mutter, "She does get bossy."

"She keeps me alive," Takeo replied in a normal tone of voice. "And I guarantee that she just heard you."

Jimmy's head slowly turned, and he peeked up at her like a child whose mother had snuck up behind him and caught him doing something wrong. He gave her a sheepish wave. Kiku shook her head and tapped on the roof of the car. Takeo got out and met her with a steely-eyed stare. In tapping the roof to hurry him, she'd overstepped, which she acknowledged with a slight nod. When he returned the gesture, she started for the restroom, and he followed.

Kiku locked the door behind them and started pulling items out of the bag—shampoo, hair dye, scissors, two small towels, dishwashing liquid ...

Takeo picked up a new pair of mirrored sunglasses. "I like these."

"You will get the chance to wear them soon enough."

"What's the dishwashing liquid for?"

"To get the grease out of my hair." She'd heard it was sometimes used to clean up birds and sea animals caught in oil spills, and hoped it would do the same for her. She was relieved to find that she was right.

When she was done washing her hair, she buffed it damp-dry. "Now for the new us." She opened the boxes of hair dye and mixed the tubes of color in the squeeze bottles with the developer.

"Well, this is something I never imagined us doing again," Takeo said.

Kiku applied the dye to his hair and then did her own. It was a deep brown that supposedly took only ten to fifteen minutes. She was hoping for the best, since the boxes looked like they'd been on the shelf for years.

"What's the new plan?" Takeo asked, laughing good-naturedly when he saw his plastic bag-wrapped head.

"We take the Trans-Siberian Railway to Moscow, then head to Finland and get a plane."

He frowned. "That's bringing us straight into Novikov's den."

"I am aware of that. And that is what I want."

Kiku's hand brushed Takeo's arm. There was nothing accidental about the gesture, but he wouldn't know that. His eyes widened and he smiled that devil-may-care grin that made her desire him.

Takeo was a world traveler, and her trust in him had deepened at every step along this journey, so she ran her idea past him while they were waiting for the dye to take. He had not been happy with the Dutch Harbor plan in the first place. They quickly agreed that they were way too vulnerable in these isolated spots, and that moving toward Cade Novikov's stronghold was the last thing he or Kenzo would expect. And most importantly, on the train they could rest in anonymity, recover their strength, and move closer to civilization.

When the fifteen minutes were up, Kiku washed the dye out and was relieved to see they both had rich-brown hair. "And now you need to lose some of the punk edge." She wrapped the towel around Takeo's neck. Using the scissors, she shaped his hair into a flattering style, shorter on the sides and back, with a bit more length on top.

After they'd changed into the cheap clothes she'd picked up at the pharmacy—a plain white shirt for Takeo and a simple green dress for her—Takeo eyed her new outfit. "You could wear a potato sack and I would still want to rip it off you."

Kiku smiled. Her eyes locked with his and she saw the hunger there. She stroked his cheek, then turned her head to pack up. Takeo seized her wrist, wrapped his other arm around her small waist, and pulled her up against him. He kissed her passionately, still holding her by a wrist. Kiku was stunned. Her head spun, her primal instincts in conflict. *Fight, kill … don't stop …*

"Stop." Kiku pulled her head back, wanting him, but unwilling to get lost in this moment. "We should get going. We still need to make another stop before the train station."

"I should've made my move when we had fifteen minutes to wait for the hair color."

Kiku smiled.

Takeo pressed his lips together, and for a moment he stood where he was, his feet rooted to the floor, his eyes devouring her. Then he nodded and turned to check out his new haircut in the mirror.

At the sight of his reflection, his eyes narrowed.

"What is the matter?" Kiku asked. "Do you not like the haircut?"

Takeo ran a hand through his hair and his expression darkened. "I have seen this hairstyle before."

Kiku frowned. Where would he have seen this? She was good with scissors, but she was no professional stylist. She had simply pictured a haircut that she liked and …

Oh …

She cleared her throat and started to gather up their things. There was no use arguing about it or denying the resemblance. Kiku had actually done a fabulous job. The problem wasn't with the haircut, it was with the person whose haircut had inspired Kiku: Jack Stratton.

Takeo and Jack had met when Jack was searching for his missing ex-girlfriend. Since she was the daughter of an Italian mobster, Jack thought the Yakuza were involved. Takeo had sent Kiku to watch Jack, but ever since that first meeting …

As she brushed past him going out the door, she said, "Well, I think you look very handsome," eliciting a low growl from him.

Their next stop before they could finally escape this forsaken place was a business supply store. Grateful for the chance to escape the awkward silence in the car, Kiku parked at the curb and went inside.

Like the pharmacy, it was small and dusty, but surprisingly well stocked. She gathered the different kinds of papers she needed and headed to the remote office section, where, for an hourly fee, she had access to a computer, the internet, and a printer.

A few minutes later, Takeo sauntered into the shop, and she was grateful for the cover. While he pretended they were office workers doing a project together, made small talk, and blocked the view, she pulled up images of the standard traveling documents and printed out copies. She even created three fake passport books. Nothing she made would pass even a cursory inspection, but she didn't need it to. She wasn't forging official papers; she was making decoys. Now came the hard part: getting the real documents.

35

Kiku drove around the market square outside the train station and found a perfect spot near the outdoor information booth. Since it was still early in the day, the booth was unmanned. Better yet, a police call box stood next to the booth, with the word "POLICE" written on it in several different languages.

"Jimmy, wait in the car. Takeo, get dressed."

As Kiku and Takeo changed their look yet again, Jimmy took the driver's seat. Kiku pulled her hair up into a bun, added glasses, and put on a lanyard with a fake name and the title "Immigration Inspector"—another pickup from the business supply store. Takeo put on the police clothes they had taken from Jimmy's guard.

Kiku watched the crowd departing from the train station. She pointed. "That group of tourists. I see a match."

Takeo pulled his hat down as he got out of the car. Other than giving her help at the store, he'd hardly said three words since the hair-cutting incident, and she wanted to patch things up.

She handed him the sunglasses and smiled seductively. "I love a man in uniform."

Takeo snatched the sunglasses out of her hand and scowled. "Are you purposely trying to get me angry with *another* Stratton reference?"

Kiku shook her head, her mouth opening and closing, and for the first time in a long time, she was at a loss for words. She'd truly intended to pay him a compliment but had put her foot in her mouth. "No. I apologize."

Takeo pulled his hat lower and stormed across the square toward the Japanese tourists. Kiku headed straight for the information booth, carrying her new briefcase full of fake documents. She stood behind the booth, looking to all the world as if she worked there, set down the case, and sorted the documents into three piles. Each pile included a Japanese passport, a Russian visa, and a driver's license—the latter being nothing more than a laminated printout of an actual license she'd googled.

Takeo was now engaging the tourists. All six were shaking their heads. Soon he marched the group over to the booth where Kiku was waiting and gruffly ordered each one to produce their travel papers for inspection. The tourists started digging through their bags without hesitation.

Kiku felt a little guilty about ripping off these naive tourists, but when she saw how thoroughly they had prepared their travel documents, she felt better. Each one had a sealed plastic bag, neatly organized, everything from visa and passport to health information and insurance papers. If they were that meticulous, surely they would have printed out backups of everything and placed them in their luggage. They would be all right.

Takeo made sure to take documents from only three of the targets, and one at a time. Kiku pretended to examine the documents, while she was actually switching them out with her fakes. She was careful to insert the fake visa, passport, and driver's license between the health and insurance papers, so that if the tourists looked, they wouldn't immediately see her crude forgeries.

In minutes, the switches had been made and Takeo was thanking the group for their cooperation. But as the woman who looked similar to Kiku was placing her plastic bag of papers back in her handbag, she hesitated, then lifted them up to look at them.

Takeo stiffened. Kiku shuffled the papers in front of her, wrestling her own heart to keep a steady beat. If things broke bad, Takeo had a gun on his hip, and so did she. She could press it against the older man's back and order them to go ... where? The market square had a small bustle of tourists now, heading for the train.

Takeo turned to glare at the woman's husband. "Where are you traveling today?"

The poor man trembled and stuttered, "The Automotive Antiques Museum. We're late." He grabbed his wife's other hand, and she stuffed the papers back into her bag as he dragged her away.

Kiku breathed a sigh of relief—until she saw three police officers strolling across the square. "Hide," she ordered. Takeo moved behind the information center counter and ducked down.

Too late. One of the policemen was looking their way. Kiku wasn't sure if he'd seen Takeo, but he was certainly staring at Kiku, and judging by his posture, he was wondering what she was doing behind the information booth.

She swore under her breath. "Stay down. Here they come."

The officer called to the other two, pointed at the information booth, and said something Kiku couldn't hear. Then all three men began to approach.

"Take off your hat, uniform shirt, and tactical belt," Kiku whispered. Buttons pinged across the ground as Takeo ripped off his police shirt and dropped it. He dropped his hat, put his gun in his waistband, covered it with his undershirt, and placed the belt on the ground.

Kiku reached around her back, her fingers sliding around the grip of her gun. She did not want to kill the policemen, but she could not let them catch Takeo.

"Excuse me!" a voice practically screamed in Japanese.

Kiku looked up to see Jimmy running straight toward the police. "Excuse me!" He was hopping from one foot to the other like a little kid about to wet his pants. He had come up to the policemen from the other side of Kiku, and they all turned to face him.

Kiku didn't waste a second. She stuffed the hat, belt, and shirt in her briefcase, grabbed Takeo by the arm, and hurried out of the booth. Using the structure for cover, they quickly strode away.

"I need a bathroom," Jimmy yelled in Japanese, then tried English. "Restroom? Loo?" The policemen pointed, and Jimmy took off running toward the train station.

Kiku and Takeo were almost to the street. She pulled him into a group of people, trying to block the officers' view, then risked another glance back. The policemen were at the information booth now, looking around. The first officer had a puzzled expression on his face, but the other two were laughing and shaking their heads. After a minute, all three walked off.

Blending in with the tourists, Kiku and Takeo headed back to the car. Now they just had to make it onto the train.

36

Kiku's fingers drummed the steering wheel as she scanned the crowd for Jimmy. Takeo sat next to her, on the lookout for more police. After a minute, Kiku picked out Jimmy's bald head weaving like a salmon swimming upstream against the flow of the crowd. He hurried across the street and Kiku motioned for him to get in the back.

Kiku glanced over her shoulder and pointed down. "Look in the bag at your feet," she instructed Jimmy.

Jimmy opened the bag and frowned. "What is this?"

"That is your disguise. You are an invalid."

Jimmy groaned. "Why do I always get the crappy disguises?"

Takeo smirked, but Kiku managed to hide her smile. "Thank you for your assistance back there."

Jimmy's eyes lit up. "I saw the cops about to jam you guys up and I just went for the distraction."

Kiku let her smile grow. "How did you come up with the idea?"

Jimmy shrugged. "I don't know. It just popped into my head."

"Well, it was impressive how fast you got there," Kiku said. "One would almost think that you had already left the car, even though I had specifically told you not to, and were wandering around the square in search of a bathroom." She lifted the nearly empty, giant cup of soda out of the drink holder. "Oh, would you like your soda?"

Takeo laughed.

Jimmy turned bright red as he took the drink from her hand. "I still saved your necks."

Takeo nodded stiffly. "Thank you. I will repay the favor."

Jimmy shot Kiku a look in the rearview mirror, wiggling his eyebrows and grinning broadly, before settling back into his seat.

"Do not get comfortable," Kiku said. "You need to put on your disguise."

Jimmy huffed, set the drink down, and picked the bag back up. "It's just an oxygen mask and tubes."

Kiku grinned. "Exactly. That is your cover and ours as well. With your bald head, you are the only one who could pull this look off. Put on the oxygen mask and try to look sickly."

Jimmy made a face and began pulling everything from the bag. Kiku pulled out the travel wheelchair from the trunk and rolled it around to Jimmy's door.

"I have actually given you the pivotal role," she said. "However, you will need to let me do the talking."

"What do I say if they ask me what I'm sick with?" Jimmy said as he got in the chair and adjusted his mask.

"The doctors have not figured it out yet. That is why we are heading to Moscow—to see the head doctor at the Center of Neurology."

Takeo got out of the car and walked over. "It's a great cover. In order for Jimmy to see someone there, he would have to have powerful Russian friends."

"I hope security is as bright as you and connects those dots," Kiku said. "With the state of Russian health care, I think our odds of that are good." She started to wheel Jimmy toward a dingy little shopping mall outside the train station.

"We need to complete our look," she explained as she picked out a suitcase, a large gym bag, and a change of clothes for each of them.

Between the cash they had taken off the tow truck driver and the sizable amount Takeo had given her, they had enough for the train tickets, but funds were running low.

As Kiku rolled Jimmy toward the train station, Takeo at her side, she ran down their cover names and information from their stolen passports and had them repeat them. The biggest issue with their cover story was their destination. The hospital wasn't on their stolen Russian travel visas.

Still, purchasing the tickets went without a hitch. The woman behind the counter was pleasant and provided them with a handful of brochures and tips for enjoying the train. Unfortunately, she said the last two cars had been taken out of service because of a faulty heater; the woman cheerfully claimed that wouldn't cause crowding on the remaining cars, but Kiku suspected that was unlikely.

Kiku wheeled Jimmy up to security, and Takeo rolled their suitcase up behind. A gray-haired security officer approached them and asked to see their papers. Kiku had everything ready and smiled quickly at him before placing a comforting hand on Jimmy's shoulder.

The security officer skimmed through everyone's documents but stopped when he hit Jimmy's passport. His eyes traveled back and forth between the passport photo and Jimmy's face. Kiku had been afraid that might happen. The tourists who owned these passports looked similar enough to Kiku, Takeo, and Jimmy, with one exception: Jimmy was clearly ten years younger than his tourist doppelganger. The security officer rubbed his forehead, his wrinkles deepening.

"The one good thing about whatever he has," Kiku said in staccato Russian, "is that the water retention makes him bloated, so he looks more like my brother than my father." She tenderly stroked Jimmy's head.

Beads of sweat formed on Jimmy's forehead as the security guard glared down at him.

Kiku switched to Japanese and told Jimmy to smile. *"Sumairu, Otōsan."* She squeezed his shoulder.

"Do I make him nervous?" the officer asked.

She spoke in Russian again. "Nervous? No. It's ... urine. Pee-pee. Not sweat. He's so backed up, he—"

"I get it. I get it." The security guard stepped back, handed the papers to Kiku, and motioned for them to move along.

Kiku pushed Jimmy past the security gate with Takeo close behind. Takeo started coughing, but she could tell he was trying to cover a laugh.

"We good?" Jimmy whispered.

"Shut up," Kiku whispered back sweetly, forcing herself to smile.

"How long till we get to Moscow?" Jimmy asked.

Kiku leaned down to whisper in his ear. "Seven days. But if you open your mouth again before we are in our cabin, I will throw you off this train well before that."

They couldn't be too careful. Not only were the Russian police looking for them—so was Cade Novikov. His ruthless reach extended everywhere in Russia, and his smuggling network cast a net around the globe; he would certainly have men working the train. And Kenzo had ways to get whatever information Novikov had.

Kiku's throat was tight as she traced their route in her mind. Four thousand miles would bring them to Moscow. It was a long journey, and when they got there, they would still be far from their final destination.

Takeo flashed her a scoundrel's smile and a quick wink. The simple gestures of goodwill were infectious, and she grinned back. Yes, they were being hunted, but they were far from helpless. Let the police try to catch them. Let Kenzo send his best men. Let Novikov order his finest ex-soldiers to track them down.

They would find out that Kiku Inazuka was *not* easy prey.

37

In the little first-class cabin, Kiku sat on the edge of the bed, watching Takeo sleep as the train slowly rocked. The way he was lying—on his back, with his hands folded across his chest—she couldn't help but think of him laid out in a casket.

She knew both of them would die violently one day. It was the fate of almost everyone in the Yakuza. There were exceptions, but not many. Live by the sword; die in a hail of bullets. At least, that was how she wanted to go—a weapon in her hand, battling an unstoppable horde. She'd be happy with such an end.

But there were other possibilities. Torture. Sniper. Poison. She didn't want those. She wanted an honorable death, not a shameful one. And she would never allow herself a cowardly one; whoever found her corpse would find her with dirt in her eyes, because she'd died with them wide open.

Whenever she had these fantasies, she told herself she was just preparing for the inevitable. But the truth was, she craved death, and it was never far from her thoughts. The obsession had started when she was very young, with the passing of her parents. But when Akari died and her spirit soared to Heaven, Kiku felt like she plummeted straight into Hell.

While Akari was alive, Kiku had rarely known pain, because Akari, her protector, had always shielded her from harm and made the world beautiful. If Kiku fell, Akari would scoop her up and bandage her wound. Whenever Kiku was afraid, the light of Akari's presence always drove away the darkness. When Akari was murdered ... the world Kiku found herself in was Hell on Earth with glimpses of the Hell to come.

"Thank you for saving my son."

Takeo's soft words made her jump. His eyes were still closed and he had not yet moved.

Kiku leaned forward, unsure if she had only imagined that he had spoken, but his next words were clear and firm. "Forgive me for doubting you."

"We need to get word to the men who are still loyal."

Takeo's eyes snapped open and a slight grin curved his lips. He rolled over onto his side, gazing at her quizzically like he was solving a puzzle. "Do you accept my apology?"

"If I had not accepted it, I would not be here. Nor would I have had sex with you."

Takeo cleared his throat and sat up. "About that ..."

Kiku shook her head. "Now is not the time to discuss ... our tryst." Her eyes locked with his and she slowly licked her lips. "My desire for you is so strong that if we speak much more of this, I would be forced to take you."

Takeo's mouth dropped open.

Kiku smiled like a vixen and teased, "Do you see my dilemma?"

Takeo took a moment before responding. He brushed back his hair and leaned forward, resting his hands on his knees. "No. No, I do not," he said, shaking his head and grinning.

"We are currently in a foreign land being hunted. It would not be prudent."

"Those were the same conditions on the cruise ship."

Kiku's eyes narrowed. "Your appetite for sex will get you killed."

"Then let it be said that I died with a smile on my face."

"What a colorful eulogy. Is that really what you want someone to say about you at your funeral?" Kiku shot back.

Takeo shrugged. "No. I'd rather someone say, 'Wait, look! He's still alive!'"

Kiku laughed. She couldn't help herself. In a moment Takeo was on her, his strong arms encircling her. His body was hard, but his lips were soft. Kiku pivoted and swept Takeo onto the bed, on his back. The sudden move caught him off guard, and his eyes widened. Kiku grabbed both sides of his handsome face and kissed him with a passion that she intended would warm his chest when he remembered it as an old man.

A tremor rippled up his body and his arms tightened around her. Grinning, Kiku broke away and stood up.

"That was very pleasurable, but we must stop until I get you back to America safely." She straightened her shirt. "You will arrive there disappointed and, I suspect, somewhat frustrated, but you will be breathing."

Takeo jumped to his feet, anger replacing the desire in his eyes. "'Still breathing'? That's your inside joke with Jack. What is it between you and Stratton?" he demanded.

"He is a friend who is about to marry another dear friend."

"And if he weren't getting married? Would he be more to you?"

"I might as well speculate about what would happen if the earth had two moons. Who knows?"

"*You* do."

Kiku thought for a moment, then decided what to say. "It is not hard to imagine loving Jack. But"—she held up a hand to silence Takeo's indignation—"if we are playing the game of possibilities ... another condition would have to be met before I could ever be with Jack."

Takeo waited for her to continue, but she was waiting for him to ask. She saw the muscle in his jaw throb, and she knew she was playing a dangerous game. Not that he would lash out or hurt her in any way. No, the risk was that he would close himself off from her forever. Takeo was the kind of man who when wounded could never forgive the person who'd wielded the knife. But more and more lately, she was beginning to think that Takeo was also the kind of man who would forgive her almost anything, as long as she did not betray his trust.

He inhaled deeply and let his breath out slowly. When he finally spoke, his voice was calm. "What would that be? What else would stop you from choosing Stratton?"

A mischievous smile that Kiku had been repressing appeared. "I will tell you once we get to America. I need to sweep the train now."

She slipped out into the hallway and closed the door. She had taken only a few steps when she heard the sound of splintering wood inside the cabin, and she knew that when she returned there would be a fist-sized hole in the wall.

Good. Hopefully, his anger would make him focus on their goal: getting back to the States. They still had a long way to go, and absolute focus had to be the priority.

Anything less would get them killed.

38

Over the next three days aboard the Trans-Siberian Express, Takeo continued to brood. It made for a tense and awkward atmosphere, especially considering they never left their room, other than to use the bathroom at the end of their car. To avoid the risk of being recognized or drawing attention, they even had their meals delivered.

But in time, Kiku realized their reclusiveness was having the opposite effect. The train had an almost cruise-like atmosphere, with passengers looking forward to socializing with one another, and the whispers and glances Kiku received when wheeling Jimmy to the restroom made it apparent that they had become a subject of curiosity, and possibly suspicion.

In order to quash that interest, Kiku decided that the three of them needed to make at least one appearance in the dining car—if only a brief one. They sat down, ordered their meal, and nodded graciously at the other diners. But after only a few minutes, Kiku called the waiter over and asked for their food to be wrapped up and taken back to their room because Jimmy was not feeling well. Jimmy hammed it up by coughing and grimacing, and Takeo acted frustrated and put-upon. They all played their part in the charade well.

Kiku rolled Jimmy back to his room, and she and Takeo returned to theirs. Takeo quickly buried his nose in a train brochure that he'd been pretending to read for days. Kiku hoped he'd get over his wounded pride soon, or it was going to be a very long trip.

A knock sounded at the door, and Takeo got to it first. He checked the peephole. "Food."

"I will get it," Kiku said, but Takeo scowled and slid the door open.

Standing in the hallway was their waiter, but he was not alone. He was accompanied by the purser and two security officers, all three of them large, burly men.

The purser stepped forward quickly and pressed a Glock-17 against Takeo's chest. "Easy," he warned in Russian.

The waiter quickly walked away, looking eager to have no part in this.

"My boss wants to speak with you," the purser said, grabbing Takeo by the upper arm and jerking him out into the hallway. He pressed the pistol into Takeo's side. "You"—he glared at Kiku—"come out and walk in front of us. Remember, at this distance, I cannot miss."

The purser walked Takeo back a few steps, and the two security men stepped in front of them. Kiku stepped into the hall and started walking. There was nothing she could do now but wait for an opportunity.

Over her shoulder, she asked, "Who is your boss?"

"You will find out very soon," the purser said.

She expected them to stop at Jimmy's room, but they didn't. Right now, though, Jimmy was the least of her worries. The good news was that they wanted to talk—they hadn't simply killed her and Takeo on sight. Still, she suspected that though Novikov would want Takeo alive, he probably wouldn't care what happened to her—or, rather, he would probably scream for her head. She wondered what the bounty on her life had risen to in recent days.

She walked to the end of the car, through the next, and into the dining car. There she slowed down, as if expecting to be told to stop, and glanced over her shoulder. One of the security officers pushed her forward. Stumbling slightly, Kiku swiped a steak knife off a table as she straightened back up. Tucking the weapon under her belt, she continued on, nodding and giving faint smiles to the diners who glanced her way.

They passed through two more cars before Kiku realized they were going all the way to the rear. She wondered if the heating system in the last two cars was *really* malfunctioning, or if this trap had been in place even before they boarded.

The sudden drop in temperature when they reached the second-to-last train car answered her question. At least the Russians hadn't been two steps ahead of them. Still, they had the drop on her now, and she needed to correct that situation. She ran through several ways of killing the security officers, but they all ended with Takeo dying before she could free him.

They continued on to the last car, where half of the seats had been removed, pushed to the back, and covered with dirty tarps. A single table sat in the middle of the car, with one man seated at it and two more standing nearby. On the table were a bottle of vodka and three glasses.

Kiku felt her carotid artery throb.

Six men. One knife. Poor odds.

The man at the table—a huge bear of a man, with a bushy beard—beckoned Kiku forward. "Come! Come, sit down."

Kiku walked up to the table, pulled out a chair, and sat. The two security officers following her moved to stand on her right side.

The big man nodded to Takeo. "My apologies, Nakumora, but my orders are not to speak with you. Novikov reserves that right, and who am I to deny him? But please, join us."

Takeo sat in the other chair. The purser stepped back from Takeo but kept the pistol pointed at him.

The big man folded his arms across his massive chest. "Kiku, I am Nikolaj Peshkov. You have heard of me?"

Kiku nodded. She knew Peshkov by reputation only. He was Novikov's head of security.

"Can you please explain to my men"—Peshkov gestured around the room and smiled—"the mistakes they are currently making?"

Kiku didn't know what Peshkov's game was, but she decided to play. "Your men are facing my strong side. One of them should have moved to my back. They have also left a weapon out for me." Kiku tipped her chin to the heavy vodka bottle.

"That was at my discretion." Peshkov lifted the bottle and filled all three glasses. "I want to be a good host. Anything else?"

Kiku glanced at the bodyguard closest to her. He wore a belt with both a gun and taser. The gun was on his left hip, opposite her. The taser was within her grasp, but the weapon was useless against more than one man.

"They didn't frisk me." Kiku grabbed the steak knife hidden in her belt, whipped it out dramatically, and plunged it into the tabletop.

Nikolaj laughed and clapped his hands like a kid at a magic show. "Very impressive." With a wave of his hand, he ordered one of his men to move behind Kiku. "That is what I wish to speak with you about."

Takeo started to speak, but Peshkov held up a hand. "I was serious when I said I have been ordered not to talk with you. Open your mouth and one of my men will break your jaw. You are to speak with Cade Novikov himself and no one else. This business is between Kiku and me."

Kiku reached out and picked up a glass of vodka. It was a private label, so strong that when she sniffed it, her lip curled slightly. "You have my attention."

Peshkov pointed back and forth between them. "You, me, we're realists. And the reality is, you are going to need an employer. Takeo has lost the civil war. His father will never take you back. Join me. I'm tired of you killing my men."

Takeo's face was a neutral mask, but the clenched fists in his lap gave him away. He would explode soon. Kiku needed to make her move.

"I do not believe Novikov would ever agree to that," she said.

"He already has. The great Kiku on our side? It will mean further humiliation to Kenzo. My boss is in love with the idea." Nikolaj crossed his beefy arms again. "Of course, I would, unfortunately, have to place you under lock and key until the current situation is rectified." He nodded at Takeo.

"Of course." Kiku took a big sip of her vodka and made a disgusted face. She turned her head and spat it out. "I sit down with you in good faith and you serve me this swill?" She threw the contents of the glass in Peshkov's face, soaking his chest. All around the room, guns were instantly trained on Kiku's head.

"Stop!" Peshkov jumped to his feet and held up his right hand. His eyes traveled around the room, making certain his men obeyed his order. He ran a hand down his face, vodka dripping off his beard, and faced Kiku once more. "What are you talking about?" He seized his glass, sipped tentatively, then followed it up with a long gulp. "This is my family's label. Peshkov is the finest vodka in all of Russia."

Kiku rolled her eyes and demurely crossed her legs. "You obviously do not know your vodka as well as you think. Do you know why?"

Nikolaj looked at her incredulously—then laughed. It was a big, booming laugh, but it did little to hide the rage building in his eyes. "Tell me, *Kiku*." He said her name mockingly now, and the other men began chuckling. "What don't I know about my family's vodka?"

Kiku stood up. "Allow me to show you." She ripped the taser out of the guard's holster behind her and aimed it at Peshkov's chest. "Tell your men to drop their weapons."

Nikolaj shook his head and motioned for his men to lower their guns. He frowned. "Maybe I was wrong about hiring you. I can take being shot by a taser. We used to laugh when they used it on us in the army. You *should* have grabbed the pistol. Now, put that away and tell me what is wrong with my vodka."

"You call yourself a true Russian man?" Kiku chided. "And you do not know a thing about vodka?"

Nikolaj scowled. "Enlighten me."

"Vodka is *extremely* flammable."

Nikolaj's eyes grew huge.

"Order your men to drop their weapons or I burn you alive. Five. Four. Three."

Nikolaj's eyes hardened. She'd seen that look of determination on a dozen other faces before—and she knew what it meant. In one second, Peshkov was going to order his men to kill her. Kiku pulled the trigger.

The taser wire shot through the air. The barbs pierced Peshkov's wet shirt, embedded in his skin, and sent a blue flame racing up his chest and beard. He was engulfed in an instant.

Kiku and Takeo were both already in motion. Kiku dropped the taser and grabbed the knife just as Takeo jumped to his feet, flipping the table so it caught Peshkov and the man beside him.

Kiku heard the door behind them slide open, but she didn't have time to see how many reinforcements were entering. She pivoted, slitting the purser's throat. At the same moment Takeo yanked the pistol from the dying man's hands.

A fire alarm blared to life. Facing off against three men, Kiku stabbed the nearest security officer in the chest, breaking the blade off at the hilt. She planted her foot and kicked the second man's knee, snapping it backward. Before she could turn to face the third, she heard a thump, and saw that the door had not slid open for reinforcements but for Jimmy, who was wrestling the other security officer to the floor.

But Peshkov was not done—and now he charged. His beard still blazing a sinister blue, the huge man growled as he ran at Takeo.

Takeo fired, but at that moment the train groaned and shuddered to a stop, throwing them all off-balance. The shot missed Peshkov and struck the guard behind him. Peshkov continued toward Takeo, crashed into him, and hurled him into Kiku. Takeo and Kiku fell together to the floor, the gun tumbling from Takeo's hand. Peshkov grabbed Takeo by the hair, slammed his head into the floor, then flung him backward into the wall.

With a cry of rage, Kiku drove her heel into Peshkov's knee. Her foot struck some kind of metal brace, and she screamed as pain raced up her own leg. Grinning like a madman with smoky tendrils rising from his singed beard, Peshkov stooped over, grabbed her by the throat, yanked her off her feet, and lifted her high off the floor. Kiku ripped the hairpin from her head, but before she could jam it into his face, Peshkov slammed her against the ceiling and the metal spike slipped from her grasp.

The sound of a gunshot thundered through the car. Jimmy was still wrestling with the last security officer, trying to gain control of his weapon, and it had gone off inadvertently.

Peshkov's eyes were wild with pain and rage as he shook Kiku like a ragdoll. Takeo clambered to his feet and slammed his fist into the Russian's nose, knocking his head back. Peshkov let go of Kiku, and she fell to the floor, gasping for air. Takeo kicked the Russian in the side, and followed with a left hook to Peshkov's cheek. Peshkov countered with a right cross that would probably have knocked Takeo unconscious, but he easily ducked it. Stepping to the side, Takeo sent his fists hammering into Peshkov's kidneys, and the big bear dropped to his knees.

But Nikolaj refused to stay down. He planted both hands on the floor and started to rise. Takeo stepped on his right hand and ground his heel in. Peshkov growled in pain and glared up at Takeo, his face purple with rage.

Takeo leaned forward. "Give Novikov a message," he said. "Tell him he deals with me now. Understand?"

Peshkov nodded, just before Takeo's fist crashed down on the back of his head, knocking him out.

Kiku returned unsteadily to her feet. The train had come to a complete stop.

"A little help here!" Jimmy groaned. He was still rolling around on the floor with the security guard, but a simple solution lay close at hand. One of the legs had broken off the table during the fight. Kiku picked it up and brought it down hard against the side of the security guard's head. The man fell limply to one side, and Jimmy rolled onto his back, panting.

"Grab whatever guns you can," Kiku said. "We have to get off the train—now."

39

For the next five hours, Kiku, Takeo, and Jimmy trudged along the railroad tracks in the moonlight. They were freezing, but the glittering lights of a small Russian town far off in the distance kept them going. Kiku tried not to give in to the pain. It wasn't just the cold, but her injuries. She didn't need a mirror to know that her neck was black and blue; she could see it in the way Takeo kept eyeing her throat and wincing. He hadn't fared much better himself. The right side of his face was bruised, he was limping, and the limp was getting progressively worse. Jimmy was relatively unharmed but complained enough for all three.

When they finally got to the outskirts of the town, the first structure they reached was a house with a sprawling patchwork of additions that looked as if they had been tacked on as time or money allowed. A single light was on inside.

They crept up close and hid in the shadows of the carport. Kiku held a shaking finger to her mouth and pointed to herself and then to the front of the house. Takeo and Jimmy nodded.

Kiku swung wide, circling around to the front door. She rang the bell, knocked loudly, and waited. After a minute, she rang the bell three more times and knocked again. No answer.

She peeked in the window. The light was from the kitchen, but she saw no movement. She returned to the carport. Jimmy was peering underneath a blue tarp.

"Snowmobiles. Four of them," he said. He was shaking so hard from the cold, he looked like he was bowing.

"No one is home," Kiku replied. "Back door."

She felt as cold as he looked, if not colder. Normally, she would have picked the simple back door lock with her hairpin, but her fine motor skills had shut down. She struggled even to get the pin out of her hair. "I doubt I can pick it right now." Her teeth chattered.

"No worries." Takeo drew his pistol, waited for Jimmy and Kiku to ready their weapons, and kicked the door in.

The three of them stepped inside with weapons drawn, and quickly swept the entire house. No one was home. Photographs suggested a family lived here—a middle-aged couple and two teenage sons.

The house felt downright balmy compared to the outside, but Kiku went straight to the thermostat and cranked it up to eighty degrees. She then checked the kitchen.

"The trash is empty and so is the refrigerator," she called out. "The family must be out of town, or this is their dacha."

"Welcome to Russia," Jimmy said, wandering in from another part of the house looking like an enormous, swaddled infant. He'd found a blanket somewhere and had wrapped it around his body and over his bald head. "They probably don't have any food."

Kiku let the insult to the Russians go. She wasn't up for arguing, and his anger at them after his stint in their jail was understandable.

"But," Jimmy continued, "they do have plenty of other stuff. You're gonna want to see the storage room. It's a jackpot."

He led them to his find. It was an interior room, so Kiku risked turning on the overhead light. It was like a showroom for outdoor gear. Apparently, this family was big on camping or hunting: there were tents, sleeping bags, portable stoves—everything they needed.

While Jimmy and Takeo returned to the kitchen to scrounge up something to eat, Kiku began taking down equipment like a kid in a toy store. A plan was forming in her mind, and her body was starting to defrost. She felt even warmer when she found four white snowmobile suits. She pulled down one with a golden fur collar, held it up against her chest, and felt like Goldilocks: it was just right. Beneath the suits were four pairs of boots. *Perfect.*

By the time she returned to the kitchen, she was rubbing her hands together and had a big smile on her face. Takeo and Jimmy were sitting at the table eating tushonka right from the cans, and a kettle sat warming on the stove.

"I have a plan," she said.

"First, sit down." Takeo pointed to the chair next to Jimmy. "You need to eat something."

Jimmy opened another can of the stewed meat. "It's not that bad cold. There's some liver spread and crackers if you'd rather."

The kettle whistled, and Takeo poured three cups of tea before sitting down once more. "Okay. What's the plan?"

Kiku cradled the tea in both hands. She closed her eyes and inhaled the aroma lovingly. What she wouldn't give for a long, long bath.

Takeo cleared his throat.

Kiku looked up slowly. "After we warm up, we should all search the house for a change of clothes. Then we'll get a few hours' sleep, eat some more, and head for Perm. It's not as far as Moscow, and there's an international airport. If we cut overland, we could be there in three days. With all these camping supplies, it will be like a vacation."

Takeo crossed his arms and scowled.

"How are we going to get on a plane?" Jimmy asked.

Kiku sipped her tea and avoided looking directly at Takeo. "I have a contact in Perm. This one will not let us down."

Jimmy persisted. "He can get us on a plane in Russia?"

She nodded. "He is well connected."

"That's a big favor," Jimmy said. "What're we gonna give him for—ow!"

Kiku had kicked him underneath the table. Takeo's expression was darkening, and Kiku wanted to put a stop to further discussion of this topic.

But Takeo chuckled gruffly. "All she has to do is ask. Albert would give Kiku the world." His eyes met hers, and he added, "If she would let him."

Kiku sipped her tea. "We leave in two hours."

Jimmy started coughing as the protein bar he was now munching went down the wrong way. "Two hours? You said we could get some sleep."

"We can stay here for two hours—no more. Peshkov will say nothing to the police, but Novikov will be on our trail soon. You sleep first. I'll take first watch. Don't forget to find a change of clothes."

Jimmy plopped the last of his protein bar in his mouth and pushed away from the table. "If that's all the sleep I'm getting, I'd better get started." He stalked out of the kitchen.

"You need sleep, too," Takeo said.

"Do not worry. I will get some. I lied to Jimmy. We will leave in three hours, at first light."

"Be sure to wake me for a shift." Takeo smiled and walked down the hall. He looked exhausted.

Kiku sat there enjoying her tea. She wouldn't wake either of them. Both needed sleep more than she did. She'd use the time to pack and ready the snowmobiles.

But first she'd make another cup of tea. She put the kettle back on and looked around the counter for the tea bags. As she pushed aside a container of sugar, she froze. Sitting in a glass vase was a long-forgotten flower, dried and shriveled. A dead chrysanthemum.

It was a bad omen.

Especially for her.

40

Kiku powered up the hill on her snowmobile and crested the top. The sunset's reflection on the snow sparkled red, orange, and gold. Everything before her was still and beautiful.

Takeo and Jimmy thundered up behind her; they'd been chasing her all day. She just couldn't seem to slow down. It wasn't because she felt like demons were chasing her—quite the opposite. Here, in the frozen wilderness, she felt *alive*. In spite of her lack of sleep, an energy coursed through her.

She was invincible.

Takeo lifted up the visor of his helmet. "We should break for the night soon."

Jimmy nodded.

They both looked very tired, and Jimmy had deep circles under his eyes. The magnificent scenery of the Ural Mountains was clearly not having the effect on them that it had on her.

Kiku pointed to a frozen pond that stretched out below. "We still have enough light. We should cross the pond and camp along the treeline. There will be less wind."

Takeo thought about it for a moment, then nodded. Kiku flipped her visor down and pulled back the throttle, sending snow flying out behind her as she shot down the hill.

Jimmy raced up on her left and Takeo on her right. She knew both men were eager to make camp, but she wasn't about to let them beat her to the other side. She cranked the throttle all the way back and leaned forward. As she shot out over the flatness of the pond, she felt like she was flying.

A crack behind her was followed by several loud snaps. She glanced back and saw the ice breaking at the base of her treads.

"Move! Keep going!" she screamed.

Takeo had started to slow; he was the heaviest of the three, and his snowmobile was the most weighed down with equipment. But at Kiku's order, he cranked up the gas.

Jimmy did the same, but he also turned toward Kiku, falling in behind her.

Kiku shook her head and pointed forward as she rode. "Not behind me! Over! Over!"

But it was too late. Jimmy was now riding over the ice that she'd already broken. He slowed down to stand up on the bike and look for a safe way to go.

That was a mistake.

His front ski caught on broken ice, and his snowmobile spun nearly ninety degrees. He clung to the handlebars, but his gear at the back was shifting and then tipped over. Jimmy yanked back on the throttle and the tread cut into the ice, but it also caught on his backpack, pulling all the gear down behind him.

Kiku kept her eyes on the ice behind her. When it stopped cracking, she slowed to a stop. Takeo did the same. Kiku grabbed a rope from her gear and ran back toward Jimmy, Takeo beside her. They didn't stop until the ice at their feet started to give way.

Jimmy was still more than fifty yards away, the front skids of his snowmobile dipped down through the ice. He flipped up his visor, and fear was written on his face. "Now what do I do?"

"Get off. Slowly. Try to walk to me," Kiku said.

"Okay," Jimmy said uncertainly as he took his first step.

With a loud crack, the ice beneath him gave way, and both he and the snowmobile vanished beneath the surface. It happened so fast, it was as if he'd been swallowed by a monster.

Kiku stared at the rope in her hands. It was a mere fifteen yards at the most.

Jimmy's helmet broke the surface and his arms flailed. His scream, high-pitched and terrified, echoed around them.

Kiku started to move forward, but Takeo grabbed her arm.

"It's too far."

"Help! Help!" Jimmy ripped his helmet off. He was trying to pull himself up onto the ice but couldn't.

Kiku broke free of Takeo's grasp and started running back to her snowmobile. Her knife flashed in her hand as she slashed the ropes holding her gear. Shoving the pile off, she jumped on.

Takeo grabbed the handlebars. "You can't make it to him. The ice is too thin."

"I have a plan." Kiku reached for the throttle, but Takeo stepped in front of her.

"Let me go instead."

"That is sweet." Kiku kissed him quickly, then shoved him back so hard he stumbled and landed on his butt. She jammed the throttle down, and Jimmy's cries for help were answered by the roar of her engine.

Circling around, she cut wide, avoiding the already broken ice. She wrapped one end of the rope around her waist and tied it to the center of the handlebars, then held the free end with her left hand. She was better at throwing with her right arm, but in order for this to work, she needed her right hand to drive. She couldn't slow down even for an instant, or her skis would dip down. She knew that if she went fast enough, the snowmobile could actually travel across water, though the broken chunks of ice complicated things.

She came around behind Jimmy, lined up her approach, and gunned it. Screaming like a Valkyrie charging into battle, the snowmobile thundered across the surface of the water. Kiku shifted back in her seat and held the rope high.

Jimmy, treading water, turned to face her and waved his hands. He was still wearing gloves.

Kiku clenched her teeth. Even if she managed to land the rope right in his hands, how would he hold on to it wearing those thick gloves?

She ripped her helmet off with her left hand and stuck it between her belly and the handlebars. With the plastic face shield flipped up, she fastened the rope to the helmet's chin guard. She'd never tied a knot faster in her life.

Jimmy's head sank under the water and bobbed back up. "Kiku!"

She tossed the helmet sidearm as she flew past him. She couldn't chance looking back to see if he'd grabbed it; she had to brace herself.

The rope played out behind her. Five yards. Ten yards. The snowmobile raced forward, and still there was no resistance.

Then the rope suddenly cut hard into her stomach and yanked her back—violently. Somehow, she managed to hold on to the handlebars. Jimmy had saved her life, and there was no way she was letting him die today.

There was no way she'd let the frozen water claim her own life, either.

Snarling like a beast through the pain, she kept the throttle pinned and the ski tips up. The snowmobile continued to power forward until solid ice was once again beneath her. She slowed to a stop and turned the snowmobile, creating slack in the rope so she could unwrap it from around her waist. Takeo rushed over to her.

"I am fine," she panted.

They both looked at Jimmy. He lay on the ice, soaking wet, clutching her helmet with both hands. Blood streamed from his nose, but he smiled broadly and gave her a thumbs-up.

Kiku laughed. The laugh made her side light up like it was on fire, but that only made her laugh all the harder. Death would not have her—not today.

She looked at Takeo. "You get Jimmy. I will start a fire."

41

Jimmy's teeth didn't stop chattering until he fell asleep. They'd bundled him up in a sleeping bag and put the tent as close to the campfire as they could. Takeo had made a bed of coals at one side and had laid Jimmy's inside-out snowsuit above it, like he was slow-roasting a pig. Jimmy's clothes were hanging to one side, already dry.

"How do you like your snowsuit?" Takeo asked Kiku. "This one is still medium rare."

Kiku smiled. "I think Jimmy would prefer his well-done. But not burnt."

"Well-done it is." Takeo grabbed the blue tarp they'd used to cover his gear and tented it over the snowsuit to trap in the heat. "This should give it an earthy, smoked flavor."

Kiku sat down on her snowmobile and stared up at a zillion stars. The heavens stretched out in all directions. She couldn't recall the last time she'd seen so many cosmic lights. They unexpectedly reminded her of a verse she'd read as a child. *He counts the number of the stars; He calls them all by name. Great is our Lord, and mighty in power; His understanding is infinite.*

Takeo sat there watching her like she was a piece of art whose meaning he was trying to decipher. She wondered what conclusion he'd reached when he folded his arms across his chest and nodded approvingly.

"What were you thinking just now, Takeo?"

"You've changed, Kiku. The woman I sent to Darrington would never have risked her life for a courier."

A courier? Was that how Takeo saw Jimmy? Was that how she *should* view Jimmy?

Now it was Kiku's turn to stare at Takeo and wonder. She already knew she'd changed since working with Jack and Alice in Darrington—she just hadn't thought it had been so dramatic, or obvious. But perhaps Takeo was right. The Kiku she had been before Darrington would have left Jimmy in that pond, calculating that the risk to her own life was too great.

But the new Kiku ... she would do it again.

Why?

A grin slowly appeared on Takeo's face. "When all of this is finished, I am definitely taking you to that wedding."

Kiku returned his smile. "I look forward to it."

Takeo's grin turned impish. "Are you ready for bed?"

Kiku nodded, unsure exactly what Takeo was up to. But when she pulled back the tent flap, she understood. Jimmy's sleeping bag had sunk to the bottom of the lake, still attached to his snowmobile. Which meant they had only two sleeping bags left, and Jimmy was already using one.

"Looks like we'll be sharing," Takeo whispered in her ear. "Unless you want to share with Jimmy ... but he still looks a little frozen."

Kiku grabbed the front of Takeo's snowsuit and pulled him so close the breath from her mouth swirled into his. "Or I could insist *you* share with Jimmy."

Takeo stroked her cheek with his thumb. "And I could always say no. We have not sparred for quite some time. I have gotten much better at it. Look how I handled Peshkov on the train."

"Does it bother you knowing you would still lose?" Kiku teased.

"Not in the least. I have a feeling that wrestling with you would be worth the pain." Takeo flashed that dashing grin that cut so easily through her defenses. He was admitting she would win a fight with him, and yet his male pride was not wounded in the least. Kiku found the combination undeniably attractive.

She kissed his cheek and unzipped his snowsuit. "This sleeping bag will be a very close fit, so we will have to undress."

"I'm willing to make that sacrifice."

They disrobed and quickly slipped into the fleece cocoon while Jimmy snored loudly in the other sleeping bag, undisturbed. But when Kiku rolled on top of Takeo, he raised an eyebrow and swallowed sheepishly.

"I may have underestimated how little room we'd have." His fingertips stroked her sides, but he was unable to raise his arms.

Kiku smiled mischievously. "I can still move. And since you are unable to, this is going to be a long night for you."

42

Down a snowmobile and now moving more slowly, the trio added an extra travel day to their itinerary. After some discussion, Takeo ended up riding behind Kiku. At first he had wanted to drive the second snowmobile, but when he realized that meant Jimmy would be holding on to her, Takeo changed his mind.

Perhaps that was what had darkened his mood; or perhaps it was because Kiku had told him she was not going to keep him up all night after all, because they needed to sleep. But more likely, it was her friendship with the contact in Perm.

Albert.

She intended to minimize the time he and Takeo spent together, but she couldn't eliminate it entirely.

When they arrived at the outskirts of Perm, they swung north toward an outlying park. There they switched from the snowmobiles to a stolen car. And then it was on to Albert's, a magnificent mansion, the biggest house in the city. Stone and slate gave the sprawling structure a storybook-castle feel.

"Wow. Who *is* this guy?" Jimmy said.

Takeo frowned. "A *business* acquaintance of Kiku's."

"Albert is a well-known art dealer," Kiku said.

"Albert Arzamastsev?" Jimmy's eyes widened, and he sat forward in the back seat with such excitement you'd have thought he was a kid about to see Santa Claus.

"I was not aware you were so interested in art," Kiku said.

Jimmy made a sour face. "Art? *Of course not*. But that guy has been on, like, ten episodes of *Big Boy Toys.* He has garages *full* of cars. He has the originals of every James Bond car, a Batmobile, the Bat Helicopter, seven cars from *The Fast and the Furious*, and—"

"Take it down a notch, Jimmy." Takeo motioned for Jimmy to sit back, but Jimmy's eyes were too focused on the mansion on the hill to notice.

"That's right! His house in Perm!" Jimmy thrashed about in the back seat. "He's got a hover car here!"

"It's a prototype. Really just a glorified helicopter," Takeo snapped.

Kiku raised an eyebrow.

"You saw the show?" Jimmy asked.

Takeo scowled. "On a flight to Korea once. There was nothing else on."

Kiku stopped at the manned gate outside the mansion, powered down her window, and smiled at the security guard. "Hello. I am here to see Albert."

"Mr. Arzamastsev is unavailable," the guard said stoically. "The turnaround is there." He turned to go.

"Please check your visitors list. My name is Kiku Inazuka." Kiku missed her phone. It would have been so much easier to call ahead, but Albert would understand.

The guard returned to the booth and picked up a clipboard, and nearly dropped it. "I'm sorry, ma'am." He snapped to attention. "I'll need to see some ID and—"

"I have none. Rodrigo knows me well." Rodrigo was the manager of the house. She leaned out the window and smiled up at the camera. "Please have him check the video feed."

Nodding, the guard picked up a phone. After a minute, the gate opened.

"My apologies again, Ms. Inazuka."

"None are necessary. Have a nice day."

When they were past the gate, Jimmy whistled low. "You're on some special list. How do you know this guy, anyway?"

Both Kiku and Takeo glared over their shoulders.

Jimmy held up his hands and scooted back in his seat, mumbling, "Yeah, yeah, I know. 'Shut up, Jimmy.'"

They parked out front. As they got out of the car, Rodrigo came down the wide marble steps to greet them, with several servants following behind. He smiled broadly, but Kiku noted his puzzled expression when he looked at the old, dented car they'd arrived in.

"It is very nice to see you again, Rodrigo. These are my friends." She purposely didn't use names, and Rodrigo nodded understandingly.

"Of course. Mr. Arzamastsev sends his most sincere apologies, but his arrival has been a bit delayed. He asked if you could kindly wait inside. I've been instructed to provide you with anything you request in the meantime."

Kiku smiled and bowed her head. "That is very generous of you, Rodrigo. When do you expect him?"

Rodrigo cleared his throat. "Four hours. He's been vacationing in Oslo."

"He's not coming all the way back for her, is he?" Jimmy blurted out —then clamped his hand over his mouth.

"It is no trouble at all, sir." Rodrigo pulled down on the bottom of his suit coat and nodded apologetically to Kiku. "Please let me know how I can make you and your guests as comfortable as possible."

Kiku knew it was useless to try to stop Albert from rushing back for her. Nor could she avoid Takeo's reading too much into Albert's schoolboy-like infatuation with her.

"Thank you, Rodrigo. I would be very appreciative if you could send someone into town to pick up a few items. The most important is a phone. A discreet one."

Rodrigo nodded, completely unfazed. His employer was, for the most part, a legitimate businessman, but his dealings occasionally—and very often when Kiku visited—slipped just over the line to the wrong side of the law. Kiku knew that Rodrigo was the embodiment of discretion.

"I also have a personal request, for which I will have to reimburse you later," Kiku said. "Would you please pick up some English caramel toffee and have it gift-wrapped? It is a thank-you for Albert, so if you would send the bill on to me, I would appreciate it."

"Yes, madam." Rodrigo bowed and held his hand out toward the house.

Kiku, Takeo, and Jimmy started up the steps, but a moment later Rodrigo called after them. "I am sorry to bother you, Ms. Inazuka, but ..." He gestured back to the car, where the chauffeur stood awkwardly outside on the driver's side, shaking his head. "There are no keys in the vehicle."

Takeo tapped Jimmy's shoulder. "Go start the car." Jimmy started back down the steps.

"Rodrigo," Kiku said, "perhaps you could put the car someplace where it will not be seen ... ever again?"

The car's engine sputtered and coughed, mirroring Rodrigo's reaction. But he quickly composed himself and nodded. "With pleasure," he said, and walked back to talk to the chauffeur.

Kiku and Takeo continued up the steps and Jimmy ran to catch up with them, whispering, "Can you imagine owning all of this?"

Kiku could. In fact, it had been offered to her once. Half of it, anyway. And when Albert arrived, he would probably offer it to her again.

43

Kiku was watching from the living room window as the limousine barreled up the country road and skidded to a stop at the main gate. The driver shouted and waved his arm at the guard, who scurried over to open the gate, no doubt apologizing for not moving faster.

Takeo came over to stand beside Kiku, scowling at the new phone in his hand. "We need papers."

"I included them on the list of requested items. Albert has some of the best forgers in the world. You will see, the documents will be exceptional." She nodded at his phone. "Have you reached anyone?"

He shook his head. "Voice mail. I've made seven calls and not received a single response."

"What about Jimmy? Has he had success?"

"He's in the games room. I'll check in with him." Takeo looked out the window; the limo was just pulling up out front. "You deal with Albert."

If the situation weren't so dire, she would have attempted to make him see how ridiculous—and counterproductive—his jealousy was. But she kept her mouth shut, and Takeo stomped away.

The front door opened with a bang, footsteps echoed in the main hall, and Albert appeared in the doorway to the living room, out of breath. He was a diminutive man in his late forties with a slight potbelly, a mop of curly black hair, round glasses, and the most adorable smile. He reminded Kiku of a young boy—though she would never say such a thing to him—and she was unbelievably fond of him.

Albert rushed over to her, delicately lifted both her hands, and stood admiring her as if he was drinking her in. "You are more beautiful each time I see you, Kiku. Please forgive my delay, but it is difficult to rush airport security along. So many formalities nowadays."

Albert's father was Russian and his mother was Welsh. The resulting blended accent added to his charm.

Kiku smiled. "As always, I appreciate you welcoming me to your home."

Albert's return smile was marred by a scar that ran along his jaw. "You've brought friends. Is everything okay?"

Kiku hesitated. She never lied to Albert—at least, not anymore. The last time she had … well, that was how he'd ended up with the scar. "These are perilous times, Albert. I apologize, but I have several favors to ask."

As soon as he'd heard what she needed from him, Albert responded, clapping his hands down on hers. "You must never apologize to me. Such small favors!" The somber face he had put on to listen to her had been replaced by a radiant smile. "I am overjoyed that you came to me for assistance." He patted her hands again and stood. "I have something for you."

He got up and limped over to a large desk in the corner. The injury that had put the hitch in his gait and three metal rods in his right leg was also Kiku's fault.

He opened a drawer, lifted out a box, and set it on top of the desk. "I was in Gyeongju and thought of you."

Kiku shook her head as she approached. Albert was one of the wealthiest men she'd ever known, but unlike most powerful men trying to woo a lady, he never bought her expensive gifts. Instead, he put thought into them—so much thought that his gifts ended up being more valuable than any others.

"Albert …"

"Shhh." He opened the box and handed her a locket on a simple chain.

On the front of the locket, mother of pearl had been crafted into a beautiful chrysanthemum. But when she opened it, she felt as if she'd been stabbed through the heart.

Her breath caught in her throat and her legs buckled.

Albert awkwardly held her up and eased her into a chair.

"I'm so sorry. I didn't realize it would be such a shock."

Kiku opened and closed her mouth several times, but no sound would come out. Tears streamed down her cheeks. "This is me," she finally managed to say.

Albert nodded. "I saw the photograph and I knew. I would know your face anywhere. Do you know the other girl in the photo? Was she a classmate?"

Kiku shook her head. She felt like she couldn't breathe, let alone speak. This was the most precious gift she'd ever received. She blinked and wiped the tears from her eyes, but more rushed to take their place.

The photograph inside the locket had been taken when Kiku was nine. The girl with her was her sister, Akari. Kiku had thought she'd only see that face again in her nightmares.

"How?" she whispered.

Albert handed her a box of tissues. "There's a little outdoor market in Gyeongju that was selling handmade furniture. Quality craft work, but it was made by children from a local orphanage. When the couple in their booth told me their names—Janice and Ken Peterson—I remembered the story you told me in the hospital. We got to talking and ..." He gestured down at the photo. "She was someone special to you?"

Kiku nodded. "My sister."

With his usual impeccable timing, Jimmy chose that moment to step into the room. Kiku was expecting him to rush Albert, perhaps begging for his autograph, but clearly something else was on his mind; his face was twisted in anxiety.

"What is wrong?" Kiku asked, clutching the locket.

"Where's Takeo?"

Kiku grimaced at Jimmy's slip. They weren't supposed to reveal their real names. "He is trying to reach someone."

Jimmy shook his head. "He won't reach anyone—"

"What?" Kiku was on her feet instantly. "Excuse me, Albert." She grabbed Jimmy by the elbow and dragged him out into the large red-carpeted hall. "What has happened?"

"Kenzo knows. He figured it out and rounded up everyone loyal to Takeo."

Kiku's chest tightened. "What about Jiro?"

"Kenzo knows Jiro was helping Takeo. He picked him up. He wants Takeo to meet him in Sendai in two days. Kenzo said if Takeo doesn't come to Japan, he's going to give Jiro up to Cade Novikov."

Kiku shook her head. Takeo would go to meet his father—that was certain. There was no way he would leave his brother at the mercy of Kenzo. And if Takeo went to Japan, so would Kiku. It would not end well, for either of them.

She looked down at the locket in her hand. She might be seeing her sister again sooner than she'd thought.

44

Kiku bid a hasty goodbye to Albert on the tarmac. The kind man was beside himself with worry for her, and she was just as afraid for him. If Novikov found out he had aided her, there would be a high price to pay. And although Albert had a security force, his men were almost as pleasant and nice as he was—good qualities in a friend, but a poor combination for people tasked with protecting your life. No, Albert's men wouldn't stand a chance against Novikov's.

The only way she could think of to protect him was to get him to leave Russia, at least temporarily. Which was why she now asked him to return to Korea and find everything he could regarding the missionary couple who had been so kind to Kiku and her sister.

"I give you my word, Kiku," he said. "But is there some way that I can assist you further with your current dilemma?"

"You have already done too much. Thank you. Take care, my friend."

Albert held her outstretched hand in both of his.

Takeo walked over to them. He stopped next to Kiku and held out his hand, which Albert shook warmly. "Thank you for all your help, Albert."

Takeo turned to Kiku. "I would like to speak to Albert alone for a moment. I will meet you on the plane."

Kiku's gaze met Takeo's. Takeo was his own man and she would honor his request. She knew he would behave himself in spite of his jealousy. Still, it irked her to not be privy to their conversation.

She touched the locket on her chest, bowed, and walked to the plane. Jimmy was waiting at the bottom of the plane's stairs, running a hand over his stubbly head. He looked nervous, shifting his weight from the balls of his feet to his heels.

"What are they talking about?" he asked.

Kiku looked back. Whatever their conversation had been about, it was now over. Albert was shaking Takeo's hand and bowing low. Takeo turned toward the plane, and the congenial mask he had been wearing fell away, replaced by a look of pain. But when he raised his eyes and noticed Kiku, he feigned a smile once more.

As soon as Kiku, Takeo, and Jimmy were on board, the pilot fired up the engines. Now dressed in gray, black, and blue suits respectively, they were the only passengers on the private jet. In minutes they were speeding down the runway and on their way back to Japan.

"Go over the phone call again," Takeo said. "You're certain it was my father's head of security?"

Jimmy nodded. "I called Jiro's burner, but I'm sure it was Ryder who picked up. Australian accent, snotty attitude—definitely him. He said your father figured everything out and wanted a meeting."

"Figured everything out ..." Kiku repeated. "What *exactly* did he say?"

Jimmy took a deep breath. "I was kinda freaked out when Jiro didn't answer, so cut me a little slack. Let me think." He closed his eyes and scrunched up his face like a schoolkid racking his brain for an answer on a test. "Ryder said Kenzo had realized both of his sons were betraying him. He knows Jiro helped Takeo flee Japan and was trying to get him back to America. And Novikov is still on a tear over his son getting killed. He's hit Yakuza operations across the globe. It's a full-on war, and Kenzo wants it over. Ryder said Kenzo will give Jiro to Novikov if Takeo doesn't come and talk to him."

"And I will meet with him," Takeo said.

Kiku frowned. "I do not agree with that decision."

"My father will not harm me." Takeo gazed out the window and smiled ruefully. "Now that the operations in the US are legitimate, he needs me to access the business holdings. That is where the real money is. Kenzo can't just march in and seize assets like he can in Japan." His eyes met Kiku's once more. "You, however, are a different story. You need to stay behind."

Kiku scowled.

Takeo's eyes narrowed. "I'm telling you, he will not harm me. He asked to meet in the Palace Mall; you can't get a more public spot. It would be the last place he would choose if he wanted to attack me."

"And it's right next to the police station," Jimmy pointed out. "You step out of the mall and you're already in jail."

"You know this from personal experience?" Takeo said with a chuckle.

Jimmy reddened, which made Takeo laugh harder.

Kiku cut in. "I will not agree to stay behind. But ... if you tell me what you could possibly give your father to placate him, I will agree to watch from a distance."

"Money and a united front," Takeo said simply. "As much as it disgusts me, I have to put aside the fact that he tried to have my son killed, and promise that Jiro and I will unite behind him to stop Novikov."

Kiku's throat tightened at Takeo's slip. They had gotten so used to having Jimmy around, it was perhaps too easy to forget that he didn't know their secrets—such as the fact that Kenzo had attempted to kill his own grandson and that Alex was still alive. But the secrets were out now, and it was no use trying to hide them.

"Will your father believe that you can so easily forgive his ordering a hit on your son?"

Takeo grimaced. He had realized his mistake, too. "I will convince him."

Kiku eyed Jimmy. She trusted him, up to a point, but she also knew that given the right persuasion, any man could break and reveal secrets. Still, Jimmy seemed unfazed by Takeo's mistake. He hadn't even blinked when Takeo said it.

"It's settled then," Takeo declared. He swiveled around in his seat and stared out the window at the clouds.

"Might as well drink 'em while you got 'em," Jimmy said. He rose and started for the bar. Kiku cleared her throat.

Jimmy looked back. "What? Only one?"

"*None*. We need to stay focused."

Scowling and mumbling, Jimmy walked past the bar and entered the bathroom.

Kiku waited until the door shut behind him. "What did you discuss with Albert?" she asked.

"I thanked him."

Kiku knew there was much more to the discussion, but she would not beg Takeo to divulge it. She crossed her legs, settled back in the chair, and let it go.

Takeo's knuckles whitened on the arm of his chair. He *wanted* her to ask. Perhaps he was the one who could not let it go.

She remained silent.

"I offered Albert your security services," Takeo said finally. "If things don't go well in Sendai."

Kiku stared at him. Takeo was a jealous man, and offering her to Albert was surely an agonizing choice for him. The pain he bore was only barely visible beneath his calm expression, but like the embers hidden beneath ash, it still burned.

And she understood. Takeo was trying to protect her. He feared something would happen to him at the meeting with his father, and if it did, he wanted her under the shield of the one man on the planet with the resources to insulate her from Kenzo's and Novikov's wrath.

She rose and stepped over to his chair. He smiled up at her.

She slapped him hard across the face, just as Jimmy opened the bathroom door. Takeo leapt to his feet, his eyes blazing and his right hand twitching. Jimmy stepped back into the bathroom and quietly closed the door.

"Do not ever doubt me," Kiku snarled. "I promised to get you to America alive, and I will."

Takeo doubled down. "Even you can fail."

Kiku's left hand struck the other side of his face—hard. Takeo's block was too slow to stop it.

"Damn it, stop hitting me!" he thundered, and his hand balled into a fist.

"Stop *doubting* me," Kiku replied through tightly clenched teeth.

Takeo's body suddenly relaxed and his eyes widened, like he'd just solved a mystery. "You know you can fail. That's not why you slapped me. That's not the doubt you're talking about."

Kiku shook her head. He was wrong. He thought she would fail. That was what had angered her. *Wasn't it?*

As Kiku stared into Takeo's eyes, she understood what he was saying. He was right. There were a thousand ways a meeting with Kenzo could go wrong; she was well aware that even she could fail Takeo, and he could die. She knew that. That was not the doubt that angered her.

What had angered her so was that Takeo thought that she might *live* even if he died. That was the only way she could accept Albert's protection—if she made it out of Japan while Takeo did not.

He thought that when he was in trouble, she'd run away to save herself? How could he think her capable of such disloyalty and cowardice?

She grabbed his shirt, balling the fabric in her fist. "We are both making it to America, or neither of us is." She shook him to hide the trembling in her hands. "Do you understand? *Both* of us make it out."

Takeo's mouth twisted into a crooked grin. "Breathing?"

Kiku stepped forward until her cheek tenderly touched his. "Yes," she whispered. "Breathing."

45

Kiku, Takeo, and Jimmy sat waiting in a sedan on the second floor of the mall's parking garage. Kiku drummed her fingernails on the steering wheel while Takeo leaned casually against the passenger door. Jimmy sat in the back, his feet nervously tapping the floor.

Kiku glanced at the clock on the dashboard. Takeo was supposed to meet Kenzo in ten minutes. But everything about the meeting felt wrong.

The plan was for Takeo to meet Kenzo in the food court and arrange a truce to secure Jiro's release. Takeo was confident his father would do nothing to harm him, but Kiku wasn't so sure. Though she couldn't image Kenzo risking an end to his dynasty, she didn't trust the man, and the public location did little to calm her fears.

Sendai's Palace Mall was famous throughout Japan, and all of them had been here before, but the three of them had come by earlier in the day to scope it out in detail. They had decided that Kiku and Jimmy would stand watch from here, in the parking garage. It gave them a direct line of sight not only to the second-floor food court, about one hundred yards away—they could see it through the huge windows—but also to the ground-floor entrance to the mall, just below the food court.

Before getting out of the car, Kiku and Takeo checked to make sure their earpieces were working. They were tiny devices, invisible to anyone who didn't get right up close.

"Testing," Takeo said. "Testing, one, two, three, four. Jimmy has a foul odor." He grinned.

Jimmy didn't react. He was nervously peering out the window at the other cars in the parking garage.

Takeo turned around in the passenger seat and smiled. "Lighten up, Jimmy."

"Yeah, yeah. It's all good." Jimmy nodded.

"They both work," Kiku said. "Time to get this over with."

They got out of the car and headed to their chosen observation point. Although they'd checked the area earlier, they now did another sweep. Everything appeared fine.

Jimmy's fingers drummed the concrete; his whole body was vibrating with nervous energy.

Takeo pointed at the police station that stood adjacent to the mall. "Is this bringing back memories, Jimmy?"

Jimmy chuckled. "Yeah. I was a kid, and we did a smash-and-grab at the jewelry store in the mall. It was pandemonium, and I took the service elevator to the bottom, ran across that little street there, and followed some lady through the door."

Kiku laughed. "Straight into the morgue."

Jimmy gaped at her like she'd developed telepathy.

"I am well acquainted with the mortician," Kiku explained.

Jimmy shook his head. "Why do I find that *not* surprising?" He walked away, giving Kiku and Takeo a moment alone.

Takeo's eyes locked with Kiku's. She was so used to seeing a sea of emotions churning in those brown eyes that she was taken aback by how calm he now appeared. She wanted to reach out to stroke his cheek.

"Takeo—"

His lips curled into a slight smile, and he gave her a deep bow. Kiku was uncertain what to say—but she didn't have a chance, because Takeo winked, turned on his heel, and started for the stairway. He never looked back.

She scanned the entrance to the mall, making sure it was clear, and checked the escalators and elevators once again. There was still no sign of Kenzo.

Takeo appeared below her. He looked calm and confident, like a man shopping at the local mall. "Still hearing me?" he whispered.

"Affirmative," Kiku responded.

Takeo began to softly sing "Pretty Woman," perhaps to calm himself, but it was having the opposite effect on Kiku. Ever since Takeo had agreed to this meeting, her fears had multiplied. He might as well have had black cats scurrying across his path as he broke a dozen mirrors, passed under a column of ladders, and stepped on every crack on the path along the way.

As Takeo waited for the elevator that would take him up to the second floor, Kiku spotted Kenzo in his signature Armani suit taking a seat at a table, with Ryder taking a standing position behind him. They were right in the middle of the food court, with plenty of people around them.

It is too public. Kenzo would never make a move here. Would he?

"What? No!" Jimmy's voice rose. He was standing beside the car, his cell phone pressed against his ear.

Kiku turned.

"That wasn't the plan. No! You can't do this, Jiro!" Jimmy looked at Kiku and the phone slid from his hand, tumbled to the cement, and shattered.

Jiro?

Kiku's throat tightened. "Jimmy, what have you done?"

"I didn't know. I didn't know." He was shaking with fear.

Kiku raced over to him and slammed him against the car. "Explain!"

"Jiro lied about being kidnapped. It's a trap. He thinks you'll kill Kenzo and then the police will catch or kill you and he can take over the Yakuza." The words flew from Jimmy's mouth like bullets from a machine gun. "In case you live, Jiro hired another assassin to finish you off, someone he says is even better than you."

Kiku balled Jimmy's shirt in her fist and dragged him nose to nose with her. "But I will not kill Kenzo."

Jimmy shook his head. "You will, because ... Kenzo's going to kill

Takeo. Jiro says you already gave Kenzo what he needs to make an heir. He doesn't need Takeo anymore."

Guilt ripped through Kiku. Kenzo was going to kill Takeo—and it was her fault. When she rescued Takeo from Fumeiyo no ie, she had stalled for time by giving Ryder exactly what Kenzo wanted: Takeo's seed.

"Takeo! Takeo!" Kiku yelled into the microphone.

"Kiku." Takeo's voice was interrupted by static. "I can't—" His microphone cut out.

"Takeo? Takeo?"

But there was no response—no sound at all. Kiku ran to the railing and stared across the street. Takeo had just stepped off the elevator into the food court. Nearby, several shoppers were looking at their cell phones in puzzlement.

"They are using a jammer." Kiku drew her gun and pointed it at Jimmy. "You told Jiro everything? The cruise? The train?"

Jimmy started crying. "I didn't know. I swear. He said he wanted to help, Kiku."

"Jiro is not helping, you fool!" Kiku screamed. "He is taking over." She spun on her heel and bolted for the stairs.

"I didn't know!" Jimmy screamed after her. "I'm sorry!"

Kiku flew down the stairs and sprinted to the mall's exterior stairs. She took them three at a time and yanked open the door to the food court. Takeo was sitting at a table fifty yards away, his back to Kiku, across from Kenzo. Ryder stood six feet behind Kenzo, beside a nervous-looking Korean man. The Korean man's hands were thrust into his jacket pockets, and from the bulge it was clear he was holding a gun.

Kiku saw Kenzo's plan in her mind as clearly as if she had unrolled blueprints. Kenzo had arranged for this non-Japanese, non-Russian patsy to kill Takeo. The Korean would be arrested, and Kenzo, the coward, would simply walk away. This would allow Kenzo to make peace with Cade Novikov and carry on his dynasty.

But Kenzo had no idea that there was another player in the chess game. And why should he? No one would suspect the bookworm Jiro. Yet it seemed Jiro was a master in the art of war. He had lured *all* of them into his trap—Kenzo, Takeo, and Kiku. They would kill each other—and anyone who survived would get swept up by the police next door. It was brilliant.

And Jiro had hired another assassin, Jimmy had said. *One who is even better than you.*

Kiku's shoulders stiffened, as if she sensed a sniper rifle pointed at her head. Ignoring the unseen threat, she started toward Takeo.

Time slowed down.

Ryder nudged the Korean, and the nervous man took a step forward. Kiku started drawing her gun. A shot rang out.

It took Kiku a second to realize that the Korean had opened fire without even removing the gun from his pocket. That was crazy. No one did that.

Takeo fell sideways, his chair tipping over and clattering across the floor. Kiku fired three shots, and the Korean staggered backward and dropped. Kenzo lifted the metal table up in front of himself like a shield. As Kiku put four rounds into the table, Ryder grabbed Kenzo and pulled him behind some trash cans for cover.

Chaos erupted in the food court. Diners screamed. Everyone started running for the exits.

Two of Ryder's men rushed up from behind, drawing their weapons. Kiku killed one before he had time to aim. The other man started firing wildly. Kiku aimed for the second man and fired two shots center mass. The man stumbled sideways and dropped.

Ryder and Kenzo ran for the escalators, surrounded by panicked shoppers. Kiku didn't have a clear shot.

Takeo was on his feet, yelling something at her, motioning her back toward the stairwell she had come up. But all she could focus on was the crimson stain spreading across his chest.

Takeo crashed into a table and fell to the floor, one last cry escaping his lips. *"Run!"*

Kiku knew he wanted her to escape, but she raced to him. He was lying on his side, his eyes closed, his arm stretched out toward the stairway, pleading for her to go. His blood pooled around him on the cold tiles, but his chest still rose and fell.

She grabbed a wheeled cart used to pick up food trays and brought it over to him. Groaning, she lifted him onto the cart. She looked around. The main elevators were in use, but she spotted a sign for a service elevator. She followed the arrow down a back hallway, found the elevator, and pressed the call button.

As she waited, she examined Takeo. The shot had struck him on his right side. His shirt was soaked in blood. She pressed one hand against his wound and held her gun in the other.

She looked back down the hallway she'd just come down—and saw one of Kenzo's men pointing a gun at her. *Where did he come from?* She reacted, raising her own gun, but she was too late. A shot sounded—right next to her. Kenzo's man clutched his throat and collapsed.

She looked down in astonishment at Takeo, who had one eye open.

"Not a bad shot for ... being upside down and dying." He coughed, and the gun fell from his hand.

The elevator doors opened, and Kiku thrust the cart inside and punched the button for the ground floor. As the doors closed, she put her hand back to his chest. "Takeo! Takeo!" she called, but he didn't answer.

Gritting her teeth, cursing and muttering, she hid her gun in her waistband and waited for the doors to open.

The elevator shuddered to a stop, and the doors parted. A city policeman stood waiting right outside. "There's a triage area out here," he said, shoving open a door that led outdoors.

She pushed the cart through the open door. "I see it," she said in Japanese. "Go! There are more wounded upstairs!"

The policeman hesitated for just a moment before stepping into the elevator.

Kiku held Takeo's chest as she pushed the cart across the street to the one person who could help her. If he wasn't there, she'd have no choice but to take Takeo to the triage area—and that would be delivering him straight to Kenzo.

She pounded on the door of the morgue. It felt like an eternity passed before it opened, revealing an older man in a lab coat. He took one look at Kiku and then down to the cart, and his eyes widened.

She pressed her pistol against his chest. "Dr. Ito, in. Now!"

The doctor's voice cracked as he backed up. "Did you do all this, Kiku?"

"No. But I need your help. This man has been shot."

Dr. Ito shook his head. "I'm a coroner, not a doctor. He needs a hospital."

"You used to be a doctor. You are going to save him." Kiku put her gun away. "You owe me that much."

Dr. Ito held up his hands. "I would do anything for you, but … I don't have the right equipment. I don't—"

Takeo started to shake, and Kiku yelled, "You are going to try. Move!"

Kiku pushed the cart behind Dr. Ito as he raced down the hallway to the main morgue, and together they moved Takeo onto an examining table.

"He needs blood," Dr. Ito said. "I don't—"

"I have type O positive." Kiku bared her teeth. "You will use mine."

"Kiku, I don't know—"

"Save him!"

Dr. Ito started grabbing supplies and laying out instruments on a small table. Kiku kept her hand pressed against Takeo's wound. As the blood seeped through her fingers, she watched the color slowly drain from Takeo's face.

"I must remove the bullet before I can stop the bleeding," Dr. Ito said. "I'll need you to help me." He turned on an overhead light and walked Kiku through assisting him as he opened up the wound. Soon he was dropping a piece of metal onto the table. "The bullet must have struck something before it hit him. Bullets usually make a little hole going in and a real big one coming out. This one was already flattened out when it hit him."

It took several more agonizing minutes for Dr. Ito to clamp and stitch. When he was finally done, he pointed to another examination table. "Pull that over here and lie down on it for the blood transfusion."

"I would prefer to stand."

"Not an option. He's lost a lot of blood. We may be able to save him, but it will take so much of your blood, you will certainly pass out."

Kiku wheeled the table over and lay down on it. "If there is any question about who dies today, it is me. Take all my blood. I appreciate your help, Dr. Ito, but if I wake up and Takeo is dead because you did not use every drop of my blood, I will kill you."

Dr. Ito nodded and inserted a needle in her arm. "I understand. Now please stop threatening me so I can work on saving this man's life."

As the minutes ticked by, Kiku's eyes grew heavy, and the room appeared to be getting darker. She held up the locket on her neck and took one last look at Akari's photograph.

Footsteps echoed in the hall. Dr. Ito jumped and stepped away from Takeo, his scalpel still in his hand.

"Relax," said a familiar voice.

"Oh, it's you," Dr. Ito said. "It's been a long time."

Daichi walked into Kiku's view and smiled down at her. "You're a mess, kid."

Kiku's eyes were so heavy now. She just wanted to sleep. She tried to speak, but no words came out. How had he found her? What was he doing in Japan?

"I tried to warn you," Daichi said.

"Jiro," Kiku managed to spit out.

"I know. And I'm sorry, kid. That's why I'm here. Jiro offered me a job."

Kiku's eyes widened as she remembered Jimmy's warning. *Jiro hired another assassin to finish you off. Someone he says is even better than you.*

Daichi clamped his hand over Kiku's mouth, his fingers pinching her nose closed.

Kiku fumbled for her gun, but she was so weak her arms wouldn't cooperate.

No. Not like this. Not Daichi.

Her eyes fluttered.

Keeping his hand over her mouth, Daichi lifted the bloody locket off her chest with his prosthetic. The carved white chrysanthemum was now splattered with blood.

Then he leaned in close, like a father tucking his little girl into bed, the fingers clamped over her mouth slowly smothering her. He smiled and whispered, "Good night, Kiku."

And everything went black.

KIKU - YAKUZA ASSASSIN

ACTION-THRILLER NOVELS

Award-winning, *Wall Street Journal* bestselling author Christopher Greyson breaks the mold for action-thrillers. Join Kiku as she criss-crosses the globe from Chicago to Hong Kong, the streets of Japan, and the frozen tundra of Russia and takes on the mob, Yakuza, black market, and anyone else who stands in her way!

A BEAUTIFUL PLACE TO DIE

Protector. Lover. Assassin. — *Kiku.*

Orphaned as a child and taken in by the Yakuza, Kiku swore an oath to serve and protect the organization. But, when Kiku discovers that the 13-year-old boy she has been assigned to guard may be the son of her lover and heir to the Yakuza throne, her pledge is put to the test. With a price on the boy's head and a target on his back, Kiku must not only save him from the ruthless Russian mob but possibly from a traitor in the Yakuza itself. Torn between love and honor, Kiku must snatch the boy from the crosshairs before it's too late.

KINDLE THE FIRES OF WAR

She's outnumbered 100 to 1.
They're going to need more men.

Kiku has gone rogue. Now hunted by the Russian mob and the Yakuza, Kiku heads to Hong Kong's underbelly to rescue her lover. Faced with impossible odds, Kiku must outwit, outfight, and outrun everyone trying to capture her and collect the two-million-dollar bounty. Rats fueled by greed or vengeance, driven by ruthless leaders, run rampant, all hoping to score. The mob, Yakuza, and Hong Kong's black market—they all wanted to fight. Kiku started a war.

DANCE OF DEATH

To save the one she loves,
she'll kill them all.

Kiku's quest to rescue her lover has gone disastrously wrong. With the odds stacked against her, her enemies think she'll run and hide to save herself. They're wrong—dead wrong. Kiku decides to take the fight to them instead. Now the hunter, Kiku, will stop at nothing to protect those she loves.

JOIN THE FREE PREFERRED READER PROGRAM

Join the Preferred Reader program and get your *exclusive* copy of *FIRST PATROL*

Preferred readers enjoy:

- Advanced Notification of New Book Releases
- The Christopher Greyson Newsletter
- Special Appreciation Giveaways
- The exclusive short story: FIRST PATROL!

Visit ChristopherGreyson.com to sign-up!

ALSO BY
CHRISTOPHER GREYSON

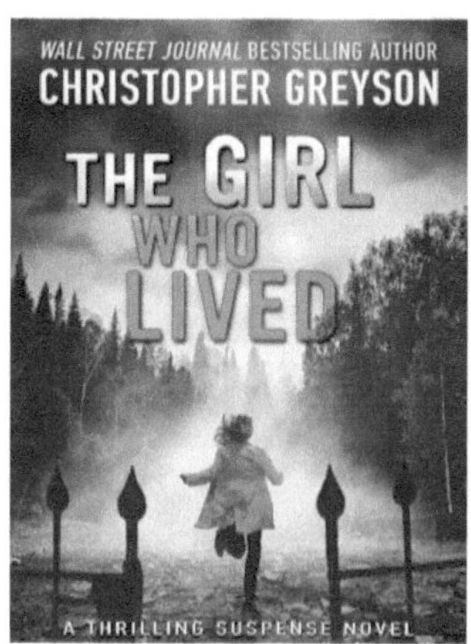

THE GIRL WHO LIVED

Ten years ago, four people were brutally murdered. One girl lived. As the anniversary of the murders approaches, Faith Winters is released from the psychiatric hospital and yanked back to the last spot on earth she wants to be—her hometown where the slayings took place. Wracked by the lingering echoes of survivor's guilt, Faith spirals into a black hole of alcoholism and wanton self-destruction. Finding no solace at the bottom of a bottle, Faith decides to track down her sister's killer—and then discovers that she's the one being hunted.

ONE LITTLE LIE

A LIE IS A WELCOME MAT FOR THE DEVIL...

Kate had high hopes when she moved to her husband‘s hometown, but her domestic bliss was short-lived. Blindsided by her spouse's public affair with his high school sweetheart, everything she worked for begins to unravel, along with her sanity. Confused, alone, and afraid, can Kate untangle the web of lies and unmask her stalker, or will she lose everything—including her life?

One Little Lie is a riveting suspense novel set in an idyllic town where money talks, gossip flows, and the court of public opinion rules. Jump on for a fun, fast-paced ride with a book you can't put down!

The Detective Jack Stratton Mystery-Thriller Series

The Detective Jack Stratton Mystery-Thriller Series, authored by *Wall Street Journal* bestselling writer Christopher Greyson, has 5,000+ five-star reviews and over a million readers and counting. If you'd love to read another page-turning thriller with mystery, humor, and a dash of romance, pick up the next book in the highly acclaimed series today:

And Then She Was GONE

A hometown hero with a heart of gold, Jack Stratton was raised in a whorehouse by his prostitute mother. When his foster mother asks him to look into a missing girl's disappearance, Jack quickly gets drawn into a baffling mystery. As Jack digs deeper, everyone becomes a suspect—including himself.

GIRL JACKED

They say a dangerous man is the one who had it all and lost it. But they're wrong, it's the one who lost everything but has a chance to get it back...

Guilt has driven a wedge between Jack and the family he loves. When Jack, now a police officer, hears the news that his foster sister Michelle is missing, it cuts straight to his core. The police think she just took off, but Jack knows Michelle would never leave her loved ones behind—like he did. Forced to confront the demons from his past, Jack must take action, find Michelle, and bring her home... or die trying.

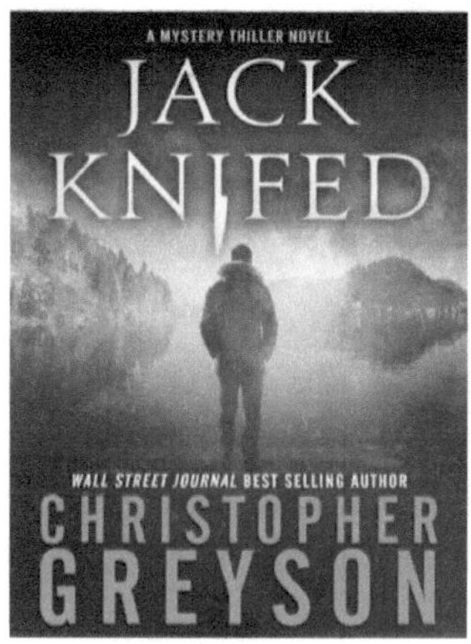

JACK KNIFED

How far would you go to uncover the truth of your past?

Constant nightmares have forced Jack to seek answers about his rough childhood and the dark secrets hidden there. The mystery surrounding Jack's birth father leads Jack to investigate the twenty-seven-year-old murder case in Hope Falls.

A heart-rending mystery-thriller about lost love, betrayal, and murder that will keep you on the edge of your seat.

JACKS ARE WILD

As the body count rises, the stakes are life and death—with no rules except one—Jacks are Wild.

When Jack's sexy old flame disappears, no one thinks it's suspicious except Jack and one unbalanced witness. Jack feels in his gut that something is wrong. He knows that Marisa has a past, and if it ever caught up with her—it would be deadly. The trail leads him into all sorts of trouble—landing him smack in the middle of an all-out mob war between the Italian Mafia and the Japanese Yakuza.

A strong hero, smart women sleuths, and more twists and turns than a piece of licorice.

JACK AND THE GIANT KILLER

A serial killer is stalking Jack's town--and no one's safe. But they don't know Jack.

Rogue hero Jack Stratton is back in another action-packed, thrilling adventure. While recovering from a gunshot wound, Jack gets a seemingly harmless private investigation job—locate the owner of a lost dog—Jack begrudgingly assists. Little does he know it will place him directly in the crosshairs of a merciless serial killer.

An action-packed thrill ride until the very end!

DATA JACK

Can Jack and Alice stop a pack of ruthless criminals before they can Data Jack?

Jack Stratton's back is up against the wall. He's broke, kicked off the force, and his new bounty hunting business has slowed to a trickle. He thinks things are turning around when Alice gets a lucrative job setting up a home data network.When the computer program the CEO invented becomes the key tool in an international data heist, things turn deadly. In this digital age of hackers, spyware, and cyber terrorism--data is more valuable than gold. The thieves plan to steal the keys to the digital kingdom and with this much money at stake, they'll kill for it. Can Jack and Alice stop the pack of ruthless criminals before they can *Data Jack*?

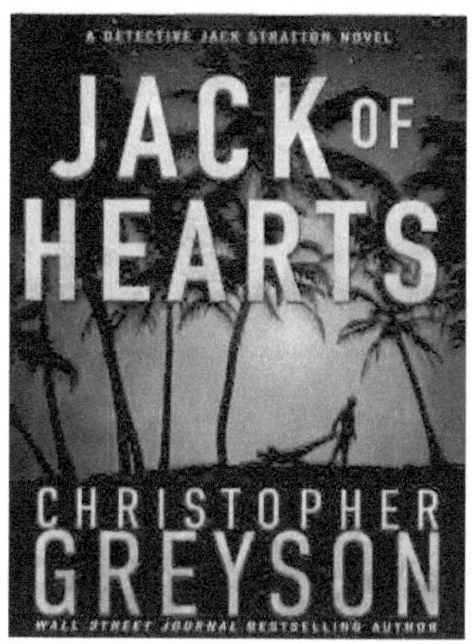

JACK OF HEARTS

Jack Stratton is heading south for some fun in the sun. Already nervous about introducing his girlfriend, Alice, to his parents, the last thing Jack needed was for the dog-sitter to cancel, forcing him to bring Lady, their 120-pound King Shepherd, on the plane with them. The dog holds Jack responsible and wants payback. On top of everything, Jack is still waiting for Alice's answer to his marriage proposal.

When his mother and the members of her neighborhood book club ask him to catch the "Orange Blossom Cove Bandit," a small-time thief who's stealing garden gnomes and peace of mind from their quiet retirement community, how can Jack refuse?

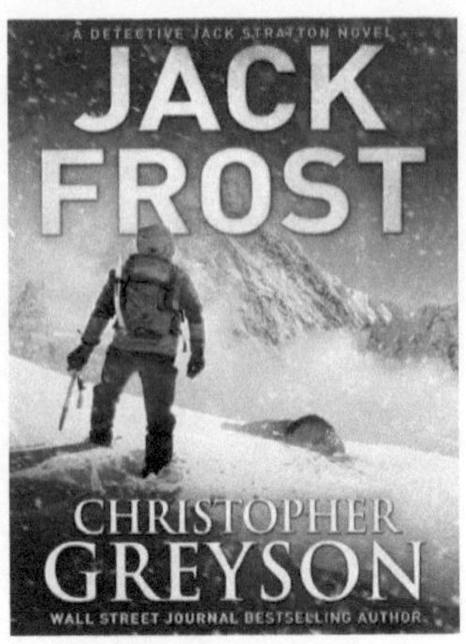

JACK FROST

What do you get when you mix the blockbuster television show Survivor with Agatha Christie's masterpiece And Then There Were None...

Jack has a new assignment: to investigate the suspicious death of a soundman on the hit TV show *Planet Survival*. Jack goes undercover as a security agent where the show is filming on nearby Mount Minuit. Soon trapped on the treacherous peak by a blizzard, a mysterious killer continues to stalk the cast and crew of *Planet Survival*. What started out as a game is now a deadly competition for survival. As the temperature drops and the body count rises, what will get them first? The mountain or the killer?

JACK OF DIAMONDS

All Jack Stratton wants to do is get married to the woman he loves—and make it through the wedding. It seems like he is finally getting his wish until he responds to a police distress call and discovers his old partner unconscious in an abandoned house. Investigators insist it was just an accident, but Jack fears there may be more to it. Sketches of women cover the walls, and among them is one sketch that makes Jack's blood run cold—a sketch of Alice, pinned up beside an invitation to a very special wedding—his own.

This time, "till death do us part"
might just be a bit too accurate!

CAPTAIN JACK

Looking forward to some fun in the surf and sand, newlyweds Jack and Alice Stratton are determined not to let something like a hurricane upset their honeymoon plans. But the storm's winds and churning tides unearthed a secret long hidden beneath the turquoise waters of the island paradise.

A local tour boat captain discovers a lost submarine and offers to sell the location to a man known only as the Dyab—the Devil. When the captain is murdered, the police suspect Jack and Alice and confiscate their passports. Trapped between the Devil and the deep blue sea, the handsome young detective and his blushing bride have nowhere to turn and everything to lose as they set out to prove their innocence and find the real killer.

Hear your favorite characters
come to life in audio versions of
the Detective Jack Stratton
Mystery-Thriller Series!
Audio Books now available on Audible!
Listen Now

Novels featuring Jack Stratton in order:
AND THEN SHE WAS GONE
GIRL JACKED
JACK KNIFED
JACKS ARE WILD
JACK AND THE GIANT KILLER
DATA JACK
JACK OF HEARTS
JACK FROST
JACK OF DIAMONDS
CAPTAIN JACK

Fantasy Adventure

PURE OF HEART

Orphaned and alone, rogue-teen Dean Walker has learned how to take care of himself on the rough city streets. Unjustly wanted by the police, he takes refuge within the shadows of the city. When Dean stumbles upon an old man being mugged, he tries to help—only to discover that the victim is anything but helpless and far more than he appears. Together with three friends, he sets out on an epic quest where only the pure of heart will prevail.

THE ADVENTURES OF FINN & ANNIE — MINIMYSTERY SERIES

In these heartwarming short stories, join Finn and Annie as they investigate their way through murder, arson, theft, embezzlement, and maybe even love, seeking to distinguish between truth and lies, scammers and victims. A Mini-Mystery series that will touch your heart and leave you craving more!

ACKNOWLEDGMENTS

I would like to thank all the wonderful readers out there. It is you who make the literary world what it is today—a place of dreams filled with tales of adventure! Word of mouth is crucial for any author to succeed. If you enjoyed the novel, please consider leaving a review at Amazon, even if it is only a line or two; it would make all the difference and I would appreciate it very much.

I would also like to thank my amazing wife for standing beside me every step of the way on this journey. My thanks also go out to my two awesome kids—Laura and Christopher, my dear mother and the rest of my family. Finally, thank you to my wonderful team, Anne Cherry, Maia McViney, Michael Mishoe, Charlie Wilson of The Book Specialist, and the unbelievably helpful beta readers!

ABOUT THE AUTHOR

My name is Christopher Greyson, and I am a storyteller. Since I was a little boy, I have dreamt of what mystery was around the next corner, or what quest lay over the hill. If I couldn't find an adventure, one usually found me, and now I weave those tales into my stories.

My love for tales of mystery and adventure began with my grandfather, a decorated World War I hero. I will never forget being introduced to his friend, a WWI pilot who flew across the skies at the same time as the feared, legendary Red Baron. I love to hear from my readers. Please go to ChristopherGreyson.com and sign up for my mailing list to receive periodic updates on new book releases. Thank you for reading my novels. I hope my stories have brightened your day.

Sincerely,

Find out more about the author and upcoming books online at www.Christopher-Greyson.com.

v.2.10.22

www.ingramcontent.com/pod-product-compliance
Lightning Source LLC
Chambersburg PA
CBHW020722310726
48979CB00004B/1023

* 9 7 8 1 6 8 3 9 9 5 1 3 5 *